THE COMFORT OF DISTANCE

A SEBASTIEN GREY NOVEL

RYBURN DOBBS

PROLOGUE

The car finally came to a stop, and the man in the trunk heard two doors open. The car rocked a little as driver and passenger alighted, slamming doors violently. Heavy steps fell on what sounded like gravel. He could hear both sets stop just outside of the trunk. The man held his breath in expectation of the trunk latch clicking free. Then, a few seconds later, it did. The trunk lid raised up just enough to let a wedge of moonlight through, casting a chalky horizontal gleam into the trunk. As quickly as the man could, he rolled from his left side onto his back, trying to ignore the lightning of pain that shot through his rib cage and into his sternum. He braced himself for the assault. It did not come.

The crunching of gravel under foot resumed, followed by muffled voices that became less audible as the moments passed. He tried to make out what they were saying, but the stifled syllables would not form words. A few more seconds passed, and the voices were gone altogether. Were *they* gone, or were they waiting to finish him off? Did they even know he was still alive? The man's mind raced, stoked by adrenaline. A few more minutes passed. He couldn't wait any longer. He must get out now and make a run for it—that is, if he could get his legs untied and if his bum knee would cooperate. But what if they were somehow tricking him? What if they were just standing out there, listening for signs of life—of *his* life? His pathetic waste of a life.

She was right, he knew. He was a good-for-nothing, and now the reaper would have him. How many times had she said that? "If you keep this up, the reaper will have you!" And how many times had he replied with, "He'll have all of us eventually —you, too!" *Eventually* can be such a comforting word, until you realize it has a shelf life. But he'd be damned if his shelf life was up. *Enough! Concentrate,* he told himself. *Stop thinking and think!* Those double-crossing bastards were gone. He'd get out of this, like all of the other times. Then it would be *his* turn to inflict the pain. Maybe he'd just wait a few minutes longer. He decided he would count to fifty. Then, if they were still not to be heard, he would make his move.

He cocked his head slightly to the left and strained to pick up any ambient signs of life. *1...2...3...4* Blood and crickets were all he could detect—the blood rushing through his ears and crickets stridulating ever so faintly some distance away. *25...26... 27...* He noticed that his counting was now synched up with the *thump-p-p, thump-p-p, thump-p-p* pulsing in his ears. But wait! Crickets! If crickets were chirping, then those two hulking idiots must be gone! It was now or never. No more counting.

Slowly, his heart pounding, he raised his bound and bare feet to the underside of the trunk lid and pressed it upward. Slowly, very slowly, after what seemed like several minutes, the trunk was filled with pale moonlight. He threw his legs over the edge of the trunk, resting the crook of his knees on the trunk's rubber seal. Then, he scooted his backside toward the rear of the Cadillac and flexed his torso upward as far as he could. Unfortunately, that was not very far. His abdominal muscles and cracked ribs were no match for gravity. He needed leverage, so he gripped the edge of the trunk with his legs and scooted his backside closer to the latch. With all his strength, he wriggled his butt up onto the trunk's edge. *What now? What if they come back and I'm stuck here? Shut up! Think!* Grabbing the farthest edge of the lid that he could reach, the man pulled himself over onto his stomach. Pain, more pain, shot through his body as he felt his right ribcage actually buckle under his own weight. Swallowing a scream, he pushed against the floor of the trunk with his bound hands. His bare knees scraped the top edge of the license plate as his body slithered out of the trunk and poured itself supine onto the gravel.

Trying to ignore the agony, he curled his torso up to find a sitting position. Despite the full moon, it took a few seconds for him to make out his surroundings. Besides illuminating the severity of his injuries, the moonlight also caught the gravel road that extended into the night. The sides of the road were thick with tall ponderosa, and patches of light reflected dully off what appeared to be exposed granite. He saw no buildings, no artificial light. *Where did they go? Are they watching me now?* He hurriedly untied his ankles but could not slip his wrists out of the knots that had, for the last few hours, bored a red furrow into the skin of his wrists.

To hell with it. He grabbed the rear bumper of the car with his bound hands and pushed his left foot against the gravel-pocked tread of the left rear tire. Holding his breath to stifle the groans of pain, he pulled himself onto his feet and quickly spun around, looking for movement. There was none. None that he saw.

The only question now was, in which direction should he go? He had no idea where he was, but based on how long they had been driving, he guessed it was some place far and unfamiliar. He must be farther up into the hills, he reasoned. The tall, dense, odoriferous pine and rocky landscape ruled out any place within a few miles of the city. It probably also ruled out finding anyone who could help him. It didn't rule out mountain lions though. *Stop thinking and think!* But the gravel road? Someone had to put it here. For what? And again, where the hell had they gone?

Just run! Anywhere away from this car. He chose the left side of the road, as he saw it. Why, he did not know. There was no reason, really; didn't need to be a reason. *Just go!*

He quickly discovered that he had misjudged his surroundings. The ground was not flat in this direction. It sloped downward sharply. The man tumbled forward, rolling through gravel, then dirt, then needles and bushes for several feet until he got lodged on the trunk of a narrow pine. Pulling himself up with the aid of the tree, the man tried to find his footing. Pinecones, needles, and small rocks punctured his feet, making the task doubly difficult. He heard the cracking of wood to his right, back in the direction of the road, and quickly spun around, instinctively ducking down against the tree as he did so. He saw nothing but noticed, for the first time, how cold it was—a slight breeze through the October air cutting like a knife, his breath diffusing into a white vapor that stood out against the dark. Maybe that's why they'd let him live, so he would freeze to death out here. Another "crack." This one from behind him and much heavier than the first. For the third and last time, he spun around.

1

Ingrid Nilsson pressed hard on the brake and the side-by-side jolted to a halt, sending a splash of liquid from her can of iced tea onto the center console. It had been a relatively dry summer, and the nimbus of dust that trailed her up the service road behind Wandering Hills RV Park now engulfed the vehicle. She set the brake, pulled a bandana out of her breast pocket, covered her mouth with it, and jumped out to clear the large tree branch that blocked her progress. Though Ingrid was in her mid-fifties, she was fitter than most and her motions bore a sort of rugged gracefulness—of muscle memory and economy of movement. The offending branch was a rather large one, and she considered it must have been the late summer thunderstorm a few weeks ago that threw the dead branch from the dead tree onto the dead earth. She chucked the branch down the slope on the east side of the road.

"Scoot over, Alice." Ingrid lovingly pushed the yellow Labrador back onto the passenger side and resumed her journey up the dry dirt road. Alice sprung back and licked at Ingrid's face, her paws pressing into Ingrid's right leg. "I love you, too, girl. We're almost there, then I'll get you some water, okay?" As if comprehending, Alice shifted back onto the passenger side and faced forward, panting heavily with her tongue lolling several inches out of her mouth.

After another fifty yards or so, the upward slope switched back sharply westward, then gave way to the flatter ground of the service area at the top of the hill. This is where Ingrid and Bill stored extra lumber and various plumbing and electrical supplies in two wooden sheds that were set about four feet back from the slope of granite and dirt that gently descended a thousand yards into French Creek Valley. The last people to rent cabin three—the family from Iowa with those insipid kids —broke the flushing mechanism on the toilet and Ingrid needed to dig through the sheds to find a spare. *They better have one! The next renters are due in two hours. Damn kids!*

Ingrid stepped out of the side-by-side and walked to the back to fill Alice's water bowl from an ancient green jug that was kept just for that purpose. Alice hopped out behind her and began sniffing around—looking for the prairie dogs, Ingrid supposed. "You're going to get bit on the nose again," she called out. "Get over here and get your water so we can get on with it and fix up that cabin." Ingrid set the filled water bowl carefully on the ground, trying not to spill any of the precious liquid.

She decided to check the smaller of the two sheds first. Ingrid seemed to recall that being the last place she saw their stock of bathroom fixtures. Several minutes went by, and Ingrid felt like she was getting closer to her quarry. She found a box labeled "misc bath" and found therein flex pipe, elbow connectors, washers, flappers, floats, fill valves and—*yes!*—flush handles. Well, one flush handle. But that was all she needed.

After re-boxing all of the parts and restacking the boxes in the order she found them, Ingrid turned to make her way back to the side-by-side. Suddenly, she became aware of a scratching noise coming from behind the shed. Alice must really want another bite on the nose, she thought. Prairie dogs were less common at this elevation, but they had made a nice little colony up behind the park, and Alice took it upon herself to be their personal tormentor.

Ingrid hurriedly made her way behind the shed to find Alice scratching and growling at what looked to be a large, angular rock. "Girl, git! Stop that!" Ingrid dropped to her denimed knees and inspected the source of Alice's fascination. She was no expert, but she also wasn't stupid. It was a skull, or at least the remains of one, stained brown, with several dark hairs clinging by a paste of mud, now long dried. The image called to mind the shell of a shucked coconut.

She searched for a stick in the surrounding landscape and, finding one, used it to poke at the skull until it broke free from the earth. Another poke and it flipped over altogether. The face of whatever this was appeared to be shattered into several pieces—a papier mâché of dried flesh keeping the jigsaw together loosely. The grotesque and desiccated visage stared back at her in a crooked gape.

Ingrid grabbed Alice by the collar and yanked the poor yelping dog all the way back to the side-by-side.

"TELL me again why you think that bone is human?" Bill asked Ingrid as they stared down at the skull behind the shed. It had taken Ingrid several minutes to convince Bill to pull himself away from rewiring the hookups at site twenty-one and come with her up to the sheds. Evidently, racing down the service road like a bat out of hell and yelling for him halfway through that journey was not enough to set Bill's alarm bells ringing. Ultimately, it was the look in her eyes and paleness of her normally tanned complexion that convinced him. He hopped in the side-by-side, they dropped Alice off with Sarah in the main office, and then they headed back up the hill.

"It's human. Look, Bill, it's a damn face. It's busted to hell, but it's a face." Ingrid was poking at the skull with the same stick she'd used earlier, trying to get it positioned, to make the "face" appear.

"Okay, Ing, I get it." Bill pulled the cell phone out of his front pocket and poked at the screen, then put it up to his ear.

"Hey-a Kathy, it's Bill out at Wandering Hills…yeah, yeah, I know it rhymes, super funny…anyway can you send someone up here? We got kind of a situation."

Ingrid was following the conversation while keeping her eyes fixed on the skull, as if it would try to run off.

"Well, Ing thinks she might have found a skull up here."

"Ing *knows* she found a skull up here!" Ingrid interjected angrily, her eyes still holding onto the twisted broken face staring back up at her.

"Yep." Bill turned and walked back toward the side-by-side, continuing his conversation. "We'll be here. How long do you think? Thirty minutes at most? Perfect. Great. We'll be down at the office waiting. Oh, and uh…could you ask them to be discreet? We got a lot of guests here, and more due to check in this afternoon. There's no need to come all sirens blazing, if you know what I mean. Perfect. Thanks so much."

Bill punched the *END* button on the phone, thanked the gods of technology for decent cell coverage this far from town, and ambled back to Ingrid's side.

"How do you think it got here?" she asked, as he sidled up next to her. "Think it's a cat that left it?"

"I have no idea," he answered.

Ingrid finally lifted her gaze off of the skull and walked a few yards down the slope, her hands on her hips, swiveling her head like a lazy sprinkler. "I wonder where the rest of it is," she called back to Bill. "It has to be here. Right?"

Bill closed the distance between them, put his arm around her shoulder, and gently drew her back toward the side-by-side.

"Let's go back down, hon. Skull or no skull, we have guests coming, and they won't like a broken toilet. I think I can get it fixed before the sheriff gets here. You found that part, right?"

"Yeah, I got it," Ingrid replied distractedly.

"That's my girl," Bill said, as they got in the side-by-side and started down the hill.

NEARLY AN HOUR LATER, Detective Sergeant Hank LeGris of the Custer County Sheriff's Office pulled the sunglasses off his head as he squatted down and stared fixedly into the dried patch of mud just in front of him. He squinted and bent his head, dog-like, as if the combination of those small movements would somehow lend clarity to the twisted and broken lump of bone that held his fascination.

"This is it?" he asked.

"Yep. We didn't touch it. Aside from Ing poking at it with a stick, that is," Bill answered.

"That stick, right there," Ingrid said, in a tone that suggested this information was somehow critical.

Hank didn't look at the stick. He just stared at the skull. After several minutes he abruptly stood up to his full six-foot-two height, put the sunglasses back on his head, and turned toward Bill. "Have you looked around for anything else? Any more bones? Anything different?" he asked.

"Not really," Bill replied. "When we saw the bone, we called you. But there's nothing different here that we can see."

"And the sheds were still locked when I came up," Ingrid added.

Hank took in his surroundings as he ran his hand through his medium length brown hair. To his immediate right was the back of the smaller of the two brown, rectangular sheds. Immediately behind the shed, where Hank now stood, was a few feet of level ground covered by dry, but once muddy, earth and low

9

grasses. To Hank's left, the level area gave way to a gentle, grassy slope descending about three hundred yards to a thick line of oak that lined French Creek. Beyond that, the valley, sparsely dotted by ranches and bisected by tenuous fences, extended a mile or so and broke at the foot of oak-speckled Mount Coolidge.

Hank pulled the radio mic from his lapel and pressed the talk button. "1Y7 to dispatch."

"Dispatch copy," the radio crackled back.

"We have a ten-five-four. We need a D unit. And have them call me. Also, when Y3 goes ten-eight, we'll need her here."

"Copy. Will have D34 call."

The cop-speak gave the whole circumstance a weight that made Ingrid nervous. What if she was wrong? What if the bone was not human? What if it was not even a bone? What had she done? Was this all a terrible mistake?

"I hope we're doing the right thing," she whispered to Bill.

Bill put his arm around her. "You did good, hon," he whispered back. "Hank and the boys will figure this out. No matter what, we had to call them."

Ingrid broke from Bill and took a few steps in the direction of the skull.

"Don't touch it!" Hank blurted out.

"I won't! I'm not dumb, ya know!"

"Sorry. We just have to keep the scene clean for the coroner. You really shouldn't even be up here."

"So, you think it is human, after all?"

"I do. We don't see a ton of these, thank goodness. And what we do see is usually old, Native remains. But I've seen enough to think that it is human. It's smashed pretty good; but like you said, it has a face."

Ingrid suddenly felt better, in an odd sort of way. Whoever this is—was—is dead. But at least she hadn't cried wolf.

"Where do you think it came from?" Bill asked. "We heard about the cat attacks. Could this be—"

The radio on Hank's uniform shirt screeched in interruption. "Y3 is ten-one-seven."

"Copy," Hank replied. He racked the mic back onto his uniform and turned to Bill. "I have no idea where this came from. I got the coroner coming, and Tiffany is heading up, too. We're going to have to have a better look around. As for the mountain lion—we don't even know if there have been any attacks."

"But we read in the paper..." Ingrid replied.

"You read that some remains were found. Which is true. But at this point the whole cat angle is just a rumor, just a story."

"There are mountain lions here, though. Everyone knows that," Ingrid replied.

"And Carmichael told me he's got sheep missing," Bill added.

"Carmichael's place is several miles away from here, Bill. You know that."

"They travel, you know *that*." Ingrid was getting irritated by the sergeant's lack of cooperation. Something about hosting a hundred and fifty guests in an RV park did not mix with a roving beast with claws and teeth. Why couldn't the sergeant understand how serious this was?

"Look, the bottom line is we have no proof that the remains were caused by a mountain lion, or lions."

"But you don't know they're not!" Ingrid spat out.

"How many remains have been found? How many bodies?" Bill asked.

"I really can't comment on that. Look, why don't you two head back down and keep an eye out for the coroner and Tiffany. Lead them up here once they arrive. There's just no point in speculating."

"Okay, Hank, we'll do that. Come on, Ingrid. We'll want to

get the coroner up here as soon as he arrives anyway. We don't need any of the guests to catch on."

～

FORTY-FIVE MINUTES LATER, the coroner's investigator, Gerry Good Crow, was gingerly holding the skull in his gloved hands. Once it was fully out of the earth, its humanness was unmistakable. The upper rear portion of the skull was draped by strands of muddied, medium-length hair. The face was smashed in a morbid jigsaw puzzle, but the holes for the nose and eyes could be discerned through the dried, desiccated skin that held forehead, face, and jaw together. To the back of the skull, near where the neck would be, was a layer of what looked to be Styrofoam.

"What do you think, Gerry?" Hank was looking over the investigator's shoulder.

"It's definitely human. It looks like a cow stepped on it though."

"Can you tell what killed him...or her?"

"No, but maybe if we find the rest of the body, we'll figure that out. The rest can't be far."

"I can get search and rescue up here, and maybe some cadets," Hank said, as he scanned the area once again.

"Okay. I'll bag up what's here. This is a mess, Hank. I hope you weren't planning on having dinner with the family."

"Same goes for you, Gerry. Any signs that this person was attacked by an animal?"

"Mountain lion, you mean? I wouldn't know what that looks like."

"No evidence from the other case, you mean?"

"Nope. Statistically it is very unlikely. But until we know for sure, it will be hard to stop people from spreading the rumors and stirring up the panic. Like I said, we just honestly don't know what that kind of thing should look like."

Something in what Gerry said rang a bell with Hank. *Wouldn't know what that looks like.* He'd said it twice, and maybe it took the repetition for Hank's brain cells to fire in just the right way.

"Well crap," Hank blurted exasperatedly and pulled out his personal cell phone.

"What's the matter, Hank? Who are you calling?"

"I think I know a guy," Hank replied, as he walked away with his phone to his ear.

2

A youngish man tepidly entered the waiting room of Christina Lucas, MD., PhD. As he did so, he quickly scanned the sterile cube of ecru walls, mid-grade carpet, and faux leather armchairs and saw only one other soul. Unless, of course, one cared to count the souls of the assortment of tang, damsel fish, clown fish, triggers, and angel fish that swam placidly through the large aquarium opposite the entrance door. But Sebastien Grey cared not to count the fish and, if pressed, would be reluctant to even count himself.

The other person in the waiting area was an older man in an oversized brown cardigan intently reading a magazine; the man showed no sign that he noticed the new arrival. Almost automatically, Sebastien calculated the relative risks involved in taking each of the eight or so open seats. Would it be better to sit behind the man, which could be construed as unsocial and rude? Or, in front of him, and perhaps force an awkward eye contact? Or even worse, conversation!

After a perfunctory check-in with the receptionist, Sebastien turned, fixed his eyes on the carpet, and took the six or seven necessary steps to the empty chair on the other side of the room, between a glass end table and one side of the aquarium. After a few moments, Sebastien's eyes could be found tracing the circuitous path of one particularly bright yellow tang. A few more moments and the ever-so-frequent self-recriminating ruminations began.

If someone had come into that waiting room, a third soul, so-to-speak, he or she would not have detected much consternation about the man in the corner by the fish tank. They likely would have only noticed a dark-haired, thinnish man of about 30 years, fastidiously dressed in blue dress slacks, butter yellow button-down shirt, brown herringbone waistcoat, and brown calfskin wingtips. In fact, the man's face would measure a few standard deviations in the direction of handsome on most scales—at least, in an everyman sort of way. And that, combined with his obviously over-studied wardrobe, gave the faint impression of an image from a menswear catalog.

The internal workings of this man were another matter, and by the eleventh or twelfth lap of the yellow tang, Sebastien's mind had fully capsized and fell onto the bed of a stormy sea, as it so often did. He simultaneously dreaded his visit with Dr. Lucas today and was grateful for it. He found himself both hoping the man in the cardigan was ahead of him in the order of clients, and praying that the man had already had his turn and just could not pull himself away from some captivating article in the magazine that continued to occupy his attention. It gradually occurred to Sebastien that he owed the good doctor some answers to questions and some homework—answers he did not have and homework he had not done. Five minutes or so later, the door to the hallway outside opened and a woman poked half of her body in.

"You ready, hon?"

The man in the cardigan closed the magazine and set it on the table beside him as he rose from his chair. "Thought you'd never get here."

"Well, I told you I had to stop by Janice's on the way in. How'd it go?"

"Fine, fine. There's stuff at the pharmacy. Let's go before they close."

The door shut, muffling a, "We have plenty of time. Would you stop worrying all the time?"

The ship of Sebastien's mind sunk deeper into the sand.

After what seemed to Sebastien to be an hour, but was probably closer to ten minutes, the woman behind the receptionist's counter opened the door that bisected the waiting area and Dr. Lucas's office. Her voice pierced Sebastien's solemn thoughts.

"Sebastien, come on in. Tina is looking forward to your visit."

Sebastien's heart began thumping a little harder and his palms felt clammy as he made his way into the inner hallway and from there through to Dr. Lucas's office—the opposite effect intended by the pleasant tone of the receptionist. But it could only be so; he had been coming to see Tina, as she preferred to be called, for seven months now, and he had only recently considered that perhaps, maybe just a little, he was a modicum less anxious about these weekly sessions. Still, spending an hour talking about himself, his loathsome self, pressed him so far outside his comfort zone that the physiological effects were unavoidable. He only hoped they had become less noticeable. He feared—no, he was sure—they hadn't.

"Sebastien, welcome. Come in and sit. Yes, there. The usual seat. How was your week?"

Sebastien had thought many times and did so again as he took Tina's hand to shake it, how unfair it was that she was so distractingly beautiful. Lowering himself into the red leather chair, he tried to take her all in without being obvious about it. Her hair was down today, a jet-black waterfall of silk cascading down her ivory cotton blouse. Her blue skirt reached to mid-calf and her shoes were simple black flats. As usual, her outfit was modest and professional, no doubt calculated to illicit no arousal or emotional response whatsoever from the damaged and lost souls that were her clientele. But her piercing dark brown eyes and flawless skin were enough to belie whatever demure affectation her wardrobe attempted to convey.

"Oh, you know, good; I mean fine, I guess." Normally, making eye contact was beyond Sebastien's capacity, but as he answered her his eyes fixed like magnets upon the dark almonds that bookended her long, thin nose. It occurred to him that she may have some Central American ancestry. One day, he would screw up the courage to ask.

"Well, that's great!" she beamed back warmly and with complete sincerity. "I'm eager to hear all about it. Let's start off by revisiting some of the goals we set for the week. Would that be okay?" Tina waited for Sebastien's nod, then continued. "I believe we talked about you doing more socializing and trying out some of the techniques we practiced. And you said something about a chamber of commerce mixer, and an opera, I think. Could you remind me about those?"

It always fascinated Sebastien that Tina could remember such details, as if she were really concerned with the minutiae of his ridiculous existence. "Well, it wasn't an opera exactly. It was a dinner thing they have for people who donate to the opera. It's called the Overture Society."

"Oh, that sounds like a great opportunity to get to know people. How did it go?"

Sebastien's eyes found the floor. "I uh...didn't go. I mean I almost went."

"What do you mean by *almost*? Would you mind explaining that a bit more?" Tina's spine straightened perceptibly; her eyes remained on Sebastien as her graceful hands opened the notebook that sat on her lap—a silver Parker pen clipped to its spine.

"Okay, so, I got dressed up and everything and, you know, when I got to the place, I saw other people going in. The men were wearing jackets. I didn't bring a jacket."

"You mean, like a blazer or sport coat?" she asked.

"Yeah, they had them on, and I didn't."

"What were you wearing?"

"Just slacks and a dress shirt and vest—this vest actually; same one I'm wearing."

"It's a very nice vest," she interjected warmly, then twisted the pen to expose the tip.

"Yeah, um...thanks. Well anyway it was hot, so I didn't bring my jacket. So, I went home." Sebastien felt the vibration of his phone in his pocket. He ignored it and hoped Tina wouldn't notice it.

"Do you need to get that?" she asked.

Of course, he thought. "No, no. It will go to voicemail."

"Great. Okay. You were concerned about being under-dressed for the occasion, you mean? I totally understand that. I think most people would be. But do you think your friends at the opera society—"

"Overture Society," he broke in, then immediately flushed with shame for correcting her.

"...Overture Society—yes, thank you—do you think your friends at the Overture Society would mind that you didn't have a jacket on? Do they seem like the kind of people who would be concerned about that?"

Sebastien noticed Tina scribbling something in her note-book. He wondered with suspicion what it could be. "Well, I've never met them."

"Oh, it was your first time? Completely understandable. Social situations can be so difficult, can't they?"

Sebastien shifted uncomfortably in his chair and Tina, catching his movement, paused her writing and looked up.

"What about the chamber of commerce mixer? Were you able to make it to that?"

"Nuh uh." Sebastien once again looked down, fixing his eyes on the burgundy quatrefoil pattern in the carpet.

"Well, that's okay. Let's talk about work. Did you get any new cases this week?"

"Not really. Well, there was this one thing—a hiker found some bones and the deputy sent me pictures from the scene. They were just bird bones though, so it was really nothing."

"That's fascinating that you can tell that kind of thing just from bones."

"Feathers," Sebastien replied.

"I'm sorry. What do you mean?" Tina's eyes narrowed.

"There were feathers scattered all around the scene."

Tina suddenly lurched and heaved into a staccato of snorting laughter. Sebastien was caught off guard. He had never heard her laugh. It seemed so contrary to the pedestal of grace upon which he placed her. He could feel his face flush red with shame and embarrassment. *What a stupid answer! You are so stupid! See? This is why you shouldn't talk about yourself!* He drove his forearms down onto the armrests of the chair as if to raise himself to his feet and flee.

Sebastien sat for several minutes in the Range Rover, replaying the appointment with Dr. Lucas over and over in his head. He had a pounding headache and his eyes stung. And even worse, he could not decide whether he should be embarrassed over-reacting to Tina's laughter, or relieved that his outburst led to a deeper discussion of how his personality disorder causes him to be overly sensitive to the slightest insult. It was something for him to work on, anyway. More information was better than less, he felt.

Just as he was about to start the car, Sebastien remembered

that he had received a phone call during the session. He produced his phone from his breast pocket and saw the missed call and message. Both from his brother. A tinge of anxiety vibrated in his chest, and he debated whether to ignore the call. After all, what could he possibly want? Finally, Sebastien decided that ignoring his brother would be of no use. Henry was stubborn. Sebastien put his phone on speaker and pressed play on the message.

"Hey, Sebastien, what's up, bro? It's Ha...Henry. Been a while. Hey, could you give me a call back? I need a favor. And I, uh, I need it kind of fast. I've got a thing here I need your help on. Anyway, please, you know, just give me a call as soon as you can. Thanks, man."

It had been almost a year since Sebastien had spoken to his brother. It wasn't that they didn't get along; they just sort of drifted apart after their mother died. It was easy, too; they were so different. Sebastien was taciturn, cerebral, and introspective. Henry was the older of the two, and much more confident, athletic, and gregarious. There just wasn't that much in common to talk about. The fact is, Henry seemed to remind Sebastien of everything he wasn't—and was fairly sure he was supposed to be. At least to their mother. Sebastien wondered whether there was something in this, something he should bring up with Tina.

Sebastien shook himself free from those thoughts and hit "call back" on the message from Henry. It was answered on the first ring.

"Sebastien, how's it going, man?" Henry's words were clipped; he sounded eager.

"Um...fine. Just calling you back. What's up?"

"Yeah, thanks for that. Hey, what was it you did for your graduate project? You know, when you went to Namibia."

"My dissertation, you mean?" Sebastien was genuinely confused. The question seemed out of left field.

"Yeah, yeah. That's what I meant."

"I was researching the impact of resource stress on the frequency of Acinonyx predation of Cercopithecines. Why?"

"Come on, Sebastien. Seriously, laymen's terms here. I don't have time for the nerd version."

"Great to talk to you, too, Henry." Sebastien reproved himself for bothering to return his brother's call. He was about to say goodbye for another year, but before he could, Henry, in a less agitated voice, broke in.

"Sorry. I just mean I'm dealing with a situation here and figured your research might help me. It was something to do with Cheetahs eating monkeys, or something like that, right?"

"Yeah, that was part of it. What could you possibly care about that?" Sebastien was still hurt, and his tone showed it.

"How would you like to come up here for a few days? It would be great to see you. We could show you the place. I know Melissa would love it."

His brother's abrupt offer alarmed Sebastien, who curtly replied, "Henry, what's going on?"

"Okay, look. We've had some strange cases up here; bodies, or parts of bodies, are being found." Henry's tone was almost desperate.

"There must be a forensic anthropologist up there, Henry. You don't need me. Besides, I'm busy." Sebastien knew he was less than honest in this reply. Despite being the consulting forensic anthropologist for several counties in the Bay Area, he still had not had a case, a real case, in several weeks. And his landlording gig, the thing that brought in the real money was essentially on autopilot.

"Busy with what? The Block runs itself, right? You don't have a job to go to. I mean...I didn't mean...I'm just saying you can spare a few days to come take a look."

"I do have case work, you know; bodies are found down

here, too, and a lot more of them I bet. You wouldn't believe the crap I get involved in."

"I know, I know. I didn't mean that. It's just that there is a bit of a panic up here. We've had parts of two bodies found so far. In fact, I'm at one of the scenes now."

No wonder Henry sounded so direct, so urgent.

"Like I said, I can't be the only—"

"It's mountain lions."

"What?"

"I mean, some people up here are saying that we have a mountain lion problem."

"It's South Dakota. You do have a mountain lion problem."

"Not like this. We sometimes have small pets or livestock disappearing. But no one has ever reported humans being killed by mountain lions up here. People are worried."

"What makes you think it's mountain lions?"

"That's where you come in. You know what a big cat attack looks like on a skeleton?"

"On monkeys, yeah. But not humans."

"Sebastien, I remember, several years ago, you lectured an entire dinner party about how humans are just primates with bigger brains."

"One of the reasons I no longer do dinner parties."

"To be honest, I don't think we have a mountain lion problem. I think someone, a person, is leaving bodies around the county. But no one here believes me. I just need you to verify my hunch that it is not a cat killing people. I think they are either homicides or accidents. Maybe even suicides."

"That's not how science works. Or detective work, for that matter. I can't take a side without looking at the evidence."

"Okay, fine. Come look at the evidence. Come see for yourself."

"That's a long way to go just to verify a hunch."

"We still need to know what we do have up here. I still need an anthropologist."

"Like I said, must be plenty of them in South Dakota."

"Not like you," replied Hank.

Sebastien gave no response, but, in truth, he was genuinely touched by his brother's compliment.

"It's been a while. And you've never seen my place. It's actually very cool. We're building stables and a corral. We're going to get a horse for Kirby. You need to see it. It's got everything."

"Including mountain lions?"

"At least think about it. But hurry, okay?"

"I'll think about it." Sebastien pressed the ignition and put the Range Rover into reverse, sensing the end to the conversation. He once told someone that he liked the way the Rover purred. Had he recalled that now, he might have appreciated the irony. As it was, he was too irritated.

"Thanks, man. Been to Mom's grave lately?"

"No." A fresh wave of guilt and shame crested.

"How's the Block? What a hassle it must be to run that place. I definitely got the better deal. I actually feel a bit bad about that."

"Don't. It's fine. Really. It suits me."

"Yeah, well, if you say so. You're happy though? Right?"

Oh, come on. Not now, he thought. "Yeah, it's all good. But hey, I'm driving so I better get going. Thanks for calling though, Henry."

"Promise you'll think about it? Oh and, by the way, it's Hank up here. Henry just doesn't seem..."

"I will. I promise, Hank." Sebastien needed no explanation and was certainly in no position to judge anyone's desire to reinvent themselves. He hit "end call" on the console at about the same time he reached the freeway on-ramp. He gunned all eight cylinders and overtook the BMW in front of him, then swung sharply into the leftmost lane through surprisingly light early afternoon traffic. Speed limit or no speed limit. He was irritated now, and now certain, as he reflected, that he had made a total fool of himself in therapy.

"Busy with what? The Block runs itself, right? You don't have a job to go to."

Sebastien called up Wagner's Siegfried on the audio system and turned up the volume. The creeping intensity of the *Vorspiel* mirrored his baleful mood. A tactile search of the console produced a prescription bottle, but it was empty.

3

Hank, Gerry, and the pathologist, Dr. Rose, stood around the metal autopsy table gaping at the hunk of mangled skull that was gaping back at them. Dr. Rose had just completed his examination and came up with precious little in the way of useful information. The lights in the autopsy suite flickered momentarily as an unexpected summer thunderstorm rolled by outside.

"How sure are we feeling that there is nothing more out there?" asked Dr. Rose.

Hank was pulling at his goatee subconsciously. "Can't be a hundred percent, but we had eleven cadets, six search and rescue folks, and a dog. We did a grid search of the entire area."

"Maybe it was brought in, planted there?" suggested Gerry.

"It's possible," admitted Hank. "Is there at least enough information from the skull to search it in the missing persons database?"

Dr. Rose began placing the skull in a small paper bag, then put the bag in a cardboard box. The lights from the ceiling reflected off his bald head as he worked. "Well, we know it is definitely human and definitely modern—the fillings tell us that. Plus, there are a few missing teeth, and those sockets have been remodeled with bone, so it may be that this is an older person. I can't tell the sex, though."

"Can we get DNA?" Hank asked, hopefully. "Like maybe from the white stuff you found on the back part of the skull."

"We can probably get DNA from the teeth or the calvarium —the top of the skull—but I don't know about that tissue. It looks like fat or something. I'll submit it to the lab along with the rest. I think, all told, we are in good shape for DNA, though."

"As long as there is a match in MISPERS," Gerry interjected, referring to the missing persons database.

"Clearly," replied the doctor. "Given the condition of the skull and the lack of other diagnostic elements, there is not much we—I—can tell. That's why I asked if we were sure that there is nothing more there."

"You mean you can't tell whether or not this person was attacked by a mountain lion?" asked Hank.

"No. There is obvious trauma with the skull being in pieces. But I can't tell if it is pre- or post-mortem, or what caused it. Like I said, I need more."

Hank's eye lit up in an idea. "What about underground? What if it was buried and the prairie dogs dug it up? There's a colony up there; I saw the holes. What's that set-up called? Ground piercing..."

Gerry shook his head and frowned, interrupting. "Penetrating Radar. Ground Penetrating Radar is what they call it. We could try, but I doubt there is anything underground. The dog should have been able to detect a burial—at least that's what I've been told."

Dr. Rose silently nodded his agreement, then offered, "I think it would be a good idea to try, though. It certainly couldn't hurt, anyway."

Gerry pulled out his phone and started walking toward the

main office. "I'll give Jenny a call. She has the gear and knows how to use it."

Hank looked at Dr. Rose quizzically.

"Geologist at the college. She's helped on some other cases. You remember the parking lot at the high school? They were digging it up to put in a new drainage system and found those Native burials?"

"Oh sure. I heard about that."

"Well, Dr. Sommers—Jenny—did the ground penetrating radar on that. It actually helped quite a bit."

A minute later, Gerry walked back into the autopsy suite, pocketing his phone. "I left a message. Can we at least tell how long it's been out there, or how long whoever it is has been dead?"

"Given the fact that the thing is mostly bone, with just some desiccated skin holding the pieces together, I would say several months at least. It has been a relatively hot and dry spring, too. That would speed things up some." Dr. Rose spoke over his shoulder, while washing his hands at the sink.

Just then, as if on cosmic cue, a clap of thunder shook through the building, causing the lights to flicker. The three men all looked up to the ceiling nervously.

Downtown Vineyard had gone through a process of gentrification over the last few decades. Buildings and streets born in the forties and fifties became sleepy relics by the eighties. But new money, squeezed from wine grapes and microprocessors, helped push affluence eastward from Silicon Valley up through the dust and weeds of the easternmost margins of the Bay Area. These winds of change resuscitated the town and transformed it into a hip, urban hub where new and quaint somehow found a happy collaboration in the form of expensive restaurants, trendy bars, and niche boutiques, all stuffed into the art deco remains of Vineyard's post-war boom. The streets, once somnolent, had given way to outright commotion.

Aside from the Worthington—a state of the art performance center hosting concerts, operas, plays, and lectures—the most notable building downtown was affectionately referred to as "The Block" by the locals. The Block, a two-storied masonry building built in 1942, occupied an entire block between First and Second streets—hence its name. The reason for the building's fame is lost to the memory of most; but the more seasoned denizens of the town know it for the heated public debate that took place in 1982, when the owner, having fallen on hard times, sought a permit to demolish the building and replace it with a strip mall.

The fortieth anniversary of the building proved to be an unfortunate time to propose such architectural violence and, perhaps not surprisingly, uproar ensued. Public meetings were held, and picketers marched up and down First Street the better part of that fall. Finally, a Canadian architect named Claude LeGris got wind of the imminent demolition and swooped in to write a check big enough to send the building's owner into a comfortable retirement. Claude rehabilitated the building, converting the second story to luxury apartments and gutting the southwest corner to make room for a small parking garage. The building had been in the LeGris family ever since and, rumor had it, Claude's grandson now ran the place. Though few people had ever seen or spoken to the man, further rumor had it that he was rather youngish and somewhat handsome. Some of the more aggressive single socialites had suggested a bounty. Of course, Sebastien himself was oblivious to the rumors of his eligibility.

After pulling into his spot in the garage, Sebastien made his way to the front of the building. The ground floor of the Block was occupied by several businesses—a Chinese restaurant, a rare book dealer, an attorney's office, an ice cream shop, a tailor, and a game shop. Sebastien looked over the façade on First Street and considered himself fortunate that his tenants were relatively easy to deal with, and they all paid their rent on time. Well, almost all.

"Sebastien! We're down here."

Sebastien turned in the direction of the voice and saw about half a dozen people sitting at a long folding table at the far end of the Goblin's Lair Cards and Games, between a display of unpainted miniature soldiers and a large cardboard dragon. The group—what looked to be a mix of teens and twenty-somethings—were busy consulting books and scribbling on notepaper. Polyhedral dice covered the table like confetti.

"You should join us, man. We just lost our healer." This from the head of the table, the proprietor and major domo of the Goblin's Lair, Eric Pool. The remainder of the table's occupants stopped what they were doing and looked up at Sebastien with apparent suspicion. After what seemed like a full minute, a pink bubble emerged from the mouth of the only girl of the group, then popped. As if prompted by the bubble-gum signal, the players rejoined their busywork.

"I don't think so, but thanks. I don't really know how to play. Plus, I have a lot of work to do still. I just came to ask if...uh... you know...if you got the, uh, invoice I left for you last week."

"Okay, cool. Oh, and on that other thing, yeah, I got it. Next week alright for that?"

"Yeah, yeah, fine." As the words came out it suddenly occurred to Sebastien how frequently he'd been lying these days.

In truth, Sebastien did want to play, or at least watch. The memory of fantasy role playing games played in the library of his middle school tugged at him whenever he set foot in the store. That may have been, indeed probably was, the last time he had friends. And as far as "that other thing" went, no, next week would not be okay. The rent was already a full month late. He really must learn to assert himself, he thought, as he made his way for the door.

"Oh hey, Sebastien." Eric stood up from the table and bounded awkwardly toward the front of the store—as if all his joints were stiff from sitting too long. "Some lady came by and left you something."

"Oh really? Who? What did she leave?"

Eric ducked behind the sales counter and emerged with an envelope in his hand. "Don't know. Never seen her before. She was old though. Pretty classy, too, by the look of her. She insisted you get this ASAP. Glad I remembered."

A mocking "barely!" came from one of the youths at the game table.

He thanked Eric and pocketed the envelope as he emerged onto the sidewalk.

Sebastien offered a silent prayer—to whatever gods there may be—that he would not run into anyone at the mailboxes. Small talk was perfect torture, and he always felt stupid and awkward trying to fake his way through it. This day the gods obliged, and he was able to check his mail in peace before heading up to his apartment. Just a few circulars, the obligatory credit card application, and a largish package postmarked from Germany. It must be the book his old colleague Hugo Drechsler had promised to send him.

He closed the apartment door behind him and, as was always the case, instantly felt himself relax. He let out an audible sigh as he twisted the deadbolt on the door. He was safe now. Perfectly, warmly cocooned. No interactions, no byplay, no social obligations. Here he was alone and invisible. Or nearly so.

"Hello, Parsifal. How was your day? Did Mrs. Kimble take you for a nice walk?" Sebastien rubbed the head of his sable corgi, which was peering at him from above the back of the couch, tail wagging violently. Parsifal yipped in response.

After taking Parsifal out to do his business and fishing through the refrigerator for something resembling a reasonable meal, Sebastien sat himself at the French partners desk—an inheritance from his grandfather—and carefully examined the envelope Eric had given him. It was fine stationary in light violet with the name "Mr. Grey" inscribed in a delicate and petit hand on the front. The flap was monogrammed "AKL."

Sebastien carefully peeled the flap away from the envelope, trying not to rip it, or its contents. He pinched the small pale violet sheet and gingerly removed it from the envelope. Parsifal stared up from between his legs—eyes large with concern.

MR. GREY,

As a valued member of the Overture Society, I would like to invite you to the premiere of Der Fliegende Hollander next Sunday at seven o'clock. There will be a special reception with the cast after the performance, and I do hope you are able to make it, as I know you were not able to attend the dinner we had this week. Your presence was missed.

With Warmest Regards,

Adeline

Sebastien felt his forehead moisten as he tucked the note back in the envelope. Adeline Lindner was both a brilliant pediatric cardiologist and the longtime president of the Overture Society. Her largess beamed over the entire institution and allowed this relatively small and regional opera company to bring in some of the world's best singers. How in the world had Sebastien come to her notice? He wasn't on the donor page of the programs—he expressly asked to be listed as "anonymous." She certainly did not know him from any of the society events since Sebastien never could bring himself to attend one. He folded his arms and leaned back in the chair, scanning the ceiling.

Suddenly, a horrific thought occurred to him. Regardless of how he had found his way into the social crosshairs of Dr. Lindner, the fact is she had somehow associated him with the game store. The Goblin's Lair! Ugh, how embarrassing! He wondered what sort of bedraggled youth were in the store when Adeline walked in. What was being said? And done?! Just as quickly, as it often happened, Sebastien's mind turned on him. *Man, you are such an elitist jerk!* He rifled the desk drawer for his spare bottle of Buspar and swallowed one.

Sebastien opened the bottom drawer of the desk and pulled out a stack of catalogues. If he was going to attend the premier of Der Fliegende Hollander—if!—then he needed to make sure he was dressed appropriately. He knew, or rather felt, that his sartorial judgement was not to be trusted. Sebastien was already several laps behind the larger field of humanity, and his clothing had to be considered carefully. The only way for him to achieve the right look—a look that would allow him to fit in without standing out—was to be a scrupulous copycat. To that end, he kept stacks of printed catalogs from just the right menswear brands, and the browser on his computer was similarly filled with bookmarks to specific looks he wished to emulate. These he would search to find the right combination of trousers, shirt, shoes, tie, jacket, etc. befitting the weather and, most importantly, the occasion. His extra-large walk-in closet was filled with the necessary pieces to recreate most of the basic looks he found amongst the pictures of ridiculously handsome models in the catalogs. And he was always on the lookout to fill in the gaps. Of course, it was all ridiculous. He knew that. Though, he had never mentioned it to Tina. How embarrassing! No doubt she would point out how silly and unnecessary it was, that it was some obsessive-compulsive trait upon which they should work. More fodder for uncomfortable conversations.

He found what looked to be a suitable outfit for the premier on page forty-three of the Brunello Cucinelli catalog—a linen three-piece suite, in crème. Fortunately, he had such a suit, although it was a cheaper brand. It will probably do, he considered. Tie? Absolutely. Brown loafers would go well, obviously, but socks or no socks? *Socks. Of course, socks. Remember, Sebastien —blending in is a subtle affair.*

4

It was the next day, Saturday, when a woman in her thirties, wearing a brown T-shirt, khaki shorts, and hiking boots, paused temporarily behind the RV park sheds to re-band her long blond ponytail—a straw hat clinched between her knees. Hank pulled up the truck just in time to see her replace the hat on her head and wipe the sweat from her forehead with the front of her shirt. He thought he detected a tattoo on the momentarily exposed small of her back.

"How's it going up here? You must be Dr. Sommers." Hank extended his hand, and the woman took it.

"Good. Call me Jenny, please. You're with the sheriff's office?"

"Yep. Sergeant LeGris. You can call me Hank, though."

"Nice to meet you, Hank the Gray." Jenny smirked.

"I'm sorry?"

"Your name. LeGris. It means *the Gray*. You didn't know that?"

"Oh, I probably did at some point. So, this is it?" Hank gestured to the contraption that Jenny had been pushing up and down the slope. It looked a lot like a lawn mower, except the wheels were much bigger, and there was an LCD screen mounted on a bar about mid-way up the handle.

"Yep. It all happens right here. I'm having a few of my students mark out meter-wide grid lines from the top of the slope going down fifty meters so we can keep track of where we've run the radar and map it out properly." Jenny pointed down the slope to a where a young man and woman were tying lines of string between metal stakes. The man was holding a measuring wheel. A third person—a young woman—stood looking on, holding a clipboard. All three were wearing hard hats—which seemed a bit unnecessary to Hank.

Jenny continued. "I've done the first three rows. There's nothing so far. Unfortunately, up here we have a low to very-low GPR index, which means it's not well suited to this kind of sensing. But the good news is that also means it's not a likely place for something to be buried. It's solid granite a few feet down."

"Well, hell."

"Dr. Sommers, do you want us to keep going down?" yelled the young woman with the clipboard. Jenny looked at Hank, who shook his head.

"No, Molly. We'll just do these rows. Could you grab the spare battery pack from the van?"

"You bet," the student called back, as she started a jog up the slope toward the area in front of the storage sheds. Her over-sized hard hat was jumping comically as her head bobbed up and down.

"This will take about an hour and a half to do properly. You're welcome to wait, of course."

This, to Hank, meant *get the heck out of the way.*

"No, ma'am, I'll let you all get back to work. Need me to bring anything? Water?"

"That's nice, but we have a cooler in the van. I'll text you and Gerry when I'm done."

"Sounds good. Thanks for the help. And stay hydrated."

As Hank ambled the Tahoe through the rain-filled potholes of the service road, he considered these latest developments in light of what had already occurred. Last month, a cell tower service crew found a human jawbone in a dry wash next to a fire road. Apparently, one of the crew members needed to relieve himself and, as he did so, saw the strange looking bone lying at the bottom of the wash, about fifteen yards away. Such a surprising discovery was supposedly common among the hiking-utility-hunting crowd. But it was the first time Hank had heard of it happening around here. So far, the owner of the bone has not been identified.

When you added this to the recent spate of livestock and pets going missing around the hills, you had the makings of a pretty good mountain lion panic. This kind of thing happened every half dozen years or so in the Black Hills. Western South Dakota was literally a breeding ground for one of the largest populations of mountain lions in the country. It also happened to be a feeder system, so-to-speak, for mountain lion dispersion throughout the Midwest and even farther. Mountain lions as far east as Connecticut, and even down into Arkansas, had been genetically traced to the Black Hills mountain lion populations. Nevertheless, the cats really didn't make that much trouble, all things considered.

But now...now, with the discovery of another body, or rather, body *part*—the skull, which had been found in a distinctly different area from the jaw—now the word was definitely going to get out, and the gun happy inhabitants of Custer County would no doubt posse-up to protect their ranches, RV parks, houses, businesses....

Hank felt a headache developing behind his right eye—a baby migraine just waiting to grow up inside his own skull. He needed to get home, get some aspirin, and check in with his brother.

SEBASTIEN WAS LYING on his balcony chaise, watching the birds spar on the roof parapet of the building opposite his. The noise of the traffic and the bustling pedestrians below lulled Parsifal into a stertorous slumber on his lap, and Sebastien himself was not far behind. The preparations for the long drive to South Dakota occupying his mind, not to mention all the uncertainty that lay ahead, was making him sleepy. What would it be like to see his brother? Would he really be able to help on the case? What if he couldn't? What if he failed and had to drive all the way home in shame? What would happen to his already strained relationship with Henry if that happened? Had he the prescience of an augur, Sebastien might have read ill omens in the behavior of the birds across the street. But telling the future had never been Sebastien's strong suit. If it were, would he be less anxious, or more?

Sebastien's ultimate decision to go was not only subsequent upon Hank's second, even more desperate call, but on the fact that the case itself, or cases, as it may turn out, could be of great interest. It had been a while since he'd had a really juicy case. The last one had been about six months ago, he reminded himself. An elderly lady had burned up in her Mercedes at the end of a dirt road. The responding fire department, and subsequently the detectives, suspected a vehicle malfunction.

The poor old woman had dementia, according to friends and family; she obviously became hopelessly lost, getting her car stuck in a dirt embankment. But Sebastien found minuscule fractures in the woman's lower arm bones, and the hyoid, the bone in the throat, was broken clean through in two places. The original pathologist attributed these to the heat of the fire, but Sebastien knew better. He knew the woman had been the victim of strangulation, and that she had fought back as best she could. Whoever murdered her then set her car on fire. It took some cajoling, but finally a fire inspector was brought in, and accelerants were detected.

Since that case, it had been the usual string of requests for his expertise—nonhuman bones found by hikers, the occasional suicide left out in the open long enough to require the skills of an anthropologist, and the ubiquitous Native American burial—these last were becoming more frequent as the suburbs forced their way farther east onto undeveloped tracts. In Sebastien's world, all these things were pretty run of the mill. He could use something new and hopefully challenging.

Sebastien had a good degree of self-awareness when it came to his own disordered thought processes. He was fully aware of the contradictory facts that he was both highly scientific and empirical, yet utterly irrational in most ways—especially in dealing with others. But, in an interesting way, this strange mix of tendencies—analytical, yet disordered—allowed him some very canny insights about himself. And it was one of these insights that ultimately tipped the scales in the direction of helping his brother.

It was an accidental discovery incident to a road trip made many years ago. Sebastien was asked to give the keynote address at the California Association of Property and Evidence annual meeting in Lake Tahoe. He had just taken over ownership of the Block, he was teaching at Cal, and his breakup with his long-time girlfriend was excruciatingly fresh. Everything was chaotic, and the pressure of all that new social interaction —with tenants, fellow faculty, and students—was eroding his sense of security. He felt wrapped in a blanket of anxiety, and his head seemed full of cement. He recalled many times driving up to the university, or even back home to the Block, wishing he could just keep going, just go right past, just disappear. But he wasn't sure why.

Then, on that road trip up to Tahoe, he had his epiphany. The farther he got from the university, the Block, and from everyone he knew, or knew him, the better he felt. He learned that the car could be, as much as his apartment certainly was, a haven for him. He just had to keep driving. The quadruple sensations of having a weight lifted, of being hidden, unknown, and unnoticed swaddled him in comfort, like a newborn, on that trip. And he never forgot it. It was the opposite of his personal status quo, in which his mind, irreversibly set to defensive mode and on high alert for danger, had no respite. To be sure, all of that returned when he got to the hotel and the obligatory mixers, dinners, and breakouts unfolded. He spent most of that conference in his hotel room looking forward to the drive back, which he determined to undertake a little more slowly.

It was not that he wanted, or needed, to be alone, to become a hermit; he was smart enough to recognize the impracticalities of a life in isolation. He did not mind being around people in the right context. Crowds did not bother him, because he could blend in. And even speaking to crowds of strangers—conference attendees, for example—did not cause him much anxiety. He was relatively good at presenting, plus he was the expert in those instances—he generally knew just a tad more than his audience, at least. And this, quite frankly, stroked his pride. It was the small talk that vexed him so. Interpersonal exchanges with anyone he knew, or was getting to know, caused him the greatest distress. He would be too busy monitoring himself and worrying about being judged to enjoy the encounter. It is impossible to be affable and charming when you are neither affable, nor charming.

And so, the farther he got from familiar people, the more comfortable he became. The social expectations decreased in direct proportion to the distance one traveled from his core area, he found. The stranger in the restaurant, the alien face in line at the gas station, the passerby—these held no terror for him, as long as he did not have to engage. The phenomenon was so reliable and consistent that Sebastien even gave it a name—the comfort of distance. And he could use some distance now. He was ready for a road trip. Of course, Hank could not understand why he wasn't just flying. It would be quicker, he had protested. "Sorry, Hank," Sebastien had said. "Beggars can't be choosers."

5

Susan Whitebear awoke to her neighbor's dogs barking, followed by insistent banging on her front door. She blindly patted the top of the nightstand until her fingertips found her glasses. She put them on and looked at her phone. 2:03. *Who the hell is beating on my door at this hour?* she thought.

She rolled out of bed, groggily wrapped herself in a robe, and took a few steps in the direction of the hall before recalling that not much good can happen at this time of night. She paused and reached under her bed, producing a twenty-gauge shotgun. The fact that it was loaded with birdshot did not bother her in the least. She'd seen what birdshot could do, the mess it could make.

"Who's there? I have a gun." Despite being terrified, she straightened her back to reach her full five-foot height and tried to make her gravely smoker's voice sound low and commanding.

A muffled voice came from the other side of the door. The words obviously being pushed through clinched teeth. "It's me. Open the door. Hurry!"

Susan removed the chain, then flicked the deadbolt and turned the knob. Mickey "Tiny" McCallister poured into her family room and quickly shut the door behind himself. Susan replaced the chain while Mickey held the door closed. It would seem he was being chased by a bear, or dinosaur.

Mickey spun around to face Susan—and the business end of a Mossberg turkey choke. "What are you doing with that thing? You're going to blow my head off," he said in full voice, as he pushed the barrel of the shotgun away.

"I didn't know it was you."

Mickey looked terrified. His nearly bald head was painted with beads of sweat. His hand shook as he pulled back the curtain and peered into the night.

"I will beat you, I swear, woman."

Susan knew that this was not an empty threat. She had been beaten by Mickey at seemingly regular intervals—especially when he was drunk, which was getting to be more frequent than when he was sober. And even when he was sober and in full control of himself, Mickey was prone to violence. He was not a man to be crossed. Not that Susan ever crossed him on purpose. No one did. Not since he'd knifed that man to death in Pierre for taking his favorite fishing spot. The twelve years in the pen in Sioux Falls had not helped his disposition in the least. The fact that he was only five-foot-three and a hundred and twenty pounds was no comfort to anyone. In fact, Susan believed it made him worse. Mickey's violence was his way of adding a few inches to his stature, she realized. Whatever the reason for the man's volatility, everyone knew not to piss off Mickey McCallister.

"What is going on? Why are you here?"

Mickey walked down the short hall into the bedroom and emerged a minute later. He was looking around nervously, obviously making sure Susan was alone.

"It's just me, Mickey. What has got you so rattled? Are you

drunk? I'll make you some coffee." Susan turned and walked the three steps required to be in the middle of the mobile home's small kitchen. As she reached to pull the coffee pot from the coffee maker, a sudden sharp pain erupted in the back of her skull, radiating forward through her eyes, which filled with fireworks.

Susan woke up on the kitchen floor. The back of her head felt like someone had drilled into it. Her ears rang loudly, and her neck was stiff. She turned herself over on the vinyl, turtle-like, and could see Mickey sitting at the kitchen table, rubbing his right fist with his left hand, a cigarette between his lips. His right knee was bouncing like a jackhammer.

It was clear he *had* been drinking again. And it was also clear that the paranoia, which seemed to have come over him these last few days, had reached a new high. Whatever he had been up to must be really bad, not to mention whomever he must be doing it with—she had never seen him so scared and on edge. His hair-trigger temper had now become a silk thread, fraying in the middle.

Susan grabbed the top of the counter with both hands and pulled herself up to her feet. Mickey showed no remorse or intention of helping her up; he just sat there staring into the table. She did not say a word, made no eye contact with the man who had just decked her from behind. The coffee pot could stay right where it was, on the floor, in a million pieces. She was going to go back to her room, lock the door, and maybe, just maybe, call the cops...for once.

Susan steadied herself with her left hand on the counter as she slowly shuffled out of the kitchen. She continued to avoid his eyes, while at the same time attempting to read his body language. Was he going to swing at her again? Or worse? The shotgun, which she had put down on the coffee table in the family room, was now sitting on the kitchen table, well within Mickey's reach.

Mickey made no movements as she approached the end of the kitchen floor and took a left turn onto the dining area carpet, between the dining room table and the end of the kitchen counter.

"Where are you going?" spat Mickey, while stubbing his cigarette out on the top of the table.

"Bed," she replied coldly, still avoiding his eyes. "I have to be at work in a few hours."

Suddenly Mickey stood up, sending his chair flying backward. He grabbed the front of Susan's robe, pulled her toward himself, then violently shoved her back into the kitchen. Susan slammed backward into the oven and once again fell to the floor, this time with a scream of pain as the oven handle bit into her back, just below her shoulder blades.

Mickey grabbed the shotgun from the table and straddled Susan. He stuck the barrel under her chin, put his mouth up to her left ear, and whispered sweetly, "You're not going anywhere until you give me some—"

About two and a half inches of coffee pot glass to the jugular turned Mickey's vile declaration into a choking gurgle. He dropped the shotgun and grabbed at Susan's hand reflexively, his eyes bulging. Blood poured down Susan's right arm as she drove the shard in deeper.

"What did you do? What happened?"

Collie Shermer gazed in stupefied horror at the pool of blood and the lifeless body on the floor. His large, jowly face had turned pale; his eyes approached the size of bread plates in his wide skull.

"He tried to shoot me! There! See the gun?" Susan pointed to the shotgun laying at the foot of the dishwasher, nearly obscured by blood.

"You shot 'em?!"

"No! I stabbed him. I had to, Collie. I swear. He knocked me down and jumped on me with the gun."

"Is he dead?"

"I think so. He hasn't moved since..."

"Where's the knife?" Collie grimaced as he steadied himself against the kitchen counter and leaned over to examine the body.

"No knife. I hit him with a piece of glass."

"Damn, Sue. Who is he?"

Susan paused, wondering whether to start lying now, or wait until later. She opted for the former.

"I don't know. He knocked on the door and barged in when I opened it. I think he was trying to rob me. Or rape me!"

"Well, we gotta call the cops, Sue. We gotta call the cops." Collie raised his hands to the sides of his head in a gesture of disbelief.

"No! No way, Collie. The cops will never believe that he attacked me first."

"Sure, they will."

Susan tried to remember how to pout. She pursed her lips, knitted her brows, and looked up at her erstwhile suitor pleadingly. Collie was desperate. He would help her. She just needed to turn it on a bit. She rushed at Collie's chest and wrapped her arms as far around him as they would reach. Collie pulled her in closer, his chin scraping the gray roots on the top of her head.

"Okay, okay. 'Course, I'll help ya." Collie patted her on the back.

"What do you think we should do?" asked Susan, looking up at him with wide brown eyes.

Collie broke free and sat down in one of the chairs in the dining area. He surveyed the body and the mess that surrounded it for several minutes.

"You got a tarp?" he finally asked.

Susan thought for a minute.

"I have one of those plastic sheets you put down when you paint. It's covering some junk behind the house."

"That'll work. Get it."

Susan returned with the plastic sheet balled up in her arms. Collie was standing now. He looked less panicked.

"I think I gotta plan. Let's get this guy rolled up. Then I'm gonna get my wrecker and bring it back here."

"I don't know, Collie. Those dogs might pitch a fit and wake the neighborhood if they hear your tow truck."

"What dogs?" asked Collie.

"You didn't hear barking when you got here?"

"No, Sue. There weren't no barking."

"Well, never mind then. My neighbor must've brought them in. So, what's your plan, anyway?"

Collie inclined his head toward Mickey's prone corpse.

"This guy's gonna steal your truck."

SUSAN REACHED in through the open driver's side window and steered as Collie pushed the old Ford Ranger from the back. It had been Shermer's idea to smash the windshield with a rock so that the gaping wound on Mickey's neck would look like it came from the windshield's flying glass as the truck careened down the embankment. But the broken bits of the windshield were everywhere. Susan was simultaneously trying to avoid getting cut and ignore the accusatorial stare of Mickey's bloated eyes as his head flopped on his shoulders.

Susan and Collie had conferred on the possible outcomes once gravity claimed the truck from the roadway, but neither had the benefit of an education in the basic principles of physics or geometry. Left to their own wits, they agreed that the key was going to be steering the truck in such a way that it would roll between a couple of ill-placed pine trees and hit the sharp drop-off to the canyon below. The truck's headlights illuminated the target zone; but Mickey's recriminating, bloodied visage was not helping.

One final "harrumph" from Collie and the truck gave way. Susan pulled her arm out just in time for the Ranger to break the apex of the slope and roll down. The truck indeed slalomed between the two large pines, and it very nearly made it to the sharp droff-off. But its momentum was far less than either expected, and the truck's progress was stopped by a particularly dense patch of fringed sagebrush.

Susan felt the rub of Shermer's shoulder against hers as she stood staring at the lane of broken vegetation and billows of dust. Shermer was panting heavily. "It didn't make it all the way down," she said.

"That's...uh...uh...okay," huffed Shermer, as he bent forward with his hands on his knees, working to keep his girth from toppling over. "Uh hm...far...enough. We uh...did... move...uh...seat, right?" Shermer's enormous head was cocked up at Susan.

"Yep. Didn't have to move it too far, though. Crazy short bastard."

Susan felt surprisingly satisfied. Like she had somehow set her world back on its proper axis.

"And...uh...rock...through window...you...uh...take it... uh...out?"

Susan hung her head and covered her eyes with her left hand. Her world was crooked again.

6

S ebastien left for South Dakota later than he had planned—he'd had to drop off Parsifal with his neighbor, Mrs. Kimble, and he wanted to let his other tenants know he would be gone.

There were only four apartments on the upper story—his large one, which took up a full third of the second story, and three smaller ones. Aside from Sebastien and Mrs. Kimble, the other permanent residents of the Block included a younger couple—professionals who kept largely to themselves, and Mr. Shelby, whose rare book shop was one of Sebastien's commercial tenants. How Shelby managed to afford the rent on both places, Sebastien did not know. But he paid on time.

The young professionals did not answer when Sebastien knocked, but Shelby emerged from his apartment just as he was headed in that direction.

"Sebastien, my friend. How are we on this fine Sunday? Are you coming to see me? I was just heading down to open up the store. I have a customer coming in—big fish; a big, big fish. He's going to clear out my Dickens and Faulkner, and I think I can talk him into one or two other things."

Shelby was a larger man, in his mid-sixties, spectacled, bald on top and gray around the edges. He gave the impression of a monk—which Sebastien reasoned was pretty much appropriate considering the man's chosen occupation.

"That's great! I'm actually heading out myself. I'm going to visit my brother in South Dakota. He needs my help with a few things."

"You never told me you had a brother! Lovely! You need me to take care of anything around here, like send a mafioso to collect the rent from Eric?" Shelby's eyes gleamed mischievously.

"Ha! No thanks. Just keep an eye out. Mrs. Kimble has Parsifal."

"Will do, old man!"

Sebastien turned to watch Shelby shuffle down the hall towards the stairs. He wondered whether the sophisticated and worldly bookman realized that he was still in his bathrobe and silk boxers. He considered asking, then decided to leave it alone.

"Oh, Sebastien, I forgot to mention," Shelby turned around just before he reached the corner at the end of the hallway, "I found a brilliant copy of Rossini's complete works. One volume—octavo in half leather. Published in 1869, the year *after* he died, as you know. It includes *Musique Anodine*. I don't have to tell you how significant *that* is, do I? Of course, it is currently in the possession of a dealer in Munich. Complete ass, and he *will* try to gouge anyone who walks by his shop. Come see me when you get back, and I'll show you the particulars. Bon voyage, Sebastien!"

Sebastien had no opportunity to respond before Shelby disappeared around the corner. What would he say anyway? The whole monologue seemed so weird coming from a man whose hirsute chest was pushing through a paisley robe while his boxer fly was open a few centimeters wider than good taste would permit—even in this day and age.

DESPITE THE LATE START, Sebastien was making good time. Although, it occurred to him somewhere around Sacramento that he was in no particular hurry. It also occurred to him, at about the same time, that he was almost recreating that momentous drive to Tahoe. In fact, it wasn't too late to make a detour and repeat the pilgrimage. He resolved to make a right turn on highway 50 and meander his way through the mountains, stopping at Lake Tahoe to breathe in some of that Sierra oxygen.

Sebastien had many times reflected that if someone ever came to him with that oft-asked poll—are you a beach person, or a mountain person?—he would most definitely register himself as the latter. It was an interesting thing, having been born and reared at sea level, with no particular sub-alpine history to speak of, that Sebastien had a great affinity for the mountains. He loved the thin air, the smell of the pine and fir, the sound of the wind stroking through needles. He hoped someday to retire, or retreat, to the mountains. And not surprisingly, green was his favorite color; it always had been. Were these predispositions? If so, were they genetic? He didn't think so.

Sebastien lingered in Tahoe for a while, and so he didn't get to Winnemucca until just before eleven. The diversion was worth it and recharged him considerably. He had stopped at a picnic area near the lake to watch the sun shimmer on the deep blue water, and even ate a late lunch at a restaurant next to Harrah's casino. He enjoyed people watching—in the crowd but not of the crowd, anonymous, hidden in plain sight.

There was a price to be paid, though. By the time he got to Winnemucca, there was only one hotel with a vacancy—a cheap, cookie-cutter franchise that could have easily changed the sign from "Hotel" to "Motel" without anyone being the wiser. It did feature a complimentary breakfast, at least. Which turned out to be worth every penny—a culinary Venn diagram where runny, tepid, and bland intersected on a paper plate. Sebastien counselled himself to stick to the name brand hotels going forward, preferably ones with stars next to their reviews.

MELISSA LEGRIS SHUT the faucet off and turned to face her husband. As she leaned against the counter, her tall frame formed a silhouette against the window over the kitchen sink. She brushed her straight blond hair from her forehead, then rested her hands on her wider than average hips.

"So, when does your brother get here?" she asked.

Hank was simultaneously digesting Melissa's pot roast and surveying the half-built stable behind the house. "Huh? Oh, uh, Tuesday morning some time. At least that's what his text said."

"How long has it been seen you've seen him?"

"Just as long as it's been for you. About two years. Mom's funeral," Hank answered.

Melissa sat down at the table. She looked earnest. "Is he staying with us?"

"Well, I thought he would. Why not? We have plenty of room." Hank moved his gaze from the backyard and fixed it on Melissa. He was afraid this might be an issue.

"Well, yes, I guess it's alright. Your brother is just so...well, he's just so..."

"Weird?" Hank finished her sentence for her.

"Well maybe not *weird*. Just a little different. I just can't read him. He never makes eye contact. It's kind of..."

"He's just shy, hon. He's harmless." Hank got up, walked behind Melissa, and wrapped his arms over her shoulders. He gave her a peck on the cheek, then spoke into her right ear. His goatee sandpapered her soft skin. "It will be fine, I promise. We're going to be working most of the time. There is a lot to do and, honestly, the investigation is completely stalled right now. I need to get some answers before total panic sets in."

"You really think Sebastien can help? This isn't just an excuse to fix the family, is it?"

Hank was a little hurt, but he let it go. "No, honey. I promise. Sebastien is a brilliant forensic scientist. I really think he can add something, and I really need you to go along with this, okay?"

"Okay, sweetheart." Melissa smiled and kissed him sweetly. "I trust you."

"Great. Thanks for understanding. Now, I'm going to go change and get some work done on the stable before it gets dark."

MELISSA once again stood at the sink as she watched her husband walk away. She did trust him, she knew. She'd just never really gotten a feel for his brother. When she'd first learned that Sebastien had a different last name than Hank, she assumed they had different fathers as well. She didn't catch the linguistic similarity between *LeGris* and *Grey*. Very clever. But was it necessary? "It's nothing, hon. He just wants to distance himself from the family a bit. There's a lot of baggage, a lot of damage," Hank had told her back then. Which inevitably led her to discovering just how onerous that baggage had been. Maybe that was her problem with Sebastien—she associated him with the family dysfunction only because he was the one who inadvertently led her to find out about it. At any rate, she was glad her husband was so resilient, that he seemed to take it all in stride, almost altogether unaffected by the death of their father, and the subsequent mental deterioration of their mother.

A figure passed in her periphery beyond the glass slider that separated the kitchen from the patio. It was Hank, in his ratty purple tank top, pushing a wheelbarrow full of tools toward the stable. His muscular arms flexed as he heaved the load over the dirt and rocks. He was wearing that stupid straw hat again—the one he'd bought to complete his scarecrow outfit last Halloween. An overpowering sense of love and gratitude welled up in her breast. She wiped a tear with the dish towel and turned again to the sink.

7

A mere few hundred yards from Hank's back yard, and at about the same time, Barry Van Lowe, of the state Department of Game, Fish and Parks, was guiding an old Jeep up a dirt road. Next to him, in the passenger seat, sat his partner Vern, who was poking a radio antenna out of the rolled-down window. A receiver about the size of two bricks was beeping softly on the seat between his legs. It was threatening to get dark, but they had tracked the cat this far and didn't want to lose it—especially as it was headed up a draw that ran between several ranches.

The mountain lion in question, the cat they had been following since about two-thirty, was none other than Male 323. M323 was a large three-year-old who was known to frequent yards and built-up areas. The state biologists had been tracking him actively for the last few days, prompted by a spike in complaints about missing pets. The goal was to dart him and relocate him farther west near the Wyoming border, but M323 was uncooperative. Unlike most mountain lions, he did not bed down and stay put during the day. He was a like a shark—always moving.

According to the receiver, M323 was about a quarter mile away, some fifteen degrees on their left. But with only about thirty minutes of daylight remaining, the mission might have to be called for the day.

"He stopped moving. He's somewhere up there," Vern said, extending his arm diagonally over the steering wheel. Go up a few hundred yards or so and park it."

Barry obliged and parked the Jeep farther up the road. Both men got out, and Barry retrieved a tranquilizer rifle from the back seat. Vern hung the radio receiver around his neck with a nylon strap and lifted the antenna over his shoulder. The men regrouped and started walking cautiously deeper into the draw.

The crackling sound of dry vegetation stopped them in their tracks. Barry pulled out some binoculars and scanned the trees. He saw nothing.

"We should have brought the dogs," whispered Vern.

"Just keep an eye out. You said he was, what, about ten o'clock." Barry pointed ahead and to his left a bit.

"Yep. He's got to be hiding in that patch of oak." Vern also pointed.   .

"Okay. Follow me," instructed Barry.

"You have the gun. Of course I'm going to follow you."

Barry headed to the left, perpendicular to the road. Leaving the road was noisier, with all of the deadfall, grass, and other vegetation crunching under their feet. But sticking to the road was not going to get them close to the cat, either.

About twenty-five yards off the road, Barry stopped, knelt, and brought the binoculars up to his eyes.

"Look there, under that big oak with the wonky branch." Barry passed his binoculars to Vern, who knelt next to him.

"Man, he's a big sucker. Looks about 160 or 170. That's way up from last year. Our boy's eating well."

From their location, the men were not covered at all. The mountain lion would surely be able to see them, not to mention smell them. Their best shot would be to get close enough to shoot the dart before they were noticed. Unless they had already been noticed.

Barry stood up and, in a hunched over position, walked toward the copse of oak. Vern followed slowly, nervously. Just as they were nearing the dart gun's range, both men heard the crack of a branch somewhere ahead, to the right. It sounded like it came from way on the opposite side of the road.

Vern looked through the binoculars. The mountain lion must have heard the noise as well; the cat was staring fixedly to their right. The cat got up and stalked off in the direction of the noise, which must have sounded to the lion like dinner.

"He's spooked. He's headed in the direction of the road," Vern said.

The men slowly doubled-back to the dirt road. The Jeep was parked about seventy yards behind them at this point. The receiver indicated that the cat was still up ahead to their left, and still moving. The pair of biologists, made a left up the road, trying to be as quiet as possible. There was no visual sign of the mountain lion, but both were looking hard, squinting their eyes in the growing grayness of the dusk. Vern checked the binoculars again, but they were becoming less and less helpful as the minutes passed.

About five minutes later, Barry paused in the middle of the road and straightened his back, which was beginning to stiffen. Vern sidled up next him, looking around nervously.

"Where is he? You still picking him up?" asked Barry, as he looked up the road in front of them.

"Good question. Let me loo—uh, Barry, look at this." Vern's whisper was urgent.

Barry looked down at the box, which hung from his partner's neck. "What the...." Both men reeled around quickly, looking for affirmation of what the receiver was telling them, and had been trying to tell them for the last ten yards or so.

There in the middle of the road was a massive mountain lion—cougar, Puma concolor, catamount, ghost cat, whatever you wanted to call it. It had been stalking them silently.

The cat was crouched, its huge leg muscles terminating at massive paws, its large, unblinking yellow eyes fixed like lasers on the men. It looked like a missile with big canines. The sight sent an adrenal rush through both men, who froze in fright.

Several seconds went by before Barry regained his wits. He raised the rifle and pointed it at the mountain line, trying to steady the barrel in his shaking hands.

"Jump up and down, make noise," he said, softly but urgently.

"Hey, cat! Hey, boy! Git! Go away! Boogey, boogey, boogey!"

Vern hollered and leapt in place like a lunatic, frequently bending down to scrape up some road dirt and toss it in the direction of the lion, who just stood there, like a statue, unphased by the antics before him.

Barry shuffled to his left while keeping the rifle trained on the mountain lion. The head-on angle was not going to allow him to get the dart placed where it needed to be. The lion's attention now looked to be split between Barry's shuffling and Vern's hopping. The tracking collar around its neck shook as its huge head moved left to right, trying to keep track of these strange creatures.

A resounding *ssht crack* echoed through the draw when the trigger on the tranquilizer rifle was pulled, the noise bouncing between the upward slopes on either side. Unfortunately, Barry had forgotten to load a dart—a mistake that, despite swearing his partner to secrecy, would haunt him for several years and be retold around many a campfire.

The noise jolted the mountain lion from his hunting mode and startled him enough to back up and hiss defensively at the men.

"What the hell happened?" Vern literally yelled.

"No dart! No dart!" cried out Barry.

The lion took two steps toward the men, ducking its head and hissing once more.

"Load it! Load the gun!" Vern shouted, as he bent down to scrape more dirt in the lion's direction.

"The darts are in the Jeep!"

The lion reared back and pounced. Barry screamed and dropped to the ground, throwing his feet in the air to repel the predator. It was unnecessary. The cat did not jump at them; it sprung just to their right and thirty feet beyond, into the brush on the east side of the road.

HANK HAD MADE RATHER good progress on the stable, he thought, as he stood back and surveyed the evening's work. Nearly two-thirds of the east side was now covered in reclaimed barnwood. He wondered silently, for probably the fourth time, whether he should stain it when all is said and done, or leave it as is. For the fourth time he decided to leave it unstained.

As Hank began cleaning up for the night, he thought he heard some voices coming from down in the trees behind his ranch, maybe even beyond the road at the bottom of the valley. It was hard to tell. It sounded like someone was yelling. It certainly wasn't a turkey; he was pretty certain of that. A sudden snapping sound rang up the draw, followed by a scream. It was definitely human.

He stopped loading the tools in his wheelbarrow and took his stepstool to the fence that bordered his property. On the opposite side stood a few sturdy oak trees. He squinted through the leaves and branches but couldn't see much farther. He waited, listening for a minute. It was difficult to tell through the ambience, but the distance muted sounds he thought could be human speech. If it was, it definitely was not yelling. It didn't sound like anyone was hurt or in trouble. Hank stepped down from the stool and resumed cleaning up his construction zone.

8

It was early the next day, Monday, when Hank was parked in his Tahoe at the intersection of Highway 16 and Avenue of the Chiefs, next to the little shack that stood guard over the tiny turn-out by the road. He was looking for red light runners and speeders, although he'd left his radar gun at the station, so all but the most obvious of the latter may get a pass this time around. Traffic wasn't his job, but ever since that kid got killed at this intersection a few years back, he'd gotten in the habit of parking here while he ate his breakfast.

His mouth was full of Danish swimming in lukewarm coffee when his cell phone rang. All he could manage for a salutation was a "umo."

"Hank, is that you?" It was Detective Tiffany Reese, his protégé and the rising star of the detective bureau.

He quickly swallowed the entire contents of his mouth, leaving a painful, doughy bolus in his throat. "Yeah, yeah. It's me. What's up, Tiffany?"

"We just got a call from Parole. Mickey McCallister's parole officer just tried to do an early morning check on him at Val's house, but he wasn't there. He was asking if we'd picked him up. I told him we hadn't, but I would check with you to see if you've seen him."

"No, I haven't seen him. He's probably just sleeping off a bender, though. Do you want me to run through town and check the garbage bins?" Hank was only half-kidding.

"If you don't mind. I'm heading out to Val's now. The PO said she's pretty worried—hasn't seen him since Saturday afternoon."

"Tell you what, I'll check town and meet you there."

"Sounds good. Thanks, boss."

Hank hung up the phone, stepped outside of the truck long enough to brush the crumbs from his shirt onto the pavement, then got back in and radioed his plans to dispatch. Exiting the lot, he turned left on 16, racing the yellow light.

It didn't take Hank long to run through Custer. The small town happened to also be the oldest European settlement in the Black Hills, and the birthplace of the Gold Rush there, yet it was not much bigger than back in those days. The downtown consisted of low one- and two-story buildings, circumscribed by pine-covered hills. Some of the buildings were original, with their establishment dates proudly carved into limestone and brick. Most had been converted into shops, bars, and restaurants that were the beneficiaries of a strong tourist industry.

After snaking his way through town—5th Street, right on Mt. Rushmore, left on 2nd Street, left on Washington, left on 5th, right on Custer—Hank could see no sign of Mickey. He even got out and fished through the dumpster behind the Rented Mule, but none of the bar's clients could be found reposing in the rubbish. He also checked in at the café and some of the souvenir shops, which were now beginning to open, but no one to whom he spoke had seen the county's least favorite son.

Farther east on Custer, he saw Homeless Mike, who had just emerged from Mickelson Trail and was heading toward him. He slowed the Tahoe, lowered the passenger window, and called out, "Hey-o, Mike!"

Mike's dirty face smiled wide as he walked up to the window, dragging a filthy unrolled sleeping bag behind him. "What's the word, Sarge? It's a fine morning."

"Yes, sir, it is. You doing okay? I see you coming out of the trail. Lots of people use it; I wouldn't want you getting run over by a bike. I recommend you stay out of there."

"Great minds, Sarge. I was just heading to Nan's. I won't be on the trail no more."

"Good, well hey..." Hank reached into the breast pocket of his uniform and pulled out a folded bill. "You take this, okay? Get yourself some pancakes at the café. I was just in there. They got their A-game going."

"Ah thanks, chief! You're the best cop who ever 'rested me." Mike unfolded the bill and smacked his lips lustily at Andrew Jackson.

"No problem. Hey, tell me, have you seen Mickey?"

Mike looked confused.

"I mean Tiny. Have you seen Tiny?"

"Oh, Tiny! That bastard! No, I ain't seen him for a few days. He almost ran me over! Light was red, too! Bastard!"

Hank put the Tahoe in park. "When was that, Mike? Do you remember? What day?"

"Well," Mike tucked the twenty-dollar bill down the front of his pants and rubbed his chin, "things kinda run together these days. Let me see. What day did we have the wood thing in town?"

"The chainsaw art show? That was Friday, Mike. Three days ago. Was it Friday you saw Tiny?"

"Nope, but the chainsaw guy paid me ten bucks to unload his truck."

Hank pulled off his sunglass and started to speak. "What does..."

"Hang on, hang on, captain. The chainsaw guy gave me ten, and it lasted until breakfast the next day."

"Ah, I follow you. So, the ten lasted until Saturday morning?"

"Yep. Of course, by that time I only had enough left for a coffee at that fancy place next to the rock store. You ever been in there? Three-fifty for a cup of coffee. Three-fifty!" Hank breathed out noisily, prompting Mike to continue. "Well, anyway, at around lunch time, this nice man—Oregon plates I think—was handing me a five when he was stopped at the light. Tiny ran between us on a motorcycle, right through the damn light, like a bat outta hell. Almost knocked that poor guy's mirror off. And you know what else? I didn't even get the stinkin' five! It blew away, and the guy took off."

This was interesting, thought Hank, as he watched Homeless Mike disappear back into Mickelson Trail through the Tahoe's side mirror. Mickey did not have a motorcycle, that he knew of anyway. He wondered whether he could have crashed somewhere in the hills. There were lots of twists and turns on these roads—which is why they were popular with riders in the first place. Maybe the Karma Department finally pulled Mickey's ticket and sent him flying over some precipice to his just desserts. He made a mental note to ask Val about the motorcycle as he pulled up to her small house and parked next to Tiffany's cruiser.

"Mrs. McCallister, I understand you haven't seen your son for a bit." Hank joined Val and Tiffany, notebook and pen in hand, on the front porch of the small house. Val's face was deeply wrinkled from years of hardship, most of which had been caused by her son. Hank couldn't tell whether the worried look in her eyes was new or a permanent feature.

"He's always coming and going," she offered. "But he's never been gone for more than a day or two. Except for, you know, his time in Sioux Falls."

"Speaking of Sioux Falls, when did he get out of prison? How long has he been staying with you?"

"Well, he came back from Sioux Falls last fall, around October, I think." Val was clearly dealing with some deep denial based on her choice of phrase, Hank noted. "But he was only here about six months. He got a job opportunity up north on one of those oil rigs, he said."

"Oh, he doesn't actually live here, with you?" Tiffany asked, looking a little confused. "His parole officer seems to think this is his address."

"Oh, it is now, dear. He showed back up a few weeks ago, and he's been staying here ever since."

Tiffany nodded in understanding and scribbled in her notebook.

"Well, of course, he told the man from parole that he was here now. He's really trying to clean up his life. I promise, he really is!"

"I'm sure he is," lied Hank. "Well, it's really only been a few days since you've seen him, hasn't it? That was, what, Saturday?" Hank looked over at Tiffany, who nodded. Val seemed to take no comfort in the observation.

Hank continued. "What time was it exactly—I mean approximately?"

"I got back from my hair appointment around three or so, and he was here—in the living room." Val gestured toward the front door. "We talked for a bit, then I went to lie down for a while. When I came back out, he was gone."

"What time was that?" Tiffany asked, pen at the ready.

"It was only an hour or so that I was resting."

"Sometime before four is when he left here, then," Hank surmised.

Val nodded.

"Did he tell you where he was going, or say anything to indicate his plans before you went to lie down?"

Val shook her head.

"How did he seem? You know, did he seem like anything was bothering him?"

"Not really. He was in his usual foul mood."

At this point, Tiffany spoke up. "Val, tell Sergeant LeGris what you told me, about the phone call, I mean."

"Oh, well, yes, that was odd. It was the Friday before last, in the evening. I was watching the TV when the phone rang—"

"I'm sorry, Val, the phone? Which phone? Your cell phone?"

"No, no, the one in the kitchen."

"The landline, you mean?"

"Yes, that one. I have a cell phone—one of those folding ones—but with my heart condition I thought it made sense to keep the home phone. You know, for calling nine-one-one."

"Sure, that makes sense. So, what about this phone call?"

"It was a man on the line. I didn't recognize the voice—not that I would have. Well, anyway, the man asked for Mickey. When I told him that Mickey was not home, he asked if I could take a message. I said sure. And the guy said, and this was a little weird, the guy said, 'Get a pencil and a piece of paper.' I told him I had one, right by the phone, and he said to write down a message for Mickey. So, I did."

"Well that doesn't sound too weird." Hank looked at his watch distractedly. He suddenly wondered how Sebastien's trip was going. "What did the message say?"

Val looked at Tiffany, who produced a small white piece of paper from between the sheets of her notebook and handed it to Hank. The paper appeared as though it had been balled up at some point, then flattened out. But the writing on the page was perfectly clear:

"Hey you Fatboy magit the boys in rapid are waiting those other fellas wont be the only ones"

"Okay, that is strange for sure." Suddenly Hank's attention

became less divided. "And you are sure this is the message the caller gave? Was there anything else?"

"The guy on the phone made me read it back to him."

Hank glanced over at Tiffany, who looked at him with an expression that said, *I know, right?*

"Hmm. And did you show this to Mickey?"

"Yep, the next morning when he woke up."

"And what was his reaction?" asked Hank, handing the note back to Tiffany.

"He just crumpled it up and threw it at me. I put it in the trash."

"But, I mean, did he say anything? Did he seem upset by the note? Besides throwing it at you, I mean?"

"Rude, by the way," offered Tiffany with a frown.

"Yes, well...I couldn't tell. He just put his boots on and took off. Didn't even eat before he left."

Hank suddenly snapped his fingers. "That reminds me. Does Mickey have a motorcycle by chance?"

"Why, yes. How did you know?"

"Do you know where he got it? Did he have it when he came back from up north?"

"No, he showed up with it a few days ago. I asked where he got it, but he wouldn't tell me. He didn't steal it, though, I'm sure of that. Like I told you, he's cleaned himself up. He's really trying."

"Okay, well, thanks Val. We'll keep an eye out for him. I'm sure he's around somewhere. If you happen to get any more calls, can you just let me, or Tiffany, know. Here's my card. Tiffany..."

"Yep, I gave her mine when I got here," Tiffany interjected.

"Great. Just give us ring if he calls back, or if you can think of anything else. And, of course, if Mickey shows up."

Tiffany was giving a teary Val McCallister a gentle, concerned hug on the porch as Hank walked toward the Tahoe, his feet crunching the dirt and rock under his feet. He was walking slowly, trying to conserve energy for his brain, perhaps. Something about this brief interview bothered him; it was something he wanted to ask but forgot. Hank lingered at the driver's side door, fingers under the latch, for an extra second before he pulled it open. And, just before he stepped in, it came to him. He spun around sharply, making a grinding sound with his boot heel. "Hey, Val. One last thing. The guy who called, did he ask for Mickey, or Tiny?"

Val brought her forefinger to her pursed lips and knit her painted-on eyebrows as she thought back to the mysterious phone call. "Well, now that you mention it, he asked for Tiny."

ABOUT AN HOUR OUT OF CASPER, the tedium of high desert tans and browns succumbed to sporadic irrigated green patches, signaling the outskirts of Wyoming's version of civilization. The final notes of Wagner's Götterdämmerung coincided with a rest stop, so Sebastien availed himself of one last bladder drain before reaching the Marriott in town.

He shook his hands vigorously upon exiting the restroom—there were no paper towels—and as he did, he caught sight of a large herd of pronghorn in a field a mere fifty yards away. He had never seen pronghorn in person before. He got as close as he could until a barbed-wire fence kept him from proceeding beyond the rest stop boundary. Watching the antelope hop around gracefully, coupled with the smell of sage, made him rethink this little adventure. He was incontrovertibly in foreign territory, clearly not home. The air was thick with uncertainty and, despite the beauty of his surroundings, a sediment of unease began to accumulate at the bottom of his mind.

One of the pronghorns got spooked and broke off from the herd, bounding and galloping farther from the rest area.

Sebastien looked to his right and saw a man walking a large dog next to the fence line, which apparently spooked the antelope. The lightning fast escape of the skittish pronghorn triggered a sudden impulse to flee, go back to Vineyard, and shut himself in his apartment. But he had come this far. It would be stupid to go back now.

9

s promised, Sebastien phoned Henry when he left the hotel in Casper on Tuesday morning, letting him know that he was less than a few hours out. Henry seemed genuinely happy and anxious to get started. He gave Sebastien the address to the coroner's office and asked him to go right there. *Good,* thought Sebastien. *No familial formalities. Let's get right to business.*

The drive from Casper to Custer took Sebastien through a moonscape of high plains punctuated by limestone bluffs and rifts, with the occasional patch of low pine to break up the monotony. Sebastien spotted a few more herds of pronghorn, and even saw what he took to be a coyote loping placidly about twenty-five yards to the west of the highway.

The road began a gentle ascent after he turned east onto Highway 18. The greyish limestone was shortly overcome by green prairie grasses and more pine trees—these much taller than those he saw earlier in the day—perched on hummocks on either side of the road. Low, dark humps in the distance signaled the pediment of the Black Hills themselves. Sebastien quickly grasped how they had gotten their name.

His meditations on the natural beauty of the place must have slowed his pace considerably. A line of motorcycles passed him noisily on the left, engines revving, unhelmeted heads shaking their disdain. A woman on the back of the last bike to pass him offered a parting middle finger. As the hills grew ever larger in the windshield, Sebastien wondered whether this was a portent of things to come.

THE LADY at the front desk of the coroner's office seemed to be expecting him. She smiled brightly when he introduced himself through the reception window and promptly hit a button somewhere, precipitating a buzzing sound, accompanied by a latch clicking free. "Come on in," she said, pleasantly.

There were four people in the autopsy suite when the receptionist led him in. Henry-slash-Hank was leaning against a counter where scales, jars, boxes of gloves, and other accoutrement of the death investigation business were kept. His brother looked older, of course—his brown goatee flecked with gray, his hair longer now, swept back rather than parted. He was perhaps a little softer around the middle, too. But he still looked strong and athletic, manly even.

"Nice beard," Sebastien declared, his hand extended as he walked toward his brother. Hank took it then pulled him in for a one-armed hug. Sebastien felt exposed and awkward and broke it as quickly as he could.

"You look great, little brother. Nice togs."

Sebastien looked down at himself briefly, wondering if his choice of clothing was eliciting genuine approbation or ridicule.

"Let me introduce you around," Hank said. "This is Dr. Rose, our pathologist. And this is one of our coroner's investigators, Gerry Good Crow. And Tiffany Reese here is one of our detectives."

Sebastien shook hands with each. "It's uh, good to meet you all. Thanks for inviting me up."

"We've heard a lot about you. We're looking forward to the help," said the woman, who struck Sebastien as looking a bit like the dark-haired lady from that improbable forensic television show—the name of which he could not recall. She was rather tall—probably approaching five-foot-eight—with a fit, rectangular shape. Her brown, medium-length hair was parted down the middle and bobbed just below her shoulders.

"Well hopefully Henry didn't tell you too much." Sebastien noticed Gerry's bronze face and dark eyes form a smirk. He wondered what he'd said that was funny.

"Oh hey, Sebastien, I think I may have mentioned...it's Hank up here. I wouldn't want these yahoos to think I'm too uppity, right?"

"Yeah. You did. Um...sorry." Sebastien felt like he had just revealed a secret. But it passed when everyone giggled.

"Well, you're probably tired from all the driving, Doctor LeGris. Let's get going so you can grab some rest."

Sebastien decided not to correct Dr. Rose on his name. And he was thankful that Henry, er Hank, did not either.

Dr. Rose had been standing in front of a stainless-steel autopsy table, and, as he spoke, he stepped to the side of it, revealing two cardboard boxes. "Let's do these one at a time, shall we? After all, as far as we know, they have nothing to do with each other."

"That would be one hell of a coincidence," Gerry offered.

The pathologist proffered a pair of purple nitrile gloves, and Sebastien forced his hands into them. He carefully opened the first box, exposing a clear plastic bag within. He took the bag out and set it on the table. As he was doing this, Doctor Rose took the second cardboard box and placed it on the counter to avoid having the bones accidentally end up in the wrong boxes.

Sebastien removed the remains from the plastic bag with both hands, delicately, as if it were a priceless heirloom. He scanned the skull, rotating it and lifting it in both hands. What he was looking at was probably ninety percent of a human skull. The face was fractured severely; the broken pieces were held together by desiccated tissue. The mandible, or lower jaw, was present but not attached. The back of the skull was largely intact, with a bright white substance stuck approximately where the back of the neck would have attached to the head in life. Some strands of muddy hair were stuck to the cranium. The maxilla, the upper jaw, was missing a large chunk of bone on the left side, along with the incisor, canine, and premolar that would have been set in that part of the jaw. Yes, it was trauma. Significant trauma. Horrible trauma.

Sebastien next picked up the mandible and scanned it carefully. He paid special attention to the teeth. He noted that the second molar on the right side was missing, and the socket was filled in with bone. There was a similar filled in socket on the left side were the premolar would be. The teeth that were still in the jaw showed significant restorations; fillings and crowns could be found in probably a half dozen of the mandibular teeth.

"Wow! This is absolutely beautiful, absolutely perfect," Sebastien whispered softly, after putting the jaw down and stepping back. The others heard it.

"What do you mean beautiful?" asked Tiffany. "Looks pretty gross to me."

"Yeah, what do you mean, Sebastien?" echoed Hank.

"Well, you don't often see such a perfect example in real life of a phenomena that most people only read about in textbooks." Sebastien continued to regard the skull as he gave his answer. "You see, what you have here is an absolutely perfect example of a Lefort fracture."

"A Lefort fracture?" asked Gerry.

Dr. Rose's eyes widened perceptibly as he muttered, "I didn't even think of that."

"Well, they are relatively rare because they result from a specific kind of trauma, or kinds of trauma. I've only seen it one other time. In a forensic sense, they can be difficult to identify unless the pieces of the skull, the fractured bits I mean, are found together. Which is not always the case in decomposed bodies. But here the desiccated tissue of the face is holding them together. So, we can recreate the puzzle, retrace the trauma."

"What kind of trauma are we talking about, exactly?" asked Gerry.

Sebastien opened his forensic case, which was on the counter next to Hank, and pulled out a large, square bean bag. He put it on the autopsy table and laid the skull on top of it. With the skull propped up on a soft, malleable surface, Sebastien fit the jaw into the sockets under the skull, then set about fitting the pieces of the face together as best he could. This process took him a good ten minutes. The others were transfixed.

"Okay, so you see, I was able to put the face back in anatomical position, for the most part. But even though the whole thing looks like an eggshell broken into pieces, if you look carefully, you can see that there are actually three major breaks."

Dr. Rose approached the skull and brought his face in for a closer look. He scanned over Sebastien's handiwork for several minutes, making a popping sound with his tongue and occasionally repeating, "uh-huh." Suddenly, he stood erect and said, "Transverse through the naso-frontal and maxilla-frontal sutures and the orbital wall; pyramidal from the nasal down through the alveolar ridges on both sides; and horizontal through the maxilla. Yep, I see it now."

"Wait, what?!" Hank had no patience for the technical talk. "Can you just tell us what happened?"

"This person has been beaten in the face so hard that the upper jaw has been separated from the middle of the face, which has been separated from the upper face, which has been separated from the forehead. And look here, in the mandible." Sebastien picked up the lower jaw in one hand and used the forefinger of the opposite hand as a pointer. "You see this part on the left side of the mandible? This is called the ascending ramus, and it connects to the skull in the temporo-mandibular joint, the TMJ."

Gerry subconsciously put his left fingers on the side of his jaw and opened his mouth repeatedly as he listened.

"Well, anyway," continued Sebastien, "see here, the ascending ramus is cracked, just below the condyle—I mean where the jaw would connect to the skull."

Indeed, the others saw it clearly; there was a crack about half of an inch long.

"If you press gently on the crack, you can see part of the bone push inward, then sort of 'bounce' back. This was not postmortem. This fracture happened to fresh bone."

Sebastien was hitting his stride now. This was definitely worth the trip. They needed him, and he knew it. "Let me show you something else," he said, placing the jaw back on the table. "Look here in the maxilla, the upper jaw, I mean. Notice, it is completely missing about an inch square of bone. My guess is it's..." Sebastien paused to look in the bag and box in which the skull had been stored, then continued. "Yep, the piece that broke off is still out there somewhere."

"We looked everywhere. We even had a dog searching," offered Hank.

"How do you know this person was beaten and all this trauma is not just part of decomposition, or maybe a cow stepped on it?" asked Tiffany.

"No, no. That is not possible. Skulls do not just fall apart like this." It was a disquisition now. "In the early nineteen hundreds, a French doctor named Renee LeFort experimented with cadavers. He wanted to see what kind of trauma would result from blunt force to the face. So, he literally beat the cadavers in the face from different angles and with different objects."

"That is horrible," said Tiffany, puckering her face in disgust.

"Yes, well, it was also very useful. Anyway, what Lefort figured out was that with the right kind of trauma, the upper jaw could be separated from the face—that was called a *Lefort one* fracture; the midface, essentially the nose area, could be separated from the upper face—that is called a *LeFort two*; and the entire face could be separated from the forehead through the eye sockets, which is a *Lefort three*."

Dr. Rose chimed in. "We have a Lefort three here. Dr. LeGris is right. This person was beaten in the face."

"Gosh, that's horrible." Tiffany's face grew pallid. She looked like she might be sick.

"If it helps any, I think the person who did this was right-handed." Sebastien was smiling, like he'd just found a hundred-dollar bill in the pocket of an old blazer.

"So, can we rule out a mountain lion?" asked Gerry.

Sebastien twisted his lip in thought.

"Technically, it's trickier than that. While what I am seeing in the skull tells me that this person was beat in the face, without the rest of the remains, I can't make that conclusion. Though, admittedly, it seems likely that we can rule out a mountain lion. But I would not commit that to paper at this point."

"That's very scrupulous of you," offered Dr. Rose.

"That's my brother. Captain Scrupulous," joked Hank.

Sebastien felt himself flush. He hoped it wasn't noticeable.

"Well, what can you tell us about this person? Age? Sex?

Race? And can you give us an estimate of how long it's been out there?" asked Hank.

"It's definitely male. The areas just over eye orbits—the supraorbital ridges—are slightly elevated. Here, if you run your finger just above where the eyes would have been you can feel them."

Only Dr. Rose volunteered, nodding as he swiped his fingertip over the area where Sebastien indicated.

"And there are two other places that indicate male. Here, just behind the ear canal, this bump is called the mastoid process. It's larger in males and tends to protrude a bit. This is an anchor point for muscles that go down to the collarbone and sternum—the sternocleidomastoid muscles; it's the rope-looking muscle in the side of the neck. Anyway, males usually have larger muscles than females, and thus larger muscle attachments. The mastoid processes on this person are pretty large."

"You said two more places. What's the other?" Gerry asked, as he ran his finger down the right side of his neck, trying to find his sterno-whatever muscle.

"Same concept. In the back of the skull, just under this fatty tissue..."

"So, it is fat," said Dr. Rose, grateful that he got something right.

"Absolutely. And just under it is the nuchal torus, the bump at the back of the skull. Again, this is where muscles attach, and, again, this person's is pretty big."

Tiffany began to forget about the horrible way the owner of this skull died as the fascination of the science overtook her. "And what about race?"

"Race is a cultural construct; it's not real."

Hank shot him a look. "That doesn't help us."

"I know, I know. I'm just trying to educate the public. Anyway, by far the most diagnostic area for determining biological ancestry—race—is the skull. But here, the skull is too deformed for reliable measurements. I do see a couple of traits that indicate potential Asian inheritance, though. That nuchal torus in the back of the skull has a little 'hook' in the bottom of it. See?" Sebastien picked up the skull in both hands and held it up to each of the others. "And the ear canal is somewhat ovoid, oval in shape. Also indicating Asian."

"So, you're saying this guy is Asian?"

"No, Hen...Hank. I'm exactly not saying that. What I am saying is that this person has some traits that are indicative of Asian ancestry. Yes, he could be Asian, but he could also be Native American or Hispanic—two groups that share Asian genes going back several thousand years. Heck, he could also be Caucasian or even Black. Humanity is just a big genetic jumble at this point."

Hank looked a little irritated, and Sebastien considered that he had probably been too direct. This was one of his bigger flaws. Tact and diplomacy were not part of his genetic inheritance for sure.

"What about age?" asked Tiffany.

"Tooth eruption gives us a fully grown adult, as does the fusion of the spheno-occipital synchondrosis—that's a small suture between bones at the bottom of the skull. The sagittal suture—the line from front to back on the top of the skull—is still mostly present, so probably not elderly. I know that is not immensely helpful, but the best parts of aging a skeleton are still out there somewhere."

All four of the others nodded, even though only one of them understood the jargon.

"This is all super helpful, actually. It definitely gets us further than we were before. What about postmortem interval?" Dr. Rose asked.

Sebastien carefully turned the skull upside down—it was still in his hands—and stuck his nose in the hole at the bottom, where the spinal cord connects to the brain. He then took in a big whiff, like an oenophile would do to an Egon Muller Riesling.

"You did *not* just stick your nose in that skull and smell it!" Tiffany exclaimed, with a sour face.

Hank visored his eyes with his right hand. Gerry and Dr. Rose were both belly-laughing.

Sebastien turned red and inwardly raged. What the hell did they expect him to do? If they didn't want his help, then he'd just go home.

Hank must have picked up on Sebastien's half-stifled anger. "That's okay, Sebastien. Hey, whatever works, right? So, any ideas?"

"Not more than about six months or so. There's still a strong smell of decomposition, and the bone itself is still oily."

"Perfect. Well done, doctor. How about we now take a look at the jawbone that was found—what would you say, Hank, about six miles from where the skull was found, as the crow flies?" Dr. Rose spoke as he replaced the skull in the bag and box and traded it out on the counter with the smaller box the jawbone was kept in.

"That's about right," said Hank. "This was found off a fire service road. Some utility workers were checking on a cell tower when they stopped to take a leak. As they were doing their business, one of them spotted it at the bottom of a dry creek a few yards away."

Dr. Rose pulled the jaw out of the bag and box and handed it to Sebastien. Sebastien eyed it carefully for a minute, then said, "Not much I can tell here. The mental eminence—or chin —looks pretty square, and the bone is large overall, which indicates a likely male. The third molars have fully erupted, which means the person was over eighteen or nineteen at death. It's not ancient, or prehistoric, based on tooth wear, and the fact that there are several fillings, some of which are gold. That would indicate an older person probably, early middle-aged at least. They don't do gold fillings much anymore. The dental work also suggests someone who, at least at one time, had enough resources to access decent dental care."

"Oh really? Is that all you can tell," said Gerry with a laugh. The rest followed suit. Except for Sebastien, who was trying to figure out what the joke was.

"Any idea if this bone and the skull are about the same age? You know, have they been out there for about the same length of time?" This from Tiffany.

"There is nothing to indicate that one is much older or younger than the other. These were both surface finds, correct?"

Hank and Tiffany both looked at Gerry for help with the terminology. "Yes. The jaw was on the surface of the creek bed. We assume it got washed down from farther up the creek some time during the spring."

Sebastien frowned skeptically and shook his head.

"What?"

"Nothing. Just thinking. What about the skull?"

Gerry continued. "The skull was stuck in some mud, but not buried. It was visible. The lady who owns the property saw it there."

"Her dog, actually," corrected Hank.

"Yeah, her dog."

"Well, this has been very enlightening." Dr. Rose started packing up the jaw. "But I am due in court this afternoon. Call me if the rest of the remains decide to make an appearance— either one. I'm too old to be picky. It was nice meeting you, Dr. LeGris. We really do appreciate you coming all the way up to our little patch of heaven and helping us out. I trust you will write up your findings for us?"

10

That same morning, at around eleven o'clock, the staff at the Game, Fish, and Parks office were having a great time. As usual, Vern couldn't keep his big trap shut, and by mid-morning everyone knew about Barry forgetting to load the dart and letting M323 slip away. By 11:00 am, the surface of Barry's desk was completely covered with unfilled dart syringes, left there by his colleagues as a reminder of his faux pas. One of the more creative staff members had even printed a two-foot by three-foot picture of M323 with the words "Miss Me?" printed along the top, and pinned it to the wall over Barry's desk. Of course, it would all blow over, Barry knew. He deserved the ribbing, and, quite frankly, if it had been Vern who had forgotten the dart, he would pretty much have taken the same approach—humiliation. Barry was a real philosopher. Although, whoever made that poster really was a bastard.

The thing that bothered Barry more than the office hazing, and the thing he couldn't get through the thick heads of the others, was M323's behavior, it's boldness. That cat had stalked two grown men, both nearly two hundred pounds and both approaching six-foot-tall, and then just stood there when its cover was blown. That was not typical mountain lion behavior. Mountain lions are opportunity hunters and ambush predators. They don't attack when outnumbered and usually don't attack things much bigger than them—or at least, in this case, taller. And when they lose the advantage of surprise, they usually, *usually*, retreat, unless the prey is a lot smaller or sick. But M323 just stood there, staring at them like it wasn't bothered. And the sound of the dart gun did not send him scrambling either. He just casually bounded up the draw when the trigger was pulled. This was bothersome. M323 was trouble, and these chuckle heads were too busy laughing to the listen to the facts—the *real, important* facts.

Barry suddenly got an idea. He walked over to Vern's desk and picked up the trashcan that was sitting next to it. Vern sat there and watched in disbelief as Barry emptied the entire contents of the can onto the top of Vern's desk—soda cans, crumpled paper, gas station sandwich wrappers, and more than one paper coffee cup holding a dark mixture of saliva and chewing tobacco. Barry swept all of the dart syringes from his desk and into the newly emptied can. He then sat down, put his earphones in, and hit "play" on his iPhone. *Heartache and Misery* by Clutch blasted into his non-ovoid ear canals.

Barry worked the mouse quickly, anxious to see whether his hunch was correct. He opened the last two week's tracking data for M323. It took him several minutes to analyze everything and make sense of what he was seeing. But it became just as clear on his computer screen as it was in the draw last night: M323 was hugging to the margins of the residential areas and ranches, moving in a northerly direction—Hot Springs—Pringle—Custer.

Next, he opened the email he'd received from Custer County with a listing of all the missing pet reports. He would need to put in a call to Fall River County to see what reports they had down there, but the data he did have painted a compelling picture. M323 had no fear of populated areas and was in or near the location of seventy-four percent of the missing pet reports in Custer County. This was alarming. The occasional missing pet or report of lion wandering into civilization was one thing. But M323 was actively subsisting on pets, it seemed. Would a small child be next?

～

THE SUN WAS BLINDING their dilated eyes as Sebastien, Hank, Tiffany, and Gerry emerged onto the parking lot of the coroner's office. Gerry put on a large pair of aviator sunglasses with gold rims as he gestured them all into a huddle.

"So, Sebastien, do you think it would help if you saw the areas where the remains were found? Any insight it would give you?"

"I would definitely like to, if it's not too much trouble," he answered.

"Oh, it's not too much trouble at all," cut in Hank. "That's our next stop after lunch. "Gerry, Tiffany, coming with?"

"I could kill a bison burger," Tiffany mumbled through her teeth, which were gripping the temple of her sunglass frames while she gathered her chocolate brown hair in her hands behind her head, working a rubber band over the resulting ponytail.

"I'll have to meet you there," said Gerry. "Say about one thirty?"

"That works. We'll see you up at Bill's."

As Gerry walked to his truck in the employee section of the parking lot, Hank turned and started for the Tahoe. "Let's take my...holy crap! Is that your car?" Hank pulled the newly situated sunglasses off his head and pointed at the green Range Rover parked between his Tahoe and Tiffany's cruiser.

"Ho-ly crap," Hank repeated. "Look at you, little brother. Maybe I was wrong; maybe you got the better deal."

"Deal?" asked Tiffany.

"My little brother here inherited a building from our mother, while all I got was a bunch of cash."

"I don't recall you complaining at the time," offered Sebastien.

Tiffany turned toward Hank. "Wait, you're rich?"

Hank ignored the question, put his face up against the driver's side window of the Rover, and whistled. "Leather. Nice. Looks like a luxury jet. I bet it handles like one, too. What's the exterior, forest green?"

"Spectral British racing green, actually."

"Of course it is," said Hank.

"What's that supposed to mean?" Sebastien bit back.

"Oh nothing, nothing. You just always were a lot classier than me. Nice ride. So, everyone hop in." A chirp came from the Tahoe as Hank unlocked the doors with the key fob.

"Screw that!" exclaimed Tiffany. "I'm going with Sebastien." Before either of the men could comment, Tiffany was making her way for the passenger door of Sebastien's car.

"Sure, I can drive us," offered Sebastien, not feeling like he had a choice.

"You two ride together. I'll take the Tahoe. *One of us* should actually be in our county vehicle since we are *both* on duty." Hank was smirking. Tiffany stuck out her tongue at him and hopped into the Rover.

"So, which way? Did you say something about a bison burger?"

Tiffany was running her hands along the leather seat and dashboard and looking around like she might find drugs in the car.

"Oh, yeah. Turn right here, then left on the main street up

there. There's a burger joint in Pringle. Well, it's more like a bar, but they have great food."

Tiffany directed Sebastien to highway 89 where he made a left and headed south. As usual, Sebastien was stuck for what to say to this relative stranger who was feeling up his car. Fortunately, Tiffany was not so afflicted. "So, this has been a very surprising day. Lots of new information."

"Well, I'm glad I could help. I think you have plenty to get started on a possible ID at least. And you can be fairly sure it was a homicide. That usually helps when it comes to resources and manpower, I've found." Sebastien spoke from experience.

"Oh yeah, sure. Definitely helpful. But I'm also talking about you and Hank, or should I say Henry." Tiffany was smiling wide as she looked forward through the windshield.

For a split second, Sebastien saw her not as a law enforcement officer but as a woman—a pretty, young woman, maybe just a few years younger than he was. He took in her profile, her check structure, the way her zygoma protruded just enough to give her a slightly flatter face than the average Caucasian. He wondered whether she could be Native, like Gerry, or even part Native. Although, her skin was a warm ivory, her nose slight and turned upward, her lips lavish and wide. Sebastien seemed to do this a lot—analyze faces and visualize the skulls beneath them. Was that ghoulish or inappropriate? he wondered. Probably. He should ask Tina.

"I had no idea my boss was a wealthy heir," Tiffany continued.

"I wouldn't say that we're wealthy. Before our mom died, she had burned through most of what our grandfather left by collecting husbands and boyfriends." Tiffany did not reply, and, after a few minutes, Sebastien added, "Sorry, that was probably too much information."

"Oh no. I'm sorry. I didn't mean—"

"No, it's fine. There's a lot of dysfunction in the family, and

I'm probably the poster child for it. Anyway, Hank and I did okay. I just got pretty lucky because real estate in the Bay Area went ape after the recession of 2008 settled down. So, the building is worth a lot and brings in decent income. It is a bit of a hassle to manage, though. But I don't mind too much."

Sebastien naturally began to wonder whether he was giving too much away. But he decided not to care.

Tiffany fell into silent thought as she evidently took all this in and for the next several minutes they both sat quietly as the Rover purred down 89, passing granite and pine on either side. At about the time they blinked through Sanator, Tiffany asked, "Is that why you changed you name? The family drama, I mean."

"How did you know about that?"

"Hank told me."

"You and he seem pretty close, considering he's your boss. I like the way you give it back to him." Sebastien hoped his changing the subject would go unnoticed.

"Oh yeah, we've been lovers for years now."

Sebastien tried to hide his alarm, but he couldn't.

"I'm kidding, you dope!"

Sebastien exhaled loudly.

"We do get along pretty well though. Hank believes in me, and he treats me like a capable detective. I can't say the same about all of my colleagues."

"Because you're a woman?"

"Yes. And thanks for noticing."

Sebastien deliberately left that one alone.

"So, how did you get interested in forensic anthropology?"

"It was just something that I became interested in at school. Well, biological anthropology really. And archaeology, for that matter. Forensics is a great application of both of those things to modern problems. Fortunately, my school was pretty heavy into forensics at the time. We handled the forensic anthropology for four counties. There was plenty of opportunity to learn, plenty of cases to work."

"When my brothers and sisters and I were kids, our mother always used to ask us, 'What was your favorite thing?' Every time we went on a date, to a dance, to a movie, or on a family vacation, she always wanted to know what we liked best about it. Heck, she still does, for that matter."

Sebastien wasn't quite sure where this was going. His face must have showed his lack of understanding.

"What is your favorite thing about forensic anthropology?"

"Oh, sorry. Yep. Umm. Probably just the fact that so much information can be gained from a skeleton. You can recreate who the person is—was—and what their life was like, to a certain extent. It's like a big puzzle. I'm very empirically minded. I like facts. Hank will probably tell you that I'm too analytical. He thinks I see facts where there are none."

"Wouldn't that make you crazy? Like, insane?" Tiffany made a goofy face, pulling back her lips to expose her beautiful straight teeth, crossing her eyes and crinkling her small nose.

Sebastien laughed. "You have no idea."

"It is really fascinating, though," Tiffany continued. "There was a time I wanted to be a crime scene investigator, but I was horrible at chemistry, and apparently that's an important thing. Whatever."

They both laughed. Sebastien found it heavily ironic that she reminded him of the girl in the forensic show when they first met. The resemblance was less marked to him now, but the collision of facts could not be ignored.

"So, what about you? Why police work?" he asked her.

"When I washed out of science, I changed my major to criminal justice. It made sense since I come from a law enforcement family. My father was the sheriff until a few years ago, and my brother is a lieutenant in the jail." Tiffany must have noticed a hint of thought in Sebastien's face. "And, no, neither of them got me this job, thank you very much. Top of my class in the academy."

"I believe it," he replied, utterly serious.

"Here, up ahead on the right."

Sebastien slowed the car and put on his signal. He could see Hank's Tahoe in his sideview mirror doing the same. The parking lot of Fortney's Roadhouse was almost full, but both men found spots for their respective vehicles and the three joined up at the front door to the bar.

The place was very dark, the walls covered with reclaimed barnwood, stained russet. Vintage metal signs spackled the walls and scarcely reflected the pale-yellow light that emanated from several crude wagon wheel chandeliers hung from the ceiling. Sebastien scanned the room and instantly felt over-dressed. He committed to himself to wear jeans the rest of the trip, feeling glad that he'd decided to bring a pair at the last minute.

A woman appeared from the darkness carrying menus. "How many? Three? This way," she said, leading them to a table on the wall next to the massive U-shaped bar.

"Wow, you guys are busy today," remarked Tiffany, as she sat down.

"Yep. It's the rally," advised the hostess.

Sebastien looked questioningly at the others. "Rally?"

"You haven't heard of the Sturgis Motorcycle Rally?" asked Tiffany, incredulously, as the hostess retreated into the murk.

"No, I haven't. I'm not sure why I would have."

Hank looked up from his menu. "It's only the biggest motor-cycle rally in the world—at least, that's what I've been told. For ten days each August, six hundred thousand motorcycle enthu-siasts storm Sturgis on the northeast edge of the Black Hills. It's one big party."

"By *enthusiasts,* your brother means bikers."

"Well, yes. But the overwhelming majority of them are the

weekend warrior types—hardworking nine-to-fivers who see the rally as a chance to cut loose. Not the outlaw motorcycle gang types. Although, we get plenty of those as well."

"I bet it gets crazy, all the same," suggested Sebastien.

"Oh yes, it does. If you are law enforcement, like Tiffany and me, it can be hell. Especially if we volunteer, or are volun-told, to work the rally. But down here, in this county, it really just amounts to added motorcycle traffic and more people walking around town. Up in Sturgis, it's drunken fist fights and puke-covered streets."

"Sounds charming."

"It's also a lot of fun. You should take Sebastien up there while he is in town. He looks like the type who would love it." Tiffany snickered a bit.

"Well, the last I checked, they weren't doing any operas up there. Are we ready to order?"

Sebastien was a little hurt at Tiffany's sarcasm and embarrassed by Hank's reference to opera. He suspected it was intended to insult. He buried his face in his menu and pretended to mull over his choices.

"Bison burger for me," said Tiffany.

Hank waved the server over. A young man in his early twenties with a small metal bar through his right eyebrow and spiked blond hair responded to the table. "Hey there, Sergeant LeGris, Detective Reese."

"Hello, Todd, how's business?" Hank responded.

"Crazy as ever. No trouble, though. So that's good."

"Were you expecting trouble?" asked Tiffany.

"Well...you know my dad. He's sure the Huns are coming over the hill any minute."

"Hey, Todd, this is my brother Sebastien visiting from California. Sebastien, this is Todd Fortney. His folks own this place."

"Yeah, you kinda look like you're visiting, ha ha."

"Nice to meet you," said Sebastien, reaching out his hand and trying to suppress further embarrassment.

"So, what will it be. Bison burger for you, right, Detective Reese?"

"Todd, I babysat you for three years; call me Tiffany for crying out loud."

Once all of their orders were in, and Todd left them, Sebastien fell mute. This happened to him quite often when he found himself in new surroundings or in small groups. It was one of his principle fears that kept him from attending the opera functions. It wasn't that he did not know what to say—well, not entirely, that was a problem, too—it was more that he literally could not speak. The words would not form, his mouth would not open. Tina had said something about self-monitoring usurping his brain power and causing the social awareness functions to shut down. Okay, she probably had not used the term *usurp*. But as Sebastien reflected on all this now, he felt it was an appropriate verb.

The clang of the drinks being placed on the table roused Sebastien from his thoughts. He became aware that Hank and Tiffany were in deep conversation. He focused his attention, trying to get caught up.

"...so, I'm thinking Mickey just left town. Went back up north," Tiffany was saying.

"Maybe," conceded Hank. "But would he do that without telling his PO? He faithfully reported his new address, or Val's address, anyway. Why would he just skip town?"

Tiffany considered this a moment. "Maybe it has something to do with that call. It was clearly a threat. Oh hey, that reminds me, I meant to ask you, why was it important that the caller asked for *Tiny* and not *Mickey*?"

Hank whisked his iced tea with a straw as he replied. "Well, that rounds it down, doesn't it? There are certain people who call him Mickey—mostly his mother, law enforcement, some of the older people around town. But other people, the ones he tends to get in trouble with, call him Tiny. See what I mean?"

"Definitely makes sense," replied Tiffany, lifting her eyebrows and nodding.

Sebastien was now listening earnestly, impressed at his brother's logic, even though he didn't know what they were talking about at all.

"You know what, we may as well do some business while we're here." Hank stood up and left the table in the direction of the kitchen.

"What's he doing?" asked Sebastien.

Tiffany shrugged while drawing down her Coke through a narrow red straw. The relative strangers sat in silence for a few minutes until Todd arrived with their food. Hank followed shortly after.

"What was that all about, boss?" asked Tiffany, as she removed the top bun from her burger and began painting it with ketchup.

"I just talked to Dave Fortney. He said he saw Mickey here with a female a few weeks ago. It must have been shortly after he arrived back in town, because Mickey hadn't been in here for months before that."

"Did he know the female's name, or recognize her?"

"Negative."

"Well, that doesn't help us much."

"No, but it does corroborate Val's version of recent history. Eat up, Sebastien. Those ribs are world famous."

11

After lunch, Hank followed Sebastien to his hotel so he could check-in, change, and drop off his car. Hank seemed a little irritated that he was not staying at the ranch, but Sebastien knew it was for the best—for his best, anyway. He required isolation to decompress, and he assumed he wasn't that welcome anyway. What was that line from Das Rheingold? Something about misfortune befalling the grudging host.

Tiffany was following them in her cruiser as they drove through the entrance to an RV park, where the road became a mix of dirt and fine gravel. Sebastien was grateful to have changed his clothes; plumes of dust rose up like mist on the paddy as assorted trucks, motorhomes, and side-by-sides navigated their respective ways around the property. An older woman was yelling into the driver's side window of an absurdly large pick-up truck as the driver was attempting to back a fifth-wheel trailer into one of the sites. Sebastien could not hear what she was saying, but it didn't require lip-reading skills to make out the string of expletives being levied at the poor old man at the wheel.

Hank parked the Tahoe in front of the park office and told Sebastien to hang tight while he went in. A few minutes later, Tiffany emerged at the passenger's side window and knocked gently, startling Sebastien, who jumped in his seat. He lowered his window as Tiffany laughed hysterically.

"Sorry to scare you, Sebastien! Or not. That was awesome!"

Sebastien grew red-faced. "It's okay. I was just thinking."

"About what?" she asked, resting her forearms and chin on the door and looking at him with interest, her dark bangs draping her forehead. Sebastien was a bit taken aback by the casual posture of the detective.

"Is there a river near here, or creek, or pond? I don't see water anywhere."

"I don't think so," she replied. "Not here in the park anyway. Why?"

Before Sebastien could answer, Hank emerged from the park office, followed by a tall, thin man with graying hair. They approached the Tahoe.

"Sebastien, this is Bill Nilsson. He owns the RV park. Bill, this is our forensic anthropologist, Dr. Sebastien Grey."

Sebastien stuck his hand out of the Tahoe and the two men greeted each other. As they did so, Tiffany added, "He's not ours technically; we're borrowing him from California."

"Wow, California," said, Bill. "It's that serious, eh? We couldn't shop local, I guess?" Bill smiled and winked at Sebastien, who laughed nervously. "Come on, follow me. I'll take you to where Ingrid found the bone."

Bill hopped in one of the side-by-sides that was parked in front of the office and backed it out a few feet. Before he could put it in drive, Tiffany yelled, "Hang on," and jumped in next to him. It must be a habit, Sebastien thought. Hank got in the Tahoe, put it in gear, and followed.

Sebastien scanned the RV park as they wound their way

along the road, passing several RV sites on either side—all of which were full. The park consisted of two concentric rings of gravel roads. The inner ring, the road they were on now, had about thirty RV sites and four cabins; a grass field with a playground and a horseshoe pit filled in the center, along with a large brick and wood structure. Sebastien supposed this to be the restroom and/or laundry. A shorter gravel road on the southeast side connected the inner ring to the larger outer ring. It was difficult to see how many sites might be along this outer road; much of it was obscured by trees as it rose gently into the granite hills that bordered the south and west sides of the park. Sebastien carefully surveyed the terrain as they drove, making mental notes. He was having a difficult time making sense of things.

The side-by-side made a right onto the gravel connector road that joined the ring roads, and then a left on to the outer ring, heading northeast. Hank followed slowly. The marked sheriff's Tahoe was generating a lot of interest from the campers, and some were gathering along the road, including children on bikes. A couple, walking two long-haired chihuahuas, stopped to ask Hank what was going on.

"Nothing," he assured them. "Just a routine visit. You all having a good vacation?" After the man and woman answered in the affirmative, Hank gave them a polite wave and continued.

On the right, about fifty yards up the outer ring, was a rough looking dirt road. Hank followed Bill onto this road, which climbed up into the hills behind the park. The road steepened as they drove. To the left, the downward slope likewise became more acute. Sebastien looked around for any sign that the puzzle in his head could be solved, but so far, the missing piece was still absent. The higher they climbed the more concerned he became.

At the top of the hill, Bill parked in front of a couple of large sheds. He and Tiffany hopped out of the side-by-side, and Tiffany began to dust off her sheriff's polo—a mission that appeared to Sebastien to be wholly vain. He was glad to be in the Tahoe.

"Okay, here we are," Hank declared.

While Hank, Bill, and Tiffany disappeared behind the sheds, Sebastien took in the surroundings. The road terminated at the top of a hill, which formed something of a mesa. He followed the others and saw a slight slope descending from the back of the sheds—this slope was much less acute than the one next to the road they had taken to get here. Sebastien walked up to Bill, who was standing behind the smaller shed, pointing at the ground.

Sebastien kneeled in the area where Bill was pointing. He turned the dirt over carefully in his hands, rubbing bits of it together between his fingers. After a minute or so, Sebastien stood up and began to look intently at the ground while walking slowing around the area behind the sheds. "You had dogs out here?" he asked as he walked, without lifting his head.

"Yep," offered Hank. "We had one. And we had a geologist look for burials."

"Bad GPR index—Precambrian granite," Sebastien murmured back, then continued to examine the area in silence for another five minutes. He was working his way down the slope. Once he was about twenty-five feet from the back of the sheds, he stopped and took his eyes from the ground, shifting his gaze down the hill. He mentally calculated about fifteen degrees for the angle of the decline and noted that it ended at a thick patch, or line, of trees probably less than a quarter of a mile away. Sebastien walked a little farther down and, once again, stopped. For the next five minutes, he alternatively placed his hands on his hips or crossed his arms in front of him with his right hand on his chin, staring down into the valley below.

"What's he doing?" Tiffany asked Hank.

"No flippin' clue. Hey-a, bro. Watcha doin?"

Sebastien ignored the question. He squatted down for a few seconds, then stood back up. All the while his eyes were pointed down to the line of trees at the bottom of the hill.

Hank tried again, his voice tinged with exasperation. "What gives, Sebastien?"

Suddenly, as if roused from a trance, Sebastien turned around and put his sunglasses back on. He walked up the hill to the others and said, "It's not here." His tone was flat and matter of fact.

"What's not here?" Hank barked back. "The rest of the body, you mean? Well, where the heck would it be, then? Don't you want to look around some more?"

Without turning his body, Sebastien pointed his right index finger backward, over his right shoulder, in the direction of the decline. "It's down there."

"Okay, mystery man, could you please explain what in the hell you're talking about?"

Sebastien could tell that Hank was losing patience. What he could not know was that his little brother was in the zone. It was something Sebastien could feel in his chest. Facts, like atoms, collided in his mind, the electrons of information releasing their energy into an aurora of understanding.

The crunching of gravel broke the moment, and the group turned to see Gerry alight from his truck and walk toward them.

"Sorry I'm late. Had a hospital case. So, what do you think, Sebastien?"

Tiffany answered for him, smiling and squinting in the sun. "Sebastien thinks the rest of the skeleton is down the hill."

Sebastien noticed Hank raise his hands in an apologetic gesture.

"It must be a California thing," said Bill. "Maybe he's on the dope."

Sebastien was offended. "I'll be in the Tahoe," he grumbled, as he started for the sheds.

"Sebastien, wait, wait. We're just lost, that's all. Can you just explain why you think the rest is down the hill? I mean, that's pretty far away from where the skull was found." Hank now sounded apologetic.

Sebastien paused and turned to the four, who waited in anxious anticipation to hear the logic behind so strange a conclusion.

"Based on the line of trees in the valley down there, I'm guessing that there's a river or creek at the bottom. Am I right?" Sebastien scanned their faces while, once again, pointing down the hill.

Gerry and Tiffany both shrugged, not having an answer. It was Hank who offered a guess.

"I believe so. It's French Creek, I think."

"That's right," added Bill. "Lower French Creek, actually. It runs from north of Custer southeast along the eastern edge of the state park. There's not always water in it, though."

"As expected," Sebastien said, nodding.

The other's faces locked in anticipation.

"Do you remember the fatty substance on the back of the skull?"

It was the others who now nodded.

"That's called adipocere. It forms when fat from the body is in contact with water for an extended period, usually a few months. Based on the location of the adipocere on the skull, it looks to me like the rest of the body is lying face up in shallow water."

"Like a creek," Gerry offered.

Tiffany's eye lit up. "Oh, that's why you asked about the water earlier."

"Yep. I've been looking for it ever since we got to the property."

Hank was still confused. "So, if the rest of the body is down there, how did the skull get way up here?"

"We will probably never know that. It could have been an ambitious raptor tried to make off with it but couldn't keep ahold of it."

"Well, there's only one way to find out." Gerry turned as he spoke and made his way back to his truck. "I'm going to call in some help. But first I need a map."

Gerry spread the map out on the hood of his truck. The others gathered around and examined it thoughtfully, trying to get their bearings. Bill seemed to have no trouble. "We're right here," he said, pointing to a spot on the map. "And about here is where the creek is at the bottom of the hill."

"It looks like there is a road down there." Hank's statement came out like a question.

"Yep. That's Lower French Creek Road," offered Bill.

Hank turned to Sebastien, who was looking at the map intently. "Can you tell at all where the body might be, I mean, if it is there?"

"Nope. I'm sorry, I really can't. Except, I would expect the water it's in to be somewhat shallow. So, if we can identify those parts of the creek, it should help."

"I'm not sure that's possible," said Gerry. "Certainly not from a map. I think we just need to go down there and start looking. I tell you what, you all head to the location where the jaw was found, and I'll go back to the office and start making some phone calls. I think we can get search and rescue and the cadets, and hopefully the dog, down there tomorrow. You do think the dog would help, even if it's in water?" Gerry's question was directed at Sebastien.

"Sure. Absolutely," he assured Gerry.

"Jaw? Where was that found?" Bill asked, half smiling.

"Oh, why the hell not. Why don't you come with, Bill? Congratulations. You've just been deputized."

"Hot damn!" exclaimed the older man, as he and Tiffany got into the side-by-side.

Tiffany grabbed the roll bar and smiled at Bill. "You know that's not a thing anymore, right?"

12

About forty-five miles to the northeast, as the crow flies, Kyle Corcoran, the leader of the West Side Silverbacks motorcycle club, was holding court with some of his cronies at a wrought iron table outside of the Iron Pony in Sturgis. The August air was dry and hot, and the thousands of people crushing past on the sidewalk made it even hotter. The whole place looked like one big Saxon song; denim and leather were everywhere. In an effort to battle the heat, and keep his patrons in their seats, the owner of the establishment had fashioned a makeshift mister around the patio of the bar using drip irrigation hoses. Evidently no one told him that *drip* is not synonymous with *mist*. Corcoran was too distracted to notice, or even care about, the river of water running down his neck and back into his underwear.

"Anyone hear from Tiny yet?" he asked the others at the table. His question only prompted head shakes, so he continued. "I'll tell you what. I'm losing patience. The dumbest thing that guy did was come back here."

"Who's Tiny?" asked the only clean-shaven man at the table

—a younger guy wearing a denim work shirt with cut off sleeves.

"He's one of the rat bastards who stole my bike," Kyle answered.

One of the men at the table—bare-chested except for a leather vest with the name "Rudy" sewn approximately over his left nipple—attempted to offer a slight addendum, before wisely stopping himself mid-sentence. "Well, technically, didn't we steal if from them fir—"

Kyle shot a poisonous look at Rudy, the newest club prospect who, though good at violence, was starting to show a certain lack of situational awareness.

The man in the denim shirt asked what most would consider a reasonable question. "Why would you expect to hear from this Tiny guy if he stole your bike?"

"Because he's supposed to bring Kyle another one to make up for the one he stole back...I mean stole," offered Rudy. "If he doesn't, he'll end up like the other guys."

"Rudy! Shut the hell up!" Corcoran raised his hands and rolled his eyes as he spoke.

The men sat in a tense silence for a moment, watching the crowds go by and nursing their beers. After about ten minutes, the younger man excused himself and made way for the men's room.

"I'm done waiting. Find him. Bring Tiny to me," said Kyle.

"I know he's still in town. I followed him to that old lady's house on Saturday. I watched the place until about four in the morning. He never came out."

Kyle looked unimpressed and stared right back at the man with the bushy black beard and tattooed neck. "Rudy, what day is it today?"

"It's Tues...oh, I see what you're saying." Rudy looked down at his beer for a moment. The copper beads braided into his beard clinked against the glass mug. A second later, his face shot up in a burst of excitement. "But he was on a bike! A Fatboy!"

"Rudy, I'm going to ask you again. What day is it today?"

"It's Tuesday. I don't know what yer getting—"

Before Rudy could finish, Kyle backhanded him across the right cheek, throwing the biker's sunglasses across the patio, under the iron railing and into the sidewalk.

"You've known that Tiny was in town and that he had a bike for the last three days, and you are just now telling me? What the hell is wrong with you?!"

The fourth man at the table—the one with the shaved head and horseshoe mustache—stared down with his green eyes into his amber beer, as if not even noticing what had just played out in front of him, and the throngs of patrons and passersby. Unfortunately, his feigning obliviousness did not work.

"And what about you, JT? Did you know this?" Kyle barked at him.

"No way, man," he replied, with a relieved tone.

After a few minutes, Rudy had recovered both his sunglasses and his composure. Recovering his pride would be a longer process. "I'll go back down there and see if I can find him."

Kyle abruptly and unexpectedly felt remorse for smacking one of the men who had pledged to help him get the bike back. It was a strange feeling, and he couldn't quite figure out if it was real, or if he was just concerned about pushing too hard against one of the few people that could, in turn, push him back. Kyle knew he needed to keep Rudy close.

"That's nice of you, Rudy. And don't make me smack you no more. I feel like crap when I do that."

"I'm sorry about that, Kyle."

"And you, Sparkles. You go with him."

Rudy and JT got up and threw their legs over the iron fence

that separated the bar's patio from the sidewalk. The crowd of people parted like a bait ball for a shark as the two huge toughs made their way to their motorcycles.

Kyle took a long pull at his beer and watched his subordinate Silverbacks disappear into the crowd. The sight of all the bikes lined up down the center of Main Street only ticked him off even more. No one steals from him. No one. The fact that he had stolen the Fatboy first was totally beside the point. It was a respect thing. The clock was running on Tiny. He was smart to leave town after his two buddies went missing, but stupid to come back and stupid to think that his reckless actions would be forgotten in just a handful of months.

The younger man returned to the table and once again took his seat. "Where did JT and Rudy go?" he asked.

Kyle ignored him and just sat there with a river of moisture running down his backside.

SUSAN WAS WORKING behind the counter at the lucky stop when the uniformed deputy stepped toward the counter. A wave of panic shot through her until she noticed he was carrying several items to purchase. The deputy also looked a bit confused.

"You ready, officer?" Susan asked.

"Ah...actually, I just got a call and need to run up the road," the man said, looking apologetic.

"Well, you're going to have to put all of that back, you know," Susan snapped in response.

The deputy looked confounded. He stood frozen and befuddled, like he wasn't used to being barked at by anyone less than a sergeant.

From the opposite end of the counter the other employee on duty—a young woman—joined this battle of wits. "That's okay, Susan. I'll put the items back. Deputy, you just leave those right here with me, and I'll get them." The clerk winked and smiled sweetly. "I hope it's nothing too bad," she added.

Susan felt like punching her, but let it go.

"No, not at all. Just an abandoned car up on Deer Gap. Thanks, uh..."

"My name is Evie."

"Well thanks, Evie. Much appreciated." The big blond cop with the huge arms and thick neck blushed brightly as he backed out of the door. "Hey uh, Evie. I get off in about an hour or so. Will you still be here then?"

"Actually, I'm off in thirty minutes."

"Oh well, okay."

The dejected deputy was nearly out the door of the Lucky Stop when Evie added with another wink, "But I'll come back here, and you can pick me up. I'll be pretty hungry by then."

Ordinarily, this kind of byplay would have made Susan puke. But the information conveyed in the exchange filled her with a sense of dread.

"Hey Evie, take the counter for a sec, will you? I have to make a phone call."

"Sure, Susan."

In the darkened stockroom of the Hermosa Lucky Stop, Susan pulled out her cell phone and punched in the number for Shermer's Wreck and Tow with shaking hands.

"Collie, it's me. We might have a problem."

"Hey, Sue. What's the problem?" replied Collie.

"I just overheard a cop talking about an abandoned car up on Deer Gap Road. He's heading up there now."

"Oh damn. Alright, now. You ain't gotta panic. We figured it would be found. Just play it cool. You made a report to the sheriff, right?"

"Yeah, I did."

"Then we're good. It will be fine, I promise."

"Thanks Collie. I...you know...well, just thanks for helping me."

"You bet, Sue. And how about we get some dinner or somethin'? Or, better yet, they got this buffet up in Deadwood. Nine-ninety-nine on Thursdays."

"Oh dang, Collie. I have to work on Thursday."

"Oh? Well, okay. We probably oughta lay low for a minute anyway."

"Good idea, Collie. Let's lay low for a bit, then you can take me to Deadwood."

"That's great, Sue. That's great."

13

Sebastien was standing in the middle of the wash in the
area where the jaw had been found. It looked to him to
be a seasonal creek. The banks on either side were
steep, and both were covered with exceptionally thick brush.
There was a gravel road about fifty feet up at the top of the
bank to his left. Bill was standing up there next to the Tahoe.
Hank and Tiffany were standing next to him in the wash.

"So's here's where the bone was, approximately." Hank
stomped his right foot twice, sending a miniature cloud of dust
into momentary floatation (the brief rain from a few days ago
had longed evaporated in the summer heat). "And up there
about a hundred and fifty feet is a culvert coming out of the
side of the bank. Follow me, I'll show you."

The three of them made their way up the creek bed,
walking carefully so as not to turn an ankle on one of the
chunks of granite that bedrocked the wash. After a few
minutes, Hank pointed to the left bank, just ahead of them.

"See that? That concrete pipe drains into the creek here. It
looks like the jaw got washed down this pipe and pushed down
the creek by the water. Tiffany, how long had it been since it

rained when the jaw was found? I know we talked about that. I think we said about three weeks."

Tiffany was navigating her way up the creek, carefully negotiating the rocks, her arms out and her eyes fixed downward, like a tightrope walker. "Um...yeah that sounds about right. Two or three weeks, I think we figured."

Sebastien regarded the concrete pipe for a moment, then asked, "Did you search the creek bed?"

Tiffany gave a nod. "Sure did. We searched it all the way from the culvert down past where the jaw was found."

Sebastien looked in the direction Tiffany was pointing. "Did you bring in dogs?"

It was Hank who answered. "Nope, not here. We found the source of the water. There's a retention pond about a half a mile away that spills over into the culvert. We ran the dogs all around it and even dragged it. Nothing. Do you want to head over there?"

Sebastien shook his head and walked back down in the direction from which they had come. Despite the treacherous footing, his gait and demeanor were deliberate. "Tell me when I get to where the jaw was found."

Tiffany and Hank watched Sebastien walk back down. Sebastien could hear their conversation.

"What do you suppose he's doing?" asked Tiffany.

"I have a feeling he's about to piss me off," responded Hank, who then yelled down to Sebastien. "There. Right there."

Sebastien ignored Hank's lack of faith. He halted and looked up the slope to Bill, then back toward Hank and Tiffany. "Hen...Hank, do you have any rope in your car?"

"Yeah, it's in the back. Hey Bill, open up the back and see if you can see that rope."

Bill gave Hank a thumbs up and searched the back of the Tahoe. Thirty seconds later, he emerged with the rope. "You want me to throw it down there?"

"No, no," Sebastien hollered at Bill. "Can you move the Tahoe up about twenty feet, then tie one end of the rope off on it somewhere, and throw the other end down to me?"

"Sebastien, what gives?" called down Hank from the mouth of the culvert, his hands supine in a now familiar gesture of confusion.

"The bank is too steep to search without a safety rope," he replied.

"Wait, we're searching the bank? That doesn't make sense. The body is not going to wash down then crawl up on the bank." Hank gave Tiffany a look that said, *I told you he was about to piss me off.*

Bill looked at Hank expectantly, waiting for instructions. After rolling his eyes and rubbing his temples, Hank finally nodded and yelled up, "The keys are in there."

"Okay, I got it," yelled Bill, as he headed for the driver's door of the Tahoe.

The pair of cops began working their way back to Sebastien. About the time they joined up, Bill was tossing the end of a rope down the bank. "How do you want to do this?" Sebastien asked Hank.

"Bro, I don't even know what we're doing. Or why we're doing it. Can you at least explain what you're thinking...this time?"

Sebastien was tempted to make a sarcastic remark about Occam's Razor and the need to do a proper job, but he resisted. Maybe it was the genuine interest in Tiffany's big brown eyes that gave him pause. He was beginning to enjoy impressing her. "Sure, um...sorry."

"That's okay," Hank said. "We just want to follow along."

"Okay, the mandible—the jawbone—is classified as an irregular bone. That is, it has an irregular shape. It's not long, and it's not round; it's angular."

"Okay, it's angular," agreed Hank, with a shallow nod and another eye roll.

"Well, it's been my experience—and I have a lot of it—that irregular bones, especially the mandible, don't travel far from the rest of the body." Tiffany was about to make a point when Sebastien interrupted. "I know, I know...at the last scene the body was nowhere around. But the mandible was near the skull. Mandibles don't just detach and roll away long distances. And water does not do a particularly good job of transporting them. They're fairly heavy, as bones go, and this creek has a lot of rocks and places on which it could get caught. I don't think it would have made it this far down from the culvert. I don't think it would have even made it *out of* the culvert."

Sebastien waited a few moments for all that to sink in. Blank stares signaled that it had not, so he continued. "This is a body dump site." Sebastien pointed up toward Bill, who waved for no reason in particular. "Your body is up on the bank between us and Bill. Somebody probably parked right there on the road,"—another finger point from Sebastien and another wave from Bill—"and threw a body down."

Without saying a word, Hank picked up the rope that Bill had tossed down, spun Tiffany around at the shoulders, tied the end of the rope to her belt, and patted her on the shoulder blade.

"Wow, chivalry really isn't dead," she said, laughing.

"Hey, *you* are the department's fitness instructor."

"Not for long, depending on how this goes." Tiffany lifted her left leg onto the slope and bounced on her right toes a few times to build momentum. With a grunt, she pulled herself up with the rope and heaved her body onto the bank, tumbling forward onto her face, forearms, and knees.

Hank laughed. "Well, that was graceful."

"Screw you, boss!" she retorted, pulling leaves from her hair. "So, what am I doing, exactly?"

Sebastien looked down at his feet, then lifted his left arm upward—reminiscent of a kicker aiming for the game-winning field goal. "This is about where the jaw was found, so just work your way up the bank in a straight line right here."

"And am I looking for anything specific?"

"You'll know it when you see it."

After several minutes of searching, Tiffany put her hands on her hips and arched her back, stretching it with a grunt. "You know, it would be really nice if I had something to sift through the leaves and crap with, rather than just my hand. Maybe some gloves, too."

"There's a trowel and gloves in my bag in the back of the Tahoe," Sebastien responded, then looked at Hank expectantly.

"Really?" Tiffany gave back, looking annoyed. "Are you serious, right now?"

Hank laughed loudly, then yelled up the bank to Bill. "Hey Bill, there's a black Pelican case in the Tahoe. It has a trowel in it and some gloves. Can you grab those?"

"Much better," reported Tiffany, as she worked the trowel through the spindles of vegetation that matted the bank, forming a loose wicker over the dirt.

Sebastien was standing by to evaluate anything she found that might be of interest. He assured her that some bones could be very small indeed, and she needed to work carefully and take her time.

Tiffany had made it a few feet up the slope when she suddenly stood, holding up something for Sebastien and Hank to see.

"Look, a bone!"

"Throw it down," said Sebastien.

The bone was about six inches long with a furrow down the middle and two three-quarter circles protruding from one end. It almost looked like two bones fused together. Sebastien recognized it immediately.

"It's a cannon bone. A bone from the lower leg."

"Human?" asked Hank. Tiffany held her breath.

"*Odocoileus.* Deer. Mule or maybe white tail. I'm not sure which you have up here."

"Both," supplied Hank.

"Damn!" Tiffany resumed her search of the bank.

After about ten more minutes, Tiffany was roughly a third of the way up the bank. The vegetation was less compacted in this area of the slope, making the task a bit quicker. "Found another one!" she called out excitedly, then chucked the bone down toward the creek bed without looking.

"Hey! Be careful. That's evidence." Hank stretched out to grab the bone in midair.

"No, it's not," said Sebastien, casually glancing at the bone Hank was hoisting in a triumphant post-catch pose.

Hank hung his head and gave an expiratory, "Damnit."

Sebastien took the bone from Hank's still-outstretched hand and regarded it more closely. "It's a young bovid. Do you have mountain goats here?"

"I think so. And how do you know it's...oh, who cares."

Five more minutes in, and Tiffany stood again. This time with nothing in her hand to throw down. She wiped her forehead with the back of her glove and said, "Alright, guys, my back is killing me. It's almost someone else's turn."

"We can't put our anthropologist on the slope; he's a contractor, and we can't risk the liability. And I'm management. You're doing great. Keep going." Hank winked at Sebastien as he spoke.

Tiffany put her left hand on her hip and pointed the trowel toward her sergeant with the other hand. "You are not management. You're a supervisor. You can't get out of the hard work with that excuse."

"Okay, okay. Come on down, and I'll have a turn."

Tiffany threw down the trowel, set her feet, and grabbed the rope with both hands. As she took her first step downward, her right foot slipped on a patch of bare dirt, causing her to tumble forward and onto her face.

"Oh geez. Tiff, you okay?" Hank called up.

Tiffany sat up on the slope and brushed leaves out of her hair, cursing.

"Yeah, yeah. I need a bath and a glass of wine, but I'm—hey, here's more deer, or mountain goat, or unicorn, or whatever."

Tiffany reached into the deadfall and pulled out a bone. This one was longer, about a foot and a half in length, with a large ball on one end and a couple of knobs on the other. She held it up over her head without bothering to stand.

"Bingo!" shouted Sebastien. "That's it!"

"Wait. What?" Tiffany stood up and looked at Sebastien, her dark bangs half-obscuring her moist and dirty face. "This bone I'm holding is human?"

"Yep. Human femur, left side," Sebastien replied, beaming.

Hank looked at the bone in Tiffany's hand, then looked directly at Sebastien. "You son of a gun."

14

Lucky Stop indeed, thought Deputy Lewis Stringer, smiling to himself as he headed toward Deer Gap Road. How do you like that? Dinner with Evie. As he made a right on Ghost Canyon from Highway 36, Stringer forced himself out of his lustful stupor and put his mind back on his job. "Dispatch, this is 3X8. Is RP still on scene?"

"Affirm, 3X8. RP is Dennis Carmichael. He's parked IFO the scene in a blue Dodge truck."

"Copy. I'm two out." Stringer replaced the mic on the console and made a left onto Deer Gap Road. Tall pines stood balefully on the low hill to the left, while pastureland—Carmichael's pastureland—nudged the hills in his periphery to the right. The road wound like a lazy serpent that could only manage half a coil, ascending sharply over the valley below.

About a mile in, the pastureland on the right abruptly surrendered to a sharp precipice—one side of a gap between the road and the next hill over. Hence the name of the road. Stringer could certainly see how a car could find its way over the edge on this road. As he calculated the possible permutations and outcomes of this call, he offered a silent prayer that it would not sabotage his date with the lovely clerk from the Lucky Stop.

A man in jeans and a short sleeve, plaid cowboy cut shirt waved him down as he approached. Stringer parked behind the blue Dodge and rolled down his window. "Hey, Dennis. What've we got up here?"

"Hey, Lew," the man replied, removing his cowboy hat to wipe the sweat off his brow with his handkerchief.

Deputy Stringer hated to be called "Lew," but he had no time for any extraneous give-and-take.

Dennis Carmichael continued. "It's down there. I saw it while I was working on the fence on the north end of the pasture—we have mountain lions, you know. Lost two sheep so far this summer. Anyway, then I drove up here to check it out."

As tempted as he was to comment about the futility of barbed wire fences stopping mountain lions, Stringer avoided taking the bait. He headed to the gravel shoulder of the road in the direction Carmichael was pointing, hoping to make this quick. Looking down, he did in fact see the back end of a vehicle—a small red truck, perhaps—about halfway down. Surveying the decline, he mentally plotted his options of approach. It didn't seem too treacherous; the abundant low bushes should provide a decent foothold and the trees were just about spaced right for him to pinball himself from one to the next and make it to the truck. Getting back up would be another matter, but the sooner he ran the tag numbers and verified that no one was on scene, the sooner he could call in the tow. Stringer wondered, just before launching himself down the hill, whether Evie would like Chinese food. He knew a nice place in Rapid City.

Upon reaching the truck—which was as easy as he'd calculated, thanks to gravity—Stringer examined the wreck. It was a Ford Ranger and was in surprisingly good shape, at least from the back. Laying on its side in the bed of the truck was a motorcycle, covered by some branches and pine needles which looked to have been deposited recently—probably windblown. The deputy wondered how long the truck had been here. Thankfully, both the truck and the motorcycle still had their license plates. He called both numbers into dispatch.

After racking his microphone on his uniform, Stringer gripped the shoulder of the truck bed and carefully made his way down to the driver's side door. Before even reaching the handle, he could see the smashed windshield. A little voice in his head, perhaps his training, told him not to touch anything else. He lifted his arms up like a man being robbed and shuffled himself toward the open window of the driver's door. As he peered into the cab of the truck, three ravens burst out through the window in a haze of black, one of them smacking Stringer's forehead with a frantic wing. The shock sent him backwards onto his butt and rolling down the hill until a particularly robust clump of juniper stopped him from going all the way down.

Once he got his bearings, Stringer crawled up the hill until he could reach the front bumper of the truck. *Screw fingerprints*, he thought to himself. He grabbed the bumper and pulled himself up into a standing position. The newly vertical deputy was now looking directly through the smashed windshield and into the cab. Glass was all over the dashboard and what looked like a mannequin was behind the wheel—an eyeless mannequin with red and black sockets, bright pink flesh exposed on the cheeks and an ascot of dried blood around the neck. Stringer fell to his knees, double-over, and vomited. His mind raced as he tried to collect himself and assimilate the facts in a professional, law-enforcement manner. He suddenly thought of Evie, thought of their date, thought of Chinese food, then vomited again.

Dennis must have heard the heaving. He called down, "Hey, Lew, you okay? Is there anyone in the car?"

Stinger crawled, hands and knees, to the side of the truck. Dennis saw him and exclaimed, "Good grief! Hang on! I have a rope."

~

TIFFANY WAS, once again, dusting herself off as she and the three other men stood on the road behind the Tahoe. As she did so, she was also doing her best to describe what she saw after finding the femur.

"There is a pair of jeans and a piece of fabric that looks to be from a shirt, and definitely a spinal column, and a few other bones that were longish. No sign of a skull, though, that I could see."

"It's around," suggested Sebastien, as he looked reflexively toward the creek bed. "It has to be."

"You want me to go get some tools?" asked Bill.

Hank was appreciative but a little surprised by the naivete of the average citizen. "No, no, Bill. That's really nice of you. But now we just have to call it in to the coroner. They have jurisdiction over the body. We aren't supposed to touch it. Only Gerry or one of the other coroner investigators can handle it from here. I've called in one of our forensic techs, and they are going to bring some flags to mark the area. And I'm going to post someone here until tomorrow to protect the scene. There's not enough light left to do the whole job this afternoon. At least, not enough to do it the right way."

Just then Hank's phone rang. "Uh-huh. Yes, sir.... No, sir, we're up on fire road 14. Yes sir, that's right. Did the sergeant tell you we found the rest of the...what? No, sir, I haven't been monitoring traffic. Really? Do we have an ID? Whose truck is it? Really? Yes, sir, I understand. Oh, sir, I did call a tech up here to bring some flags to mark the area. Can you have them make sure they do that before handling...okay, perfect. Thank you, sir."

Hank hung up the phone, and the others looked at him with interest. All those "sirs" made the call sound important, at least from this side. Hank gave Tiffany a look and gestured for her to follow him. They walked down the dirt road about thirty feet before Hank summarized the phone call.

"That was the lieutenant. They found a truck over the side of the road on Deer Gap. There's a body in it."

"Who is it? Do they know?"

"Not yet. The body is too bloated and messed up for a visual identification. At least, Stringer couldn't tell."

"Stringer? Guy's a bozo. Did he even run the plate?"

"Be nice, detective; of course, he did. It comes back to a Susan Whitebear out of Hermosa. Evidently she reported it stolen on Sunday."

"Sounds like some joy-riding kid couldn't make the turn on Deer Gap and ended up dead."

"I'm not sure about that," replied Hank.

"What do you mean?"

"Stringer found a motorcycle in the bed of the truck. It also comes back stolen. Out of Hot Springs. On *Friday*." Hank took care to put a special emphasis on *Friday*.

Tiffany immediately registered his implication. She silently mouthed the name *Mickey*.

HALF-SPENT flares dotted the road like scarlet stitches when the Tahoe pulled up to the crash site on Deer Gap. Three men were standing in the middle of the right lane in a huddle.

Hank and Sebastien approached the three men, who each took in Sebastien warily. Hank introduced his brother—Dr. Grey, forensic anthropologist—and the man in the blue jumpsuit lit up and offered a hand enthusiastically. "Oh yeah, Gerry told me about you. I'm Investigator Miller, with the Coroner's Office. Gerry said you're some kind of savant."

Sebastien wasn't sure whether Gerry was using the term "savant" in the pejorative sense, but he assumed so. "Good to meet you." Sebastien took Miller's hand and shook it, then shook hands with the other two. The deputy did not look well at all; Sebastien wondered whether he'd been in the car during the crash.

"What brings you up here?" asked a uniformed man with sergeant stipes on his sleeves. His tone was unfriendly and suspicious.

"The L.T. called me. Thought it could be related to a misper Tiffany is working," replied Hank.

"What does this have to with that dirtbag?" the other sergeant asked, his hands digging into his hips defensively.

"I take it you aren't referring to the lieutenant."

The man sneered in response. Hank continued.

"Mickey was last seen on a motorcycle. He doesn't have a motorcycle registered to him and, if I've heard correctly"—Hank looked at Stringer—"there is a stolen motorcycle in the bed of that truck down there." Hank pointed a thumb toward the precipice. "Is the tow truck on its way?"

"We're not standing around for our health," snapped the other sergeant.

"Regular guy is busy. There's a semi versus garbage truck out west on 16. We had to call in a tow truck from Hill City," provided Stringer.

The men continued their discussion as Sebastien wandered to the side of the road and looked down. He could see the red rectangle of the truck's tailgate and the path of broken vegetation that led to it. The angle intrigued him. "Mind if I go down there?" he called back to the group. A resounding "No!" returned in unison from all parties. Deciding, wisely, not to take the answer as literal, Sebastien stayed put.

A minute later, Hank joined him at the ledge. "Looks like you came at the busy season, little brother."

"What's next up here?" asked Sebastien, still looking down at the truck.

"The tow truck is about five minutes out. Once we get it up on the road, Miller will make the call whether or not to move the body and take it to the coroner's office or leave it in the truck as it gets transported to forensics."

"Are we going to wait?"

"We don't have to. You must be exhausted."

"No more than you are. I'd like to wait. I know it's none of my business, but I have a feeling about this."

"Well, Sergeant Hudson seems to be in the mood for more help. Let's wait." Hank smiled widely and rested his forearm on Sebastien's shoulder.

"What's with that guy?" asked Sebastien. "Seems like he has a bad attitude."

"Nah. He's just mad because it's the end of his shift, and he's stuck out here."

The brothers stood together, staring into the gap.

The tow truck driver, a large-bellied middle aged man, began to descend the slope, pulling the hooked cable from the winch, which belayed him carefully downward. The five other men were perched at the top, watching nervously as the driver huffed and puffed his way to the wrecked vehicle. Sergeant Hudson turned to Stringer and ordered him to go down and help the man.

At the bed of the truck, the tow truck driver went to steady himself against the tailgate. Sebastien suddenly gave out a yell, startling the others into stochastic jerks of alarm. "Stop! Stop right there! Don't move!"

"What the hell, kid?" Hudson shouted, as he regained himself.

The tow truck driver was looking up in utter confusion.

"He was about to touch the tailgate! Did you see that?"

"What are you talking about? Settle down, Poindexter. He's doing his job."

"I know what I'm doing," called the tow truck driver back up the hill. "I pull cars outta this spot all the time."

Hank visibly tensed up. Sebastien wasn't sure whether his brother was embarrassed or getting ready to deck the other sergeant. But Hank did nothing and said nothing.

Sebastien likewise let it go. He just stood there watching the retrieval of the truck, like a stoic contemplating the fruitlessness of suffering.

Once the hook was secured and the tow truck driver was back up at his truck, the winch was turned on. The atmosphere was filled with squealing and cracking as the metal cable wound around the winch drum and the truck trampled vegetation and dead branches on its return journey from its abysmal resting place. Everyone covered their ears with their hands, except the tow truck driver, who was wearing industrial earmuffs; the bright orange cups made him look like an aspiring hipster millennial.

The winch was stopped when the front tires of the truck reached pavement. The group gathered around the outside of the cab and looked in, except for Stringer, who sat on the curb, looking like he'd had quite enough. Hank immediately focused on the body behind the wheel, while Sebastien stood just in front of the side view mirror watching carefully. The face was blue and bloated, with chunks of flesh torn away. The eyes were also missing; the optical nerves resting like lazy stamen on the man's cheeks (it was definitely a man). His neck and shirt were stained brownish red with dried blood.

Hank examined the corpse's pecked over face, then called out, "Hey, Miller, what about checking this guy for some ID?"

Hank stepped back to let Investigator Miller access the body. Miller, who was already gloved himself, pulled out a pair of nitrile gloves and handed them to Hank. Sebastien paid special attention as Miller unfastened the seat belt that kept the man in place against the seat.

"Push him over a bit, and I'll check the back pockets," the coroner investigator said.

Hank complied and gave the body a gentle press on the left shoulder. The man's head lolled toward the passenger seat. Miller kneeled and slid his hand under the somewhat elevated butt of the deceased. "Ah. A wallet. Can you lean him forward a bit?"

With an "aaand...there," Miller produced a brown wallet from the jeans of the dead man and stood up. The others gathered around to look over his shoulder as he fished through the wallet for some identification.

15

Detective Reese was enjoying her much anticipated bath, although she changed her usual routine and opted for beer instead of wine as an accompaniment to her relaxation. The bathroom sconces were dimmed down, and the dancing shadows thrown by the beeswax candle against the subway tile made her eyelids heavy.

Subconsciously working her big toe in and out of the bathtub faucet, Tiffany's mind drifted between the highlights of this remarkably interesting day, not the least of which was meeting Hank's brother. Sebastien was definitely different. His intelligence was obvious, and he was even a little handsome. Not in the way Hank was—rugged and manly. Sebastien was softer. It was as if the features of his face were in the right place, all the right shape, all symmetrical. But his handsomeness didn't jump out at you, didn't take your breath away; it just sort of crept up. And it was curious to see two brothers who were so different, not just in looks but in confidence and presence. Maybe it was that thing with their mother? In any case, she was fascinated by watching the quirky anthropologist work. The next few days should be a hoot, she mused.

The next few days! There was a lot of work to do. And even more depending on the ID of the guy in the truck on Deer Gap. She hoped Stringer didn't screw things up too badly on the scene. She had wanted to go up there and see things for herself, but Hank directed her to call it a day. Maybe it was for the best. It certainly felt like it was for the best from the comfort of her bathtub. She closed her eyes and let the first stages of sleep percolate through her muscles.

It didn't take too long for the bathtub water to cool, but Tiffany did not notice. She began to dream: her mother was calling her, but every time she answered the phone it just kept ringing. This went on and on. In her dream she began to panic, thinking that something was wrong with her father. How could she know if she couldn't answer the phone?

A light scraping sensation on her right hand, as it hung out of the tub, roused her from her dream. It was her cat, Mist, licking her gently. Shaking off the sleep, she realized that the ringing sound persisted. Her actual phone was actually ringing.

"Hello? Yes, I'm here. Sorry, I was napping." She felt slightly awkward talking to her sergeant while naked and dripping wet in the bathroom. "No, no...it's okay. What's going on? Oh? Really? Do we have a positive ID? Okay. Yep, I will be there. No, really. Don't even worry about it. See ya."

Tiffany's list of things to do tomorrow had just gotten a little longer. And her first item of business was to attend the autopsy of Mickey McCallister.

HANK HUNG up the phone and turned to Sebastien. "So, can you tell me what all that was about, back there?" Hank made a right from Deer Gap onto Ghost Canyon. It was nearing dark, and he was tired. Not to mention that he still had to deal with the lieutenant before he could head home. He was not in the mood for drama, but he was genuinely curious. "Why did you yell at the tow truck driver? Sorry for Hudson, by the way. He's an ass."

Sebastien's eyes were fixed on the dusky valley through the passenger window. "Did you see the angle of the truck?"

"What do you mean? The truck as it went down the canyon?"

"Yes. It was perfectly perpendicular to the road."

"Okay. So?"

"That means it was heading directly for the edge when it went over. If the driver lost control while going up, or down, that road, he should have hit the edge at an angle."

"Well, what if he were swerving from hitting a deer, or racoon, or something?"

Sebastien turned his head to look at Hank, flattened his hands, and used them as visual aids. "He would still hit the edge at a slight angle, at least. Think about it. Let's say the truck was heading down the hill. That would put it in the lane farthest from the edge. Even if an animal ran out in front of him, and he swerved to the left to miss it, he still would not have enough room to strike the edge at a ninety-degree angle." Sebastien pressed the fingertips of his right hand obliquely into the palm of his left.

"Well, the accident reconstruction people should be able to calculate that."

"I didn't see any accident reconstruction people up there, did you?"

"Well, you know, when they go up to check the skid marks," offered Hank.

"There were none," Sebastien replied.

"What's the point of all this anyway? What does this have to do with you going off on the tow guy?"

"The truck was pushed over the edge, Henry." Sebastien

made no effort to correct himself. He just continued. "If the tow truck guy gets his prints all over the tailgate, you may never know who pushed it."

"Well, hold on a minute—"

"And it's not just the angle," Sebastien said, interrupting. "That slope was pretty steep. How did the truck end up in the middle of it instead of all the way down? It must have had little or no momentum when it went over. It's not like it was resting on a tree or rock. Oh, and speaking of rocks, did you happen to see the big rock sitting in the passenger's seat floorboard of the truck?"

"And here I thought you were just the bone guy. Any other observations, Poirot?"

"Since you asked, the seat belt."

Hank sighed. "What about it?"

"There was a heck of a lot of blood on that guy. Why was the seat belt strap clean if the crash caused the trauma?"

Hank let out another sigh and shook his head inwardly as he lifted his radio mic from the console. "1Y7 to dispatch."

"Go 1Y7."

"Is forensics 10-40?"

"Affirm. I'll have someone call."

"What was that about?" asked Sebastien.

"That's about having the forensic techs call me so I can tell them to treat this as suspicious."

In Hank's periphery, he could just about detect a slight smile on his brother's face.

THE BROTHERS each occupied a burgundy vinyl chair facing the desk in the lieutenant's office. The lieutenant was sitting at his desk with his tongue poking out from between his lips, trying to figure out how to operate what looked to be a fancy cigar cutter. Flecks of dandruff fell from his marine haircut onto the shoulders of his dark blue dress shirt. Sebastien was wondering when the man would acknowledge, or even notice, their presence. Hank seemed less worried.

After a few minutes, without looking up, the lieutenant abruptly spoke. Sebastien was not sure whether he was talking to them or the cigar cutter. "So now we have three scenes, don't we?"

Hank nodded. The lieutenant still did not look up from his fidgeting.

"Three scenes, Sergeant. *And* the herds from the rally running amok through the hills. Do you know how many people we loaned to Meade County? Do you? Not to mention, I got a mouth breather from Game, Fish, and Parks telling me to increase patrols to look out for some rabid mountain lion. Do you know what will happen if *that* gets to the media?"

Hank started to respond, but he was cut off while drawing in the breath to do so.

"So, you can see, these archaeology expeditions are pretty ill-freaking-timed."

The cigar cutter slipped from his hand, and the lieutenant leaned under the desk to retrieve it, swearing an oath.

"Sir, this is Dr. Grey. I told you about him."

The lieutenant straightened up with a grunt, the capillaries in his round cheeks practically bursting, and looked apologetically at the stranger sitting next to his sergeant. "Oh, well...no offence to you, son. I heard you've been a big help."

Sebastien offered an appreciative nod.

"He has, sir. Because of Dr. Grey, we now know that the skull up at Bill and Ingrid's is not likely the result of a mountain lion attack. And we have the rest of the skeleton from Fire Road 14. It appears to be the result of a body dump. So, we do have suspicious deaths. But I personally don't think a mountain lion is involved in either."

Sebastien almost offered a comment but remained silent.

"Good. Then you call him. You figure out what's got his britches in a twist." The lieutenant ripped a piece of note paper from the rest of the pad on his desk and handed it over to Hank. "Now, talk me through the logistics of the recoveries."

"The coroner's office is running point on the jaw site, since we know there are remains up there. They'll do the recovery and let Dr. Grey know when they think they have it all. However, I did call in an extra body on grave shift to watch the scene and keep it safe."

"Interesting word choices, Sergeant," the lieutenant mused. "Body and grave." He had given up on the cigar cutter and was now fully listening.

Hank didn't respond to the lieutenant's observation. "The French Creek search will be the bigger operation. We're not even sure if that is where the remains are." Hank looked over at Sebastien furtively, who, once again, managed to swallow his protestation. "But it *is* the most logical place, we think."

"What do you mean, 'big'?"

"Gerry already got the ball rolling on a full call-out of the search and rescue team, and the dog. With your permission, I'd like to detail a few detectives to the search, just to have extra bodies."

"That's acceptable. But keep Detective Reese on the McCallister caper. At least until we know COD."

"Of course. She'll be attending the autopsy."

"And what about cadets?"

"Cadets, sir?"

"For the French Creek operation."

"Oh. Yes. I'm not sure about that, sir. We don't know what to expect down in that creek area. The terrain could be squirrely."

"Fair enough. Dr. Grey, you came a long way to help us out.

We really do appreciate it. Did you find a place to stay? It's always tough when the rally is going."

"Yes. I guess I got lucky. I'm at the Holiday Inn," Sebastien replied.

"Excellent. Make sure Sergeant LeGris here gets the bill."

"Thank you, I will."

16

"We're out here," Melissa called from the back patio. Hank dropped his backpack on the couch, locked his pistol in the safe, and walked out to join his wife on the patio sofa. As he sat, Melissa leaned over for a kiss and a nuzzle.

"I wouldn't do that. I stink."

"That's okay, I'm used to it," she teased.

It was fully dark now, and the lights from the patio threw a pale glow halfway into the yard. Beyond that, Hank could see the chicken coop, illuminated by a single work light that he had fastened to a post near the coop. He saw Kirby down there, playing with her chickens.

"Isn't it a bit late for her to be up?" asked Hank.

"I told her she could wait for you to get home before she goes to bed. She's saying goodnight to her chicks."

Hank stood up with a painful grunt—he was sore from walking up and down the slope of the wash—and made his way toward the coop.

"Daddy!" The little girl gripped Hank's thigh tightly.

"Hello, sweetheart. Watcha doing?"

"I was telling my chickens not to be scared."

"Oh. That's nice. Why were they scared?"

"Daddy, it's dark," Kirby said, in all seriousness. "Everyone knows chickens are afraid of the dark."

"Well, if it's dark, that must mean it's your bedtime. Come on, mother chicken, I'll tuck you in."

"I'm not a chicken!"

"No? Oh, I'm sorry. I thought you were a chicken because you like to peck, peck, peck."

Hank formed his hands into beaks and poked Kirby gently as the little girl ran giggling to the patio.

"Mommy, can I have some ice cream before Daddy tucks me in?"

"No, you already had ice cream, remember? But you can have a bath."

"Aw, Mommy."

"Come on, Kirby."

"I'll be right there," called out Hank, as he went back to the coop to turn off the work light.

The faint sound of footfall on leaves gave Hank pause just after he switched off the light. There was something walking behind the fence that marked the back of the property, about forty feet from the coop. Hank stood frozen in the darkness and waited, listening. His eyes were fixed in the direction of the sound. Nothing. Probably a racoon, he thought, and made to turn back toward the house.

Hank made it a few feet before hearing the sound again. He swiveled around on his heals and looked. He could see a branch of the big bur oak on the opposite side of the fence moving against the moonlight. Something was in the tree. He squinted and looked harder, thinking that he could make out the glow of two eyes. Just then he remembered that he still had his small flashlight on his belt. As he trained the flashlight on the silhouette of the tree, a shiver ran through his body and his breath stuck in his lungs. A mountain lion—a big mountain lion—was perched in the oak. The cat's eyes glowed yellow in the beam of the flashlight, but it did not move. It just stared back at Hank, tilting its head curiously.

Hank wanted to yell, to scream out to Melissa to get the rifle. But that would scare her to death, which in turn would scare Kirby. Maybe they should be scared? Hank turned and darted for the house, not considering the possibility of being chased. He ran into the master bedroom closet and punched in the code on the gun safe as quickly as his shaking hands would allow.

As Hank ran back out of the master bedroom, and past Kirby's room, he heard his wife call out, "What's going on?" He didn't answer.

Hank stopped running when got to the patio. He instead walked slowly, carefully, with his Remington 7600 pointed ahead of him. It felt like it took an hour to make it all the way to the coop. But he had heard nothing and seen nothing. Once again, he produced his flashlight, this time holding it in his mouth to scan the tree as his hands held the rifle. The mountain lion was gone.

Hank was shaking as he walked closer to the fence—and the tree—the barrel of the rifle bouncing up and down. He stopped and waited and listened. Still nothing. He scanned the yard and the fence to his left and right but only found empty darkness and a peculiar, haunting stillness.

"Hank! What's going on?" called out Melissa from the patio.

Hank lowered the rifle and turned around.

"It's nothing, hon. Just a racoon."

"Well, don't kill it! Poor thing. I swear, you cops and your guns." Melissa shook her head and walked back into the house.

Hank pulled a chair from off the patio and positioned it near the coop. He sat there staring intently into the darkness, occasionally running the flashlight beam in an arc in front of him. Several minutes passed, and the adrenaline started to dissipate. The implications of what he had just seen, a few feet from his own backyard, began to flood through his mind. The thought of Kirby playing with her chickens a few yards from a stalking mountain lion made his blood run cold. He listened hard and tried to focus on the tree. But it was not easy through his tears.

∽

SEBASTIEN WAS TOO tired to eat and probably wouldn't have anyway; the ribs he'd had for lunch never quite settled right, and his guts felt like a mold for fresh concrete. After showering and a little reading, he tucked himself in for the night. A vertical ray from the hotel sign fluoresced into his room, falling across his chest. He got up to adjust the curtains, but they refused to come together completely. He gave up.

Sleep was slow to appear and desultory. There was too much novelty for him to digest, too many new faces, encounters, conversations, and actions for him to replay in his mind, to assess. This was the harsh self-recrimination that could only be avoided by staying away, keeping to himself as much as possible. But, on reflection, he was glad he'd come. Today had been a good day. A really good day. And, as he lay there, he found his mind drifting repeatedly to the most interesting aspect of the trip, so far. Detective Tiffany Reese.

Tiffany was a mystery. She was definitely a cop—the firearm obtruding from her tiny hip looking at the same time cartoonish and aggressive. But she also had a playful, casual side. She was clearly not afraid to give it back to Hank. That was rather fun to watch. Moreover, she seemed to be impressed by his own ability to shed light on these cases. Sebastien suddenly felt the desire to know her better, to befriend her. A friend. How would that be for novelty?

About one o'clock, Sebastien got up to relieve himself and get a drink of water. His room felt hot despite the air conditioning being nearly all the way up. He made the mistake of looking in the mirror, which made him think of body dysmorphic disorder—the obsession with perceived flaws in one's body, according to his Internet searches—and tried to remember whether he had ever brought it up with Tina. He did not think he had, did not think he would.

Back in bed—on top of the covers this time—his abstractions finally succumbed to light sleep, though he was still faintly aware of his snoring as well as the preliminary hypnogogic starts that frequently punctuated his attempts to slumber. At some point, the gravity of the day finally pulled him down into a deep, paralyzing torpor, and Sebastien began to dream.

He was standing in Dr. Rose's autopsy suite. The room was bright—much brighter than usual, he supposed, and certainly more so than necessary. He looked up to the ceiling and saw, not the recessed vapor-tight fixtures that were there earlier that day, but rather the open sky—blue and cloudless. In front of him were two autopsy tables: on the table to the left lay a body covered by a white sheet, boot toes poking out bashfully; the table on the right was nearly bare and remarkably clean, the stainless-steel reflecting blinding flashes from the sun above. The only thing that occupied it was the skull from the RV park, the jaw connected and, somehow, grinning.

In an instant, he became aware of three other people in the room, obscured by a fog that dissipated slowly, revealing the identities of the interlopers: Sergeant Hudson, Dr. Rose, and Tiffany were there, standing behind the sheeted body. Dr. Rose had his arms folded and was shaking his head in disappointment. Hudson was animated, his face red in anger. He was ripping up a batch of papers—it was Sebastien's forensic report, his as yet unwritten forensic report. Tiffany appeared morose, a tear from her left cheek catching the light for a millisecond as their eyes met. A rush of desolation overtook Sebastien, and he jerked his head toward the door, only to find that it was no longer there.

"Sebastien, over here." He turned to face the three others again. "Over here."

The voice was coming from underneath the sheet on the table. He lifted his questioning eyes to meet Tiffany's. She gestured to the sheet-covered body. Sebastien stepped forward and Tiffany rolled the covering off the corpse's face. The eyeless face of Eric Pool, from the Goblin's Lair, revealed itself. His naked neck had a deep gash, his chest, blood-stained. Suddenly the corpse shouted, "I'll have it next week! Leave me alone!"

The shock reeled Sebastien backwards, crashing through the table with the skull on it and onto the floor. The skull fell from the table and smashed into thousands of pieces. "Look what you did!" shouted Hudson, Dr. Rose, and Tiffany in unison. Sebastien, trying to stand, grabbed at his chest, his sternum suddenly on fire, the muscles of his thorax tightening around him. He could not breathe. He dropped to his knees on the floor, then fell backward. Staring up, the sky was no longer there, having been replaced by the artificial whiteness of the recessed lights. As he lay there gasping for breath, he saw his mother lean directly over him. She scowled, poked at his stinging chest with a bony finger, and yelled, "Why don't you get off the floor?!"

Sebastien jolted awake. The horror of his dream fled his mind as he realized the pain in his chest was real. His mouth was filled with thick saliva, and his face was clammy and wet. He searched the catalog of his mind for the symptoms of a heart attack, but he did not know what they were. He'd never had a reason to know. Until now?

Embracing the toilet of a hotel room was not an ideal thing to do, certainly. But he could not deny that the cold porcelain felt good against his naked chest while he spit thick gobs of saliva into the bowl. He wondered whether he should call an ambulance, then thought better of it once he realized the embarrassment and fuss it would involve. Silly, he knew. Actually, the longer he sat there, with his back against the shower door, the better he felt. It occurred to him that maybe this was all just heartburn. He remembered the ribs he'd had for lunch and felt a little more confident in this self-diagnosis. He decided to wait a few more minutes, then go down the front desk to see whether they had some antacid handy.

17

A sense of hopelessness came over Tiffany as the initial Y-incision was being made in the thorax of that poor bastard, Mickey McCallister. She always felt like this at the outset of an autopsy; the notion that, up until the moment that the scalpel was traced from the shoulder to the xyphoid process of the sternum, then so on down the abdomen, the deceased could somehow be saved. It was as if the pathologist was dealing the fatal, irredeemable blow. Absurd, of course, but the words, "No coming back now" regularly and involuntarily formed on her lips during those first moments.

In Mickey's case, the extra violence inflicted by the internal examination seemed to Tiffany to be wholly unnecessary; it was clear, or at least seemed clear from the external examination, that the two-inch long gash in his neck had sent the life-long criminal and aficionado of random violence into the hereafter. Tiffany was putting her money on exsanguination due to sharp force trauma as the cause of death. That's not to say that some surprising revelation would not result from the full autopsy—poison, heart attack, gunshot through the anal cavity. One just never knew. Patience and thoroughness were always justified in these situations. Fluids would need to be collected, wound entry locations excised, their underlying trajectories documented, organs weighed, and a host of other ghoulish tasks.

Manner of death would be trickier. The forensic tech had mentioned the large amount of glass in the truck—much of it around Mickey's body and on the dash. But that was windshield glass—safety glass, which, upon smashing, exploded into thousands of cuboid fragments no bigger than a centimeter. It was not at all likely that Mickey was done in by the windshield glass being driven into his jugular on impact; and, if that were the case, there should have been evidence of it in the cab of the truck. It certainly had not been found by forensics, nor did Dr. Rose find anything in the wound itself. Maybe it was a perfectly timed and targeted tree branch that impaled Mickey as he crashed down the slope? That didn't seem likely either, but perhaps it would be worth mentioning to forensics; maybe they should go back out to the scene and look for a bloody branch or limb? Barring that, if some mechanical force did not accidentally jab Mickey in the neck during the crash, it seemed more likely that this would be a homicide.

Interesting, thought Tiffany. That would make three murders in the last handful of months. For a county whose population was outnumbered five-to-one by deer, this seemed an odd coincidence.

"YOU LOOK LIKE HELL. ROUGH NIGHT?" Hank moved some paperwork from off the passenger seat as Sebastien clambered into the Tahoe.

"I'm fine. Those ribs I ate attacked me in the middle of the night, gave me horrible heartburn."

"We have to make a stop first. I called the guy from Game, Fish, and Parks. He's apoplectic about one of the mountain lions they're tracking. It will take a bit for Search and Rescue to get set up anyway. We may as well miss that drudgery." Hank considered telling his brother about the mountain lion from last night but decided it could wait.

"What about Tiffany? Is she coming?"

"She would eat you alive, bro." Hank smiled impishly and rubbed Sebastien's hair like his brother was a five-year-old.

"Oh, shut up! That's not what I mean."

Hank was still smiling. "She'll be there later. She's at the autopsy of the guy from last night."

Hank's smile quickly faded into a concerned frown as he regarded his brother's drawn and weary profile. "You sure you're up for this? I can take you back to the hotel and pick you up later."

"Honestly, I'm fine."

"Okay. Oh, by the way, I hope you haven't eaten yet. We're having breakfast with the mountain lion dude."

Sebastien answered with a grimace.

As the brothers entered the café, they nearly collided with a couple of bikers who were walking out. Besides nearly impaling him with the door handle, the men looked to Hank to be trouble. They were definitely not local, nor did they resemble the monied wanna-be bikers that invaded the hills from the nation's suburbs on their forty-thousand-dollar Harley's each August. The camera of Hank's mind snapped a couple of photos, just in case, as he and Sebastien slid by.

Barry Van Lowe stood up at the booth farthest from the door and waved the men over. "Sergeant LeGris. Thanks for agreeing to meet with me."

"Absolutely. We always have time for our colleagues at GFP. This is Dr. Sebastien Grey, our forensic anthropologist. He also happens to be an expert on...uh..." Hank struggled to find an apt description for something he barely understood himself. He looked at his brother for help.

"Big cat predation on primates, you could say," offered Sebastien, who then offered his hand to the state biologist.

"Hmm, interesting. Much call for that kind of thing, is there?" Barry's face betrayed genuine interest rather than sarcasm.

"Well, no. My dissertation work specifically involved cheetah predation on primates in Namibia."

"By primates you mean humans?"

"No, no. Not at all. Mostly baboons; sometimes vervet monkeys."

"That's actually fascinating. Is it important that the sheriff's office have an expert in big cat predation? Are you aware of some problem about which the GFP should be aware?"

Uh-oh, thought Hank. He had driven himself down into a cul-de-sac and was about to be jumped. "Nope. I just figured it would be important that we have someone who knows a bit about cat behavior. That's why I brought Sebast—er, Dr. Grey along. I'm just a dumb cop. I'll need him to translate for me." Hank smiled innocently as he searched Barry's face to see whether the biologist bought it. The man's right eye narrowed a millimeter and his head tilted about five degrees. *Nope. Didn't buy it.* Hank leaned over the table and looked directly into his eyes. "But evidently, the GFP is aware of something that the SO should know. Correct?"

Just then a waitress walked up to the table. "Morning, Hank!" she beamed.

"Morning, Daisy. I will have the pancake plate and a cup of coffee. Sebastien?"

"Do you have a spinach omelet?"

Daisy's pencil was poised against the order pad, but her mind looked like she was calculating the volume of a cone while spinning. "I'm sorry? Um..."

"You know what, that's fine. I'll have the pancakes, too. And water, please. Thanks."

After Barry ordered and Daisy left the table, the men resumed their conversation.

"It's not so much the GFP—well, not officially." Barry looked around to see whether anyone was eavesdropping, then lowered his voice a few decibels. "We've been tracking a mountain lion that's been getting awfully close to towns throughout the county. He's kind of using the built-up areas as his feeding grounds." Barry pulled a tan folder from the canvas messenger bag, which was on the seat next to his. From this he produced an eleven-by-seventeen printed map, which he laid on the table.

"Is that unusual?" asked Sebastien.

"Not necessarily," replied Barry. "But, if you look here on the map, this blue line represents the lion's movement. The red L's are reported livestock kills, and the red P's are missing pet reports."

Hank and Sebastien leaned over the table and studied the map carefully. Daisy stopped by the table briefly to assure them their food would be out soon, causing Barry to cover the map with his hands like it was the schematic for Operation Flashpoint and Daisy was a Nazi infiltrator.

"I don't get it. This happens all the time. A few missing pets —which could be due to just hawks, owls, coyotes, or even simple runaways—does not an emergency make. Do you have anything more specific that points to a mountain lion?" After the events of the previous night, Hank was a convert. But needed to know what the GFP knew.

Barry shook his head while he sipped his coffee.

"And, isn't it likely that missing pet reports would increase when panic sets in. Could be confirmation bias. The simplest explanation is usually the correct one, right?" This from Sebastien.

"Dr. Grey, this is South Dakota. A mountain lion *is* the simplest explanation."

"What exactly, would you like us to do for you, Mr. Van Lowe?" queried Hank.

"Dr. Van Lowe," the man corrected, looking directly at Sebastien, but answering Hank.

Sheesh, more doctors than you can shake a stick at, thought Hank. "Sorry. *Dr.* Van Lowe. What can we do for you?"

"See this pattern here?" Barry said, pointing once more at the map. "It's essentially cyclical. This is his home range. We're trying to trap the cat and relocate him, but we're having a difficult time doing that. Methods for trapping in built-up areas are more limited than the open country. What I...er, we, would like is for you to keep an eye out for signs of the cat. Pay special attention to missing pet reports—you know, get out and look for tracks, search the area. And, if you feel appropriate, warn people. Especially people with children."

The last sentence struck Hank. He looked over the map carefully and pointed to a hand-drawn green circle. "What's this?"

"That is the location where we tracked the lion last Sunday. We almost darted it, but it...uh...got away from us."

Hank didn't tell Barry that his little green circle was just to the east of the LeGris residence.

"What do you think it will take to capture this thing? Any idea how long it will take?"

"It's hard to say, Sergeant. We have a team working on it. I may be the only one who sees the urgency though. I know we see a lot of this, but this one has got me nervous. We're getting ready go out again soon. I think..."

Daisy arrived with their food, interrupting Barry's response. The conversation paused as the men dug in. It was Sebastien who broke the silence midway through their meal.

"Dr. Van Lowe, I'm curious, in my work in Africa I noticed

that the cats shifted from their standard prey items to less common food sources as a result of resource stress. You know, when developments encroach on their territory, or prey is reduced through hunting, the bushmeat market, pollution, habitat loss, that kind of thing. Is that the case here? What is your hypothesis around this behavior?"

Oh, geez. They're going to nerd it out, thought Hank.

Barry looked up from his eggs, a yellow drip of yolk dangling from the corner of his mustached upper lip as he spoke.

"There is no resource stress here. It's a smorgasbord for mountain lions. Besides about fifty thousand deer—white tail deer being their preferred diet—there are also bighorn sheep, elk, smaller mammals like porcupine, and even birds such as turkey. Not to mention the domesticated livestock and pets. Really, almost anything they can sneak up on. They're ambush predators. Not like your cheetahs who succeed because they outrun their prey. Mountain lions are shifty bastards."

"Porcupines?" questioned Sebastien.

"Oh, yes. Those cats are tough suckers. Anyway, based on estimated population numbers, there is no sign of reduction in the population; the numbers keep going up. And this is even with a lion hunting season."

"How many mountain lions would you say there are?" asked Sebastien.

"Estimated numbers are about a hundred and fifty throughout the Black Hills. Most of those—the vast majority— are in the Southern Black Hills."

"Where we are, you mean?"

"That's right."

"How diverse is the population, genetically?"

"Pretty diverse. Strong heterozygosity. There's no bottle neck that we can detect. Plus, there is molecular evidence of gene flow between the lions here and ones in the Bighorn

Mountains to the west and Laramie Mountains to the southwest."

"So, you are saying, despite a healthy population, with plenty to eat, and—"

"That's right," Barry said, interrupting. "Despite all the reasons to stay away, we have a mountain lion that likes to hang around populated areas."

Barry was stabbing at his eggs a little dramatically. Hank wondered whether it was for effect.

"Like I said, we're working on relocating him. But until that happens—maybe even after that happens—we could use your cooperation."

"Sure. We will definitely cooperate, like I said before. When did you say you are going back out to try and catch him—it is a male lion?" asked Hank.

"Yes. Three-year-old male. Approximately eight feet long and a hundred and seventy pounds. Tomorrow I think."

"Big fella! Would you mind if Dr. Grey tags along?"

Sebastien looked at his brother in bewilderment.

"Sure. We could use another expert."

Sebastien shot Hank a look of irritation. But Hank ignored it.

Hank looked at Barry. "When are you starting?"

"Sometime in the afternoon."

"Perfect," replied Hank. "Dr. Grey, give Dr. Van Lowe your number so he can text you the details."

"What did you do that for?" They were barely out of the café when Sebastien laid into his brother. "I didn't come up here to chase around with the locals in search of mountain lions."

"One mountain lion," Hank corrected. "And yes, you did. You came up here to help me."

"Help you with your forensic cases, not with your wildlife issues."

"Sebastien, here's my problem: I have no way of knowing—of assessing—whether or not that guy is bat crap crazy, or if the mountain lion they're tracking does pose a real danger to the people of this county or the surrounding counties. If I go along with them or send Tiffany or another deputy...well, then that will be noticed. People will start talking about how the sheriff's office is tracking people-eating cougars. Folks around here are already wound up. Could you imagine what they'll think if they believe that there is enough evidence for law enforcement to get involved? And, by the way, what did I ask you first when I called you last Friday?" Hank was now leaning against the hood of the Tahoe and looking at Sebastien, who was doing the same on the other side.

"You asked me to come help."

"Negative, Ghost Rider. I asked you about your research in Africa. That is why I needed you up here."

Sebastien jerked open the passenger door of the Tahoe and climbed in, pouting.

"I saw it," said Hank, through the opened driver's side door.

"What? What did you see?" Sebastien replied.

"The mountain lion. When I got home last night. I saw it sitting in a tree behind my yard."

"Oh man." Sebastien's eyes were wide with concern.

"Oh man is right. Damnit, Sebastien, Kirby was playing out there! And at basically the same time the lion was wandering around. I need to know if this thing is a real threat to humans, as Barry says, or if there is not enough stress to make him go after people."

"Resource stress," Sebastien corrected.

"See? That's exactly why I need your help."

"I'm really sorry about this, Hank." Sebastien sounded, and looked, genuine.

Hank climbed into the Tahoe. "So, you'll do this for me? You'll go with Barry and his guys?"

"Sure, Hank. I will."

"Great," replied Hank, as he snapped on his seatbelt. "I owe you one. And you know what? I'm going to repay you right now." Hank pulled his phone out of his breast pocket, punched in some numbers, and hit the speaker button. The cab of the Tahoe filled with the dialing sound.

"Who are you calling?" asked Sebastien.

Hank put his index finger up to his lips.

"Hey, Hank. What's up?" It was Tiffany.

Hank smiled. Sebastien suddenly looked worried.

"I was just checking in. How's it going on your end?"

"Dr. Rose is finishing up. We'll have to wait for toxicology, of course. But Mickey definitely bled out. He has a big cut on his neck—that's where all the blood came from."

"Could that be from the crash?" Hank asked, noticing his brother silently shaking his head in the passenger seat.

"Rose thinks not. The glass from the windshield doesn't match the wound. And for that matter, forensics didn't find anything sharp with blood on it in the truck."

"You have their report?"

"Not yet," replied Tiffany. "But I talked to one of the techs. They did collect that rock and send it to the lab. The one on the floorboard."

"What about fingerprints on the tailgate?" Hank looked over at Sebastien as he anticipated the answer.

"Just the tow guy's. And, of course, a few of Stringer's."

"Well, okay. Thanks, Tiffany. Hudson did the notification to Val, right?"

"Yep, last night. I'm going to stop there after this if you don't mind."

"That's a great idea, Sergeant."

"Don't jinx it, *Henry*. Ha ha!"

"One last thing before I go. We're having a barbeque with Sebastien at my place tonight. He asked if you were coming. I told him I would try to twist your arm, but no guarantees."

Sebastien jerked his head toward Hank, just in time to see that devilish smile again.

"Well, that is extremely sweet of Dr. Grey. What can I bring?"

"Just your cat."

"Yes, sir! See you at the search a bit later."

Sebastien began to speak. "I really wish you wouldn't—"

"Hang on. I gotta make another call." Hank started punching in new numbers right after he hit "END" with Tiffany.

"Who are you calling now?"

"Melissa. I need to tell her we're having a barbeque tonight."

"Does she know her backyard is being patrolled by a mountain lion?"

Hank pointed a finger at his brother. "No! And don't you tell her. And don't worry, I'll call GFP this afternoon and make sure the cat isn't...hey, hon, how's it going?"

18

R udy Goodwin and JT Stahl exited the café just in time to literally bump into a cop who was coming in the door, causing the man to step awkwardly back onto the sidewalk. "Excuse me, officer," Rudy said, as politely as possible. "Let me get that for you." The officer, an important and earnest looking man, nodded his appreciation as he and his companion in plain clothes passed through door. *It's best to stay under the radar of these local boys,* Rudy thought.

Custer was just about fully conscious and bustling when Rudy and JT made a left down the sidewalk and headed for their motorcycles.

"So, where to?" asked Rudy.

"I think we've done enough looking. It's time to start asking."

"What do you mean?"

"I mean, it's time to knock on that old lady's door and ask her where her son's at."

Rudy lifted his leg over his motorcycle and paused before pressing the ignition.

"Won't that blow our cover?"

"What cover is that, exactly?" replied JT, sarcastically. "We ain't exactly cruising the streets in disguise."

Rudy thought for moment, trying to work out what JT meant as he watched his partner walk his bike backward and point it east.

"What is that supposed to mean?" Rudy asked.

"Your name is on your vest, you jackass."

Rudy choked on JT's fumes as he followed him eastward on Custer St. Inwardly, he was fuming as well. If it wasn't Kyle smacking him, it was JT talking to him like he was some helpless chump. But Rudy knew he wasn't a helpless chump. The other two should know it, too. They saw what he'd done to Davis. You would think that Kyle and JT would be a little more respectful.

JT took the lead at the door, and Rudy was glad. *Good,* he thought. *Let him screw something up for a change.*

"Hey there, missus," JT said cheerfully when the woman cracked the door open a few inches, revealing her left eye behind and just under the door chain.

"Can I help you?"

Rudy tried to look behind the woman to see whether anyone else was there with her.

"We're looking for Tiny. You seen him?" replied JT.

"Why are looking for him? What do you want?"

JT glanced over at Rudy for help. But all Rudy could offer was a shrug.

"We're friends of his and he...uh...he was telling us he got a new motorcycle, and he wanted to show us."

Rudy was impressed and gave JT a look that showed it.

"Are you the man who left a message for him a few weeks ago?"

"I don't know what you're talking about, lady. We just want to know where Tiny is."

"So do I."

"Oh, you mean you ain't seen him?"

"You know I haven't seen him. You been sitting outside my house every other day. You think I don't know that? I called the sheriff, you know. I told him about the phone call. You better get out of here."

Rudy smacked the door with the flat of his hand, causing the chain to rattle and the woman to let out a shriek.

"Look, you little skank. You better tell us where he is. We're not playing," Rudy growled through the door.

JT pushed Rudy hard, with both hands against his rock-solid pecs. Rudy lost his balance and fell down into the flower bed, crushing half of the bright pink dianthus that lined the porch.

"Forgive my buddy here. He's a just a little on edge because someone stole his vest and he had to buy a used one at the thrift store. It's a little tight. Sorry we bothered you. Come on, Billy, get out of the nice lady's flowers."

Rudy waited until the lady closed the door before speaking.

"That's it! You're dead! I'm tired of your crap, JT."

JT laughed and patted Rudy on the back. "Oh, come on, man. You almost gave that lady a heart attack. That's all we need at this point. Dust yourself off, Sally. I'll buy you a beer when the bars open. Now, let's get out of here before that lady calls the cops."

Rudy put his hands on his hips and walked a few circles around his bike before getting on it. He knew he needed to be careful, as mad as he was. It wouldn't do any good to beat JT's face in right in front of Tiny's mom's place. He needed to calm down, to think.

The pair of West Side Silverbacks made a few runs through the town before heading northward to Hill City, then eastward to Keystone. They didn't spot Tiny, or the Fatboy he was seen riding, so they headed back down to Custer. At this point, Rudy didn't have too much hope for the current mission. But at least they were doing *something*. And the ride helped him calm down. There's nothing better than a ride through the Black Hills, even if you're doing it with a jerk.

The Rented Mule had just opened and was nearly empty. There were only two other patrons in the place—a couple who were wearing tight-fitting, bright yellow bicycle-riding outfits, their funny pointed helmets sitting on the table. Rudy laughed and poked JT in the ribs as he took a seat at the bar. JT looked at what was making Rudy giggle and gave off a big smile.

"These dives ain't what they used to be," mused JT. "I bet they ordered kale juice."

Rudy did not know what kale juice was, but feigned understanding.

The bartender ambled down and threw a couple of coasters in front of them.

"Hey, fellas. Let me know when you're ready."

"Ready," said JT, instantly. "Couple of beers."

"Great," replied the bartender. "If you're in the mood for something different, we have an amazing low-cal IPA, and we just started offering an APA that's brewed here in town."

"Couple of beers," echoed Rudy.

"You know what we should do, you know, while we're down here?" Rudy offered, after the bartender left to get their drinks.

"I'm dying to know."

"Since we're down here, maybe we should run by the spots where we, you know, where we..."

"You mean where we left those guys?"

Rudy nodded.

"You are out of your ever-loving mind, son. If there are two places we should never go, it's where we left them dudes."

"Well, I was just thinking, you know, to make sure it was all good still."

"Believe me, Rudy. If it were not all good, we'd know about

it. Which is why we need to get out of this place as soon as we can."

The bartender returned with their beers and said, smilingly, "Here you go, gents."

"Much obliged," replied JT, before draining half the glass.

"I haven't seen you guys in here before. Are you here for the rally?"

Rudy was afraid to speak. He waited for JT to respond.

JT's glass made a heavy "thunk" sound as it hit the bar.

"You know what? We're not from around here. We're just here to find a friend."

Rudy tried to catch JT's eyes with a "what are you doing!" stare. But JT continued.

"Yeah, he's been missing for a few days, and we volunteered to help look. His mom's in a panic. Poor lady. Maybe you know him. Goes by Tiny."

"Oh no! Poor Val!" replied the bartender, with concern. "Mickey just got back in town, too. Well, he kind of comes and goes, so I'm sure he's around."

"You do know him, then?" asked JT.

"Sure. He's been coming in quite a lot recently. Actually, come to think of it, he hasn't been in for a few days."

Rudy and JT looked at each other with eyebrows raised.

"Have you guys checked in Hermosa?"

"Hermosa? Why would we check there?" asked JT.

"That's where his girlfriend lives. Or, at least works. Come to think of it, I'm not even sure if she's his girlfriend."

Rudy jumped in. "How do you know?"

"Yeah," followed JT. "He didn't tell us about any girlfriend."

"Well, like I said, I'm not sure she's his girlfriend. I just know that he came in here with her about a week ago. While they were here, she asked if we were hiring. She said she works at a store in Hermosa, but she was sick of it and wanted something new."

"Did you get her name," asked JT anxiously.

"No."

"What does she look like?"

The bartender put both hands against the bar, looked to the ceiling, and twisted his mouth.

"Mmm...she was older, like in her late forties..."

"That ain't old, boy," interjected JT. "But, continue."

"She definitely looked Native. Short. Maybe five feet at most. Graying hair."

Just then the door opened, and a group of tourist-looking people entered the bar.

"Excuse me, fellas," the bartender said, as he went to greet the newcomers.

JT stood up and patted Rudy on the shoulder. "Pay the check, Rudy. And leave a nice tip."

"We going to check out the stores in Hermosa?" asked Rudy, as he took out his wallet.

"Yep. And it shouldn't take too long seeing as though there's just the one."

JT pushed his way through the group of tourists and out the door.

"Hey, Ginger. You're pretty." Rudy flashed his tobacco-stained teeth at the young female clerk who stood behind the counter of the Lucky Stop, refilling the cigarette display.

The girl spun around, frowning. "How do you know I'm pretty from the back of my head?"

"That's what they all say," replied Rudy, snickering and smiling lewdly.

"What? What are you talking about? Can I help you with something?" she replied with a smarmy tone.

'Never mind my idiot friend," said JT, pleasantly. His tone

betrayed an attempt at mollifying the young clerk. "He had an operation to remove the broken parts of his brain, and now the sound of the wind through his ears is driving him crazy."

Rudy shot JT a venomous look. *There he goes again.*

"What? Okay, seriously, can I help you?"

JT's smile morphed into a scowl. "You know anyone named Tiny? We heard he may know someone here."

"What do you want with Tiny?"

JT gave Rudy a fist bump underneath the counter, then said, "Tiny won a sweepstakes, and we have a big ol' cardboard check for him."

Rudy laughed at this.

"Sure. Whatever. I have no idea where Tiny is, but maybe Susan knows. She's on a break."

Rudy twisted his torso around and looked out the front windows of the store, remembering to have passed a lady out front, smoking a cigarette. He caught JT's eyes and pointed toward the door with a shift of his head. The pair exited without another word.

SUSAN WHITEBEAR WAS SITTING on the curb in front of the ice machine about two-thirds through a Salem, yellowed fingers shaking, the silver roots of her bottle-brown hair catching the sunlight. She was deep in thought, submerged in concern, wondering what the cops were thinking and what they knew. Sure, the news reports called it a single vehicle collision, with one fatality, no mention of the victim's name. But they also said, "pending investigation." *Oh lord.*

"Mind if we sit here with you?" The voice came from above and to her right. Susan looked up to identify the mouth from which the question came, but all she could see was a haloed hairy silhouette against the intense sun. She quickly squinted and looked down, waiting for the sting to leave her eyes. When she opened them, she discovered that she was now flanked on the curb by two men—one on each side—sitting next to her.

"Got a cigarette?" asked the man on her left.

Susan quickly offered him the pack, and he pulled out a white tube and put it behind his ear. Susan's mind went into overdrive.

"Thanks, lady," the man said casually, staring out of the parking lot into nowhere. The man on her right was similarly gazing into space, looking unconcerned, unburdened. Susan knew better, though. This was bad. She decided she didn't need her full break after all and got up to go back inside.

"Sit down," said the man on her right, firmly, without shifting his focus from the ether. Susan complied nervously, wishing she had peed at the beginning of her break, instead of planning to relieve herself after her cigarette.

A full two minutes passed before anyone spoke. Susan had plenty of time to think about what this all could mean. *Is this about Tiny? Are these undercover cops?* Finally, she couldn't take the suspense any longer. She took the final drag on her Salem, flicked the butt onto the asphalt, and spoke up, mustering her courage. "What can I do for you fellas?"

The man on her right, the one with "Rudy" on his vest, answered her. "Where's your man?"

Oh no, thought Susan. *This is about Tiny. This is bad, this is really bad. I knew that sumbitch was getting into trouble. Or maybe I'm the one in trouble!*

Susan did not expect the truck—her truck!—to be found so soon. She had no plan for this, had not thought it through to this point. Then it came to her, like a bolt from Heaven. *An accident! That's it! Just like it said on the news.* Fortitude suddenly found her. "I haven't seen him in days. Not since he took off in my truck. I mean, stole my truck." As Susan spoke, her courage increased. She doubled down. "Have *you* seen him?! If you do, you tell the S.O.B. to give me my truck back! I'm sick of walking to work!"

The man on her right turned and looked directly into her eyes, searching them, as if reading tea leaves afloat in the dregs. He sleekly took his index finger and rested it faintly between her eyebrows. "You tell Tiny that Kyle is waiting for his Fatboy. We know he has it. We seen it."

"Yeah, we seen it," echoed the other man.

Rudy continued, his finger still in place. "I just marked you, maggot. I just marked you."

19

It was determined relatively quickly that a search of the entire creek would not be practical—or even possible. The stream carved a curvilinear path through about two miles of the valley that lay directly in the shadow of Bill and Ingrid's sheds, and maybe another thirty miles beyond that. The searchers would have to work smart, not hard.

An examination of the map, and survey of the length of the road, revealed five locations that made sense for a vehicle to pull up relatively close to the creek, be off of the road, and be somewhat obscured from passing vehicles. Four of these five sites were located within the boundary of Custer State Park, and the remaining one was a mere eighty feet out of the park. Because of that, State Park personnel were brought in to help, providing jurisdictional cooperation, not to mention much needed augmentation to the search party.

The initial search strategy was fairly straightforward: the party would be divided into five teams, with each team searching the bank and creek at their designated site. The dog and its handler would start at the northernmost site—site one

—run the dog, then head down to the next site, and so on. As is usually the case in these things, there was some disagreement among the search team members about the chosen approach—too superficial, too random, etc. But given the fact that the whole thing could be a wild goose chase to begin with—all because of some out-of-town anthropologist—well, there was just no sense to shoot the collective law enforcement wad, was there?

Site four was designated the command post, owing to a large, treeless field that bounded the north side of the creek, providing room for vehicles and supplies. The south side of the creek was heavily wooded with ponderosa and bearberry. The road itself bisected the field and spanned the creek, dividing both into west and east portions.

Sebastien counted a dozen or so vehicles stippling the large grass field as he and Hank approached in the Tahoe. Most looked like official county or state vehicles. Many were unmarked, and likely driven by search and rescue volunteers. All were caked in dust accumulated from their respective peregrinations through the valley.

A pale green pop-up canopy shaded two long folding tables in the field between the road and the edge of the creek. Two men in camouflage BDU's were underneath it, examining a large map that covered two-thirds of one of the tables. The whole tableau presented the air of an official operation—which of course, it was. A feeling of alarm struck Sebastien as he realized that he was the cause of all of this. There were no rival causal factors for which to account. He was the prime mover. This commotion was on him.

The two men came out from under the canopy and met the brothers in the field. "Hey-a, Sarge, glad you could finally join us." One of the men, the short and stocky one with the baseball cap and wire rim glasses, gave Hank a confident fist bump as he spoke.

"Well, John, we've just been slumming it, you know. What about you guys? Nicky, how're you doing, bro?" Hank replied.

"All good here, Hank," replied the taller man, with the blaze orange T-shirt under his camo top.

Sebastien had forgotten how smooth Hank always was. So gregarious, so easy—just one of the guys. Such interactions were nearly impossible for him. Especially when they involved strangers. Usually, selective mutism took over. It was as if his jaw were wired shut. Except, of course, when pontificating on forensics. Maybe he should ask Tina about why this might be. He must catalogue this into the ever-growing mental exhibits of the Sebastien Grey museum of oddities and curiosities.

"This here is our forensic anthropologist, Dr. Sebastien Grey." Hank introduced him with an outstretched hand, like a master of ceremonies bringing out the next act. "Dr. Grey, this is John and Nicky. They coordinate our search and rescue team."

"Hey there, great to meet you," Nicky, the taller man, said, offering a hand. His tone was warm and sincere.

"What's up, Doc?" asked John, punching out his fist at Sebastien, who punched it back awkwardly, wondering whether he was doing it right. "Gerry told us about you. That's pretty cool how you found the rest of the body up by the cell tower. We went all up and down the creek there. Didn't see anything. Do you think it could have been put there, after we looked? I mean, we searched all the way up and down that creek bed."

"I suppose it's quite possible," offered Sebastien.

"Don't be fooled, fellas. We were looking in the wrong place the whole time. It was right under our noses. Seb—Dr. Grey knew within a few minutes where the remains would be. It was very impressive."

Nicky smiled widely, betraying a chipped left lateral incisor, Sebastien noted.

"Well, we are super glad you are here."

"Yeah, we really appreciate it. Hopefully, we'll be able to validate what you said about the rest of the RV park body being around here somewhere." John looked up and westward as he spoke, in the direction of the hill with the sheds.

Sebastien was beginning to feel really good. Maybe he belonged here? Maybe these guys really were grateful for the help? Maybe he was the only one skeptical of his worth and purpose? *Shake it off, Sebastien. Focus. Get to work.*

"What do we have going on here? Where are things at this point?" asked Hank.

"Come here. We'll show you," replied Nicky. The two men led the brothers under the canopy and abreast of the folding table with the map on it. An odoriferous wind—a mix of fertilizer and pine—was beginning to pick up a bit, and the map had rolled onto itself at the edge. John flattened it out and put a bottle of water on each corner to keep it from curling.

"We've identified five sites that we think are more likely to be dump locations: one, two, three, four, and five. We're at site four now." Nicky was jabbing at the map with a dirt-stained index finger.

"What makes these five sites more likely? What are your criteria?" Sebastien hoped he wasn't coming off too critical. He wasn't trying to be.

"Great question. Most of the creek is pretty far from the road and difficult to get near in a vehicle—we are assuming that the body would be transported in a vehicle. Do you agree, Dr. Grey?"

"Absolutely. Of course," Sebastien replied.

"Perfect. So anyway, John and one of the detectives drove the road and identified these five areas."

"That's right," interjected John enthusiastically. "In all five locations we were able to park close to the creek and behind tree cover. For example, in this site, just after you cross the bridge, you can make a right onto the shoulder and back into a little opening in the trees. That opening is about fifteen feet from the bank of the creek." John had turned and was pointing in the direction of where the road crossed the creek.

"Okay, we have five initial sites. How are we working them?" Hank asked.

"There's a team at each site," Nicky replied, pointing northward up the road. "The dog has been run through site one, with no indications. Dog and handler are working their way south; they're currently at site two. Each team is walking the creek and the bank, flagging anything that is a bone or looks suspicious. It's a hell of a job, Hank. I had to call in for more flags to be delivered."

Sebastien broke away from the group and made his way to the road where it crossed the creek. Looking westward over the water, he could see half a dozen men and women in hip waders, using long poles to probe for anomalies in the creek bed. Orange surveying flags were planted at various spots on either bank. Sebastien left the road and headed for the closest marker flag.

It didn't take long for him to catch up to the searchers. All of the bones that were marked with a flag were nonhuman, mostly deer with some cow, sheep, and a handful of bones from smaller mammals.

One of the searchers called over to Sebastien from midstream. "Hey there! Are you the anthropologist?"

"Yes, sir," replied Sebastien, deferentially, from the bank.

"Well, what do you think?"

"It's all nonhuman, I'm afraid to say. Mostly young deer and some livestock. Some other bits, too."

"You can tell all that?" the man asked.

"Sure."

"Hmm. Well, how far do you think we should go?"

"If we're thinking that the body would have been dumped near the bridge back there, then I wouldn't think too much farther. Did you search the creek on the other side of the bridge?"

"Not yet. Do you think we should call it on this side and move over there?" The man was now gripping the pole with both hands and leaning on it.

"I think so. But maybe check with the others?"

"We don't know what the hell we're doing on this one, son. We're depending on you."

A blanket of satisfaction rested on Sebastien as he made his way back to the canopy. These people were really nice, and they really trusted him. He was beginning to feel comfortable.

"What do you think?" John asked him, as he regrouped with the others by the map.

"Just animal bones on this side of the bridge. I think they're getting ready to move to the other side. I told them to ask you guys first."

"That sounds great," replied John.

Nicky turned and made his way for the creek. "I'll give them the go ahead," he said, as he left.

"Alright then, John. We'll leave you to it. Let's check out some of the other sites, Dr. Grey," said Hank.

TIFFANY RECOGNIZED Hank's Tahoe among the other cars on the shoulder of the road and pulled over next to it. She couldn't see anyone but heard voices from a little farther down and into the wooded area to the left. She ambled in the direction of the chatter, carrying a bottle of water, gloves, and a small garden fork she'd brought from home. She would not be scraping through the forest again barehanded.

As she penetrated the woods, she began to pick up the sound of running water—the creek, she supposed. The talking became louder, too. After another hundred feet or so, she emerged from the woods and onto a wide grassy area that made up the west bank of the creek. Opposite the creek was an expansive grassland, peppered with massive granite boulders. Looking around, Tiffany spotted Hank talking to a woman who appeared to be in her mid-sixties, wearing jeans, and a utility vest over a blue short-sleeve fishing shirt. She was holding the end of a red leash. A handsome black Labrador was sitting majestically at her feet.

"Oh, hey there! Tiffany, you remember Heather and Cooper," Hank said.

"Of course I do. Thanks for coming out to help again. And you, too, Cooper." Tiffany gave the dog a tickle under his chin. Cooper stood up and lapped at her hand happily, tail lashing against the woman's right leg.

"We're happy to. Just wish we had more success," replied Heather.

"Awe, no luck, huh?" Tiffany said, with a slight frown.

"Well, we still have three sites to search with the dog," offered Hank, optimistically. "The day is still young. How's Cooper holding up, anyway? Will he be good for the other locations?"

"Oh sure. I just have to rest him and make sure he is hydrated. This heat is a killer. I think we're ready to head to the next site now, actually."

"Okay, that's great. We'll be down there in a few minutes, too," said Hank.

"Where is Sebastien?" asked Tiffany, as Heather and Cooper walked toward the road.

Hank lifted his left arm and pointed it toward the creek. "He's searching the bank downstream a bit. They've flagged a lot of bones, and he's going to each one checking to see if it's human. So far, just a bunch of deer and other animals. Sebastien seems to think that there is, or was, a large predator in the area."

"Oh yeah? How's that?"

"I guess most of what he's finding is from young animals. Apparently, that means something."

Tiffany nodded dimly. "It's been good having him here, Hank. He's really been helpful. It was a great idea to bring him out."

"I think he has a thing for you," suggested Hank, with a smug smile.

"You're on crack, boss." Tiffany's sarcastic reply shrouded the brief flash of warmth that radiated in her chest. The feeling surprised and scared her. It was not expected. She tried to brush it off.

"So how did it go with Val?" Hank changed the subject.

"She's devastated, of course. Her sister is with her at the house, and her brother-in-law. I have to be honest; no one seems particularly surprised that Mickey ended up a coroner's case."

"Yeah, I can see that. What did you tell them about the cause of death?"

"Oh, very little. I told them it looked to be an accident, but the autopsy wouldn't be complete until all of the tests came back. Pretty much the same thing our PIO told the press."

"Good girl. Did Val, or anyone there, offer anything helpful?"

Tiffany chose not to be offended by Hank's use of "good girl." He didn't mean anything by it, she knew. He was a good soul, and good souls get the benefit of the doubt in her book. That was something she'd learned from her mother. "Yes. A lot, actually. Val's brother-in-law works at a car dealership in Rapid City, and he said he's bumped into Mickey at a bar in town a couple of times recently."

"How recently? Was he with anybody?"

"Last few weeks, he said. Just biker types. And a lady."

"That might explain the fact that he was on a motorcycle. Maybe he's trying to fit in with a different class of villain."

"Well, get this: Val said she seen a couple of bikers hanging around her house at night. And they even knocked on her door this morning looking for Mickey. And yes, I asked. They were calling him Tiny."

"Really? Hmm." Hank pulled up the mental images of the two men he saw outside the café that morning. "Interesting. Did they seem threatening to Val?"

"She said one of them got pretty ticked when she couldn't tell them where Tiny was."

Hank nodded and pursed his lips in concern.

"I got more, too. You ready for it?" Tiffany pulled off her sunglasses and hung them from the neck of her sheriff's polo.

"All ears, Detective," Hank responded, doing the same with his sunglasses, for no reason in particular.

"One of the times that Val's brother-in-law ran into them, Mickey introduced his lady friend."

Tiffany was savoring the moment, Hank could tell. "And...?"

"He didn't get a full name, but he may have gotten a first name." Another pause.

"I know what you're doing. Stop it!"

"He said it was either Sharon or Susan, he wasn't positive which, though. But Mickey introduced her as his friend from Hermosa."

Hank looked over Tiffany's shoulder and seemed to fish through his brain for the significance of what she had just said. There was no sign of it clicking, so Tiffany helped. "Remember the RO of the truck we pulled out of Deer Gap? Susan White-bear, with an address in Hermosa."

Hank met his protégé's eyes with his own and, with a look of utter sincerity, said, "You're a great detective, Tiffany."

Tiffany didn't want her sergeant to see her blush. She replaced her sunglasses and said, "I'll go fetch our anthropologist." She walked toward the creek, trying to suppress the enormous smile that was beginning to span her pretty oval face.

20

L ower French Creek meandered from north to south generally, but in some locations, it cricked its meagre neck in an east-west direction. This was the case at site three, where the road went over a short bend in the stream just before the creek resumed its usual southward march. As a result, the creek and the road ran parallel to one another immediately south of the bridge. A thick line of trees lined the banks here, but there were a few crannies amongst the pines that could be large enough to park a vehicle.

Sebastien and Tiffany were working their way from flag to flag, starting just below the bridge. There were dozens of them running about three hundred feet down both banks. At this point, most of the searchers were congregating at their vehicles on the northwest side of the bridge and, aside from Sebastien and Tiffany, only Heather and Cooper were actively working the scene. Dog and handler were nearly to the end of the line of flags and the terminus of the designated search area.

"So, can you show me what you look for? How can you tell if a bone is human or not?" Tiffany was leaning over a spot on the bank, her forearms on her thighs, a bead of sweat tracing down her slight nose.

Sebastien was on his knees sifting through the grass, looking for the bone signified by the flag. "Ah, here," he said, taking up the small bone in his hand and turning it over slowly. "This is an ulna, a bone of the lower forelimb. I used to teach my students that you can tell an ulna because, when you hold it horizontally, you can see the 'u' shape on the end." Sebastien demonstrated as he spoke.

"Hey, that's pretty slick," Tiffany replied. She could tell he lived for this kind of thing.

"Now, determining human versus non-human is usually a function of bone size and shape. Humans are one of the few mammals, and the only living primates, that are habitually bipedal—walking on two legs—and that shows in the shape of our bones. Our skeletons are flexible and generalized— meaning they allow us a wide range of movements. On the other hand, quadrupeds—animals that walk on four legs— have skeletons that are built for stability. There's less movement in the sockets of the fore and hind limbs. See here, this bone has a shorter, stubbier end where it attaches to the humerus— the upper forelimb bone."

"And how do you know what kind of animal the bone belonged to?" Tiffany queried.

"To be honest, sometimes I don't know. A lot of it is experience and studying comparative osteology. This looks like a canid to me, probably a fox of some sort."

"Osteology?"

"Yep. Osteo is bones. Anyway, the good news is that as long as we know it's not human, that's usually all that matters."

"You mentioned some of these animals being young. How can you tell that?"

"See this little line here, in the bone." Sebastien pointed to the "U" with his gloved pinky. "This line is where the end of the bone, the epiphysis, is fusing to the shaft of the bone, the diaphysis. When the individual is fully grown that line will have disappeared. Or, if the individually is really young, the end of the bone will not be attached at all. What connects them during the growth phase is cartilage, which decomposes relatively quickly. There are other methods for determining age, but epiphyseal union is a pretty good one."

"Hey, do you think you could use a hand when you do your examination of the remains from the wash? I'd really like to see how you do it and learn some more."

Sebastien began picking at the dirt and grass as if something interesting was still to be found—which it was not. "Sure, uh...of course. I could use some help." Looking up from the ulna, he was shocked to see Tiffany staring intently at him as he spoke, her amber eyes fixed on his own.

Tiffany evidently caught his surprised look and giggled before her full lips came together in a thoughtful crease. "You know, you're a bit of a mystery, Dr. Grey."

"How is that, Detective Reese?"

"You're not nearly as awkward and shy as your brother said you were."

Dammit, thought Sebastien, blushing through his already crimson and sweaty face and pursing his lips. "We'll, I guess you could say I'm in my element," he replied, with an unmasked tinge of resentment.

"Are you referring to working with bones, or being with me?" Tiffany smiled playfully, like a teasing child.

Come on, Sebastien, don't screw this up, he thought to himself. "Both," he said, suddenly glad his brother was such an ass sometimes. Suddenly proud of himself.

Over Tiffany's left shoulder, Sebastien noticed that the searchers, who had all been sitting on camp chairs, tailgates, and the grass a few minute ago, were now walking toward the creek in an animated ferment. "What's going on?"

Tiffany turned around to see what Sebastien was seeing. The searchers were gathering up their tools and walking their direction, en masse. She punched in Hank's cell number and put it on speaker. It was answered on the first ring.

"They got something!" Hank was speaking excitedly, audible chatter from the searchers could be heard in the background.

"Where?" This from both Sebastien and Tiffany in unison.

"Just past the end of the search area. Heather was about to turn around and run Cooper back up the other side of the creek, but the dog picked up on something and kept going. Just a minute." Hank's voice muffled as he evidently covered the phone and spoke to someone nearby. A moment later he got back on. "Yep, it's a body. Cooper found the body."

HEATHER AND COOPER were sitting under a large pine on the west side of the bank when Sebastien and Tiffany arrived. Cooper was lapping from a collapsible water bowl as Heather stroked his head lovingly. The group of searchers were gathering around their find.

About three hundred and fifty feet downstream from the bridge, an errant tap root—from the very pine under which the dog and handler sat—breached the wall of the bank and lunged into the creek. The interceding root caught hold of a pair of jeans belted to a skeletonized torso. The ribs and corroded belt buckle were pointing upward. One of the arms was tangled in the ribcage, the other bobbed in the current listlessly, pointing downstream like the hand of doom.

Sebastien stood staring at the grotesque display as the rest of the team were patting each other on the back and speculating about the various circumstances that brought such a poor wretch to such a poor spot. For Sebastien's part, he was actually stupefied, completely amazed that he had been right. Sure, the logic all worked in his head, and certainly it was sound reasoning on his part. But now that he was looking at the broken frame in the creek, the vastness of the valley around him, and the distance to the hill over the RV park, he realized what a long shot it all was. The thought of what could have happened had they never found the body stretched around him like icy fingers. He suddenly felt cold and so wandered off to find a patch of sun amongst the trees.

For the next several minutes, Sebastien watched as the searchers fell into what was clearly a well-practiced rhythm. It was as if someone had put on music, and they all knew the dance. Distances were being measured, sketches made, copious photographs taken. A man and a woman in blue jumpsuits with "CORONER" in lurid yellow letters across their backs were unfolding a green body bag and carrying it toward the creek. Others were setting up sifting screens, along with plastic buckets; still others were searching the bank and creek bed downstream from the body.

Sebastien noticed Hank and Tiffany break from the bustle and swiveled their heads as if looking for something, or someone. Tiffany caught sight of him and smacked Hank on the arm. They both approached.

"Wow, dude. I mean seriously. You're a game changer, you know that?" Hank sat next to Sebastien on the grass and Tiffany followed suit.

"There's a lot to do now," Sebastien replied, drily.

"What do you mean?" Hank flexed his knees up to his chest and crossed his arms.

"You have two bodies now. That's a lot of lab time."

"I told you, I'd like to help," reminded Tiffany.

"Hey, we're in no hurry," said Hank. "Before yesterday, and today, we'd have a skull and a jaw sitting in the coroner's freezer for the next twenty years, waiting to be cremated as soon as space was needed. Now we have evidence, bodies, a case. We can certainly wait."

"Probably two cases," added Tiffany.

"That's true," conceded Sebastien.

"How much time are you thinking, anyway?" Hank asked.

"A good day, at least. But you have me going out with the biologists tomorrow."

"Oh, don't worry, bro. There's no rush on the autopsies. I know how much you're looking forward to chasing mountain lions through the hills."

"Well I do have a life, you know. I have a friend watching my dog, plus tenants, and cases. I can't stay up here forever."

"Oh crap. Is that a news van?" Hank got up and scurried in the direction of the makeshift parking lot upstream near the bridge. Both Sebastien and Tiffany watched the sergeant walk away. Sebastien saw no van.

"What was that stuff about mountain lions?" Tiffany asked, leaning back on her hands to let the sun wash over her face.

"Apparently people are freaked out about mountain lions..."

"Oh, I knew that," Tiffany interrupted.

"Yeah, well, your boss offered me up to the state biologist, to help them find a lion they've been tracking."

"Are you a mountain lion genius, too?"

"Not at all. But he thinks my work on cheetah predation can somehow help. Which, it cannot. I also think he wants to use me as a plant in the GFP. He's hoping that I'll figure out if they know more than they are saying."

"What are they saying?" Tiffany asked.

"Just that one of their collared lions, a big male, is stalking the cities and towns, eating pets and livestock."

"Dang. Do they have proof of that?"

Sebastien chose his words carefully, supposing that if Hank didn't want Melissa to know about the cat near his house, he might not want Tiffany to know either. That didn't really make sense, but he'd rather not risk causing issues.

"They have a map of the lion's movements, which shows that his home range includes several inhabited areas, and he spends most of his time in, or near, those places. They also plotted the reports of missing pets, which overlaps the lion's movements. Seems fairly circumstantial to me, though."

"In what way?" Tiffany asked, sounding genuinely interested.

"Well, looking at it like it was a murder, or murders, you would never charge someone just for being near the scene of the crime, would you?" Tiffany nodded, and Sebastien continued. "You would need evidence that points to one person, or in this case, factor, over the others. What other factors could be in play here? Tons. Too many to count. Not to mention that missing pets are not necessarily dead pets. But, hey, that's just me. Remember, I'm in the body business. What?" Sebastien would have been tired of her wry smirks by now if she weren't so pretty while in the act.

"You really do live for this stuff, don't you? Hey, I get it. I think it is a good thing. I mean, where would we be if you weren't so...so..."

"Strange. The word you're looking for is strange, Detective."

"What is that line from Sherlock Holmes? It is a capital mistake to theorize before one has evidence." Sebastien's face lit up and Tiffany continued. "Maybe Hank is right—sometimes. Maybe you do see some facts that aren't really there at all."

Sebastien's countenance fell.

"Your brother really respects you, you know. I mean, I don't know what things were like when you were kids. But you are one day in up here and look what's happened already."

Sebastien nodded diffidently but made no reply.

"Well, Sebastien, I think we should go join the others."

Tiffany hopped up, dusted off her backside, and put her hand out to help him up. "We need to make sure everything they flag is flexible and generalized, not built for stability," she said with a wink.

Sebastien took her hand, then took his sweet time getting to his feet.

IT WAS deep afternoon when the coroner investigators and forensic technicians were loading the grim findings into their respective vans: body parts and everything attached thereto for the coroner, and other items of potential evidence for the forensic techs. The search and rescue folks were collecting their flags, and other equipment, and retreating north to civilization in their personal vehicles. Gerry, Hank, Tiffany, and Sebastien were in a now-familiar huddle next to the coroner's van.

"Looks like we got most of the body, according to my people, anyway," said Gerry. "Of course, Dr. Grey, you'll tell us what we may have missed, and we can come back for a second look."

"I'd be surprised if you have everything. I rarely see everything recovered. But I will certainly let you know."

"And how did it go at the jaw site?" asked Hank.

"Good," replied Gerry. "Very good. We found a skull, along with the legs, spinal column, and hips. Both arms, too, although those were several feet away on the slope."

"Probably pulled off by scavengers—that's usually what happens to the appendicular elements," offered Sebastien.

"Sure. Well, anyway, you were right on. Damn right on if I do say so myself. Great job. Really just incredible."

Sebastien blushed and reminded himself what Tina had instructed him about taking compliments. "Thank you very much," he replied, simply.

Gerry began again. "So, we'll have both sets of remains set aside in the freezer for you. Any idea when you will be able to take a look?"

"Sure. I'll come in tomorrow morning."

"Great. Thanks."

"Well, I'm going to leave you meddling kids and head back. Some of the search crew and forensic people are going to meet at the Rented Mule for a celebratory drink. You should join us," Gerry said.

"Thanks, Ger," replied Hank. "But we have an appointment with my barbeque tonight. I'm going to show these two amateurs how it's done."

"Suit yourself." With a wave, Gerry was off to his van.

"Unless of course you two would rather hit the bar?" Hank asked, turning toward Tiffany and Sebastien.

"I've been to your house, Hank. Compared to what you got, the Rented Mule is a place where you go to die of thirst," joked Tiffany.

"I'm not a huge drinker, myself," said Sebastien, instantly regretting this confession.

"Good. I need a designated driver. You can pick me up in your fancy car. Hank, give your brother my address."

As Tiffany walked away, Hank put his arm around Sebastien's shoulders and softly repeated his earlier admonition. "Eat. You. Alive."

21

Sebastien carefully laid out on the bed every piece of clothing he'd brought with him. It looked like his suitcase threw up, had rejected all contents submitted. Nowhere in his sartorial calculations had he included a variable for a social event with a woman to whom he had become surprisingly and undeniably attracted. This was disconcerting. Unforeseen developments always caused him distress.

Twenty minutes, and several ensembles later, Sebastien regarded himself in the full-length mirror affixed to the wall in his hotel room. The khaki chinos, wine-colored cotton tee, and leather sneakers seemed somewhat appropriate to the occasion, if not the company. In any case, it was the best he could do.

Just as he was stepping out of his hotel room, he thought about the mountain lion, and the relative probability of being the barbeque instead of eating the barbeque. He dialed up Hank.

"What's up, bro? You're still coming, right?"

"Yep, on my way now. I was just wondering if you checked with the biology people about the uh…"

"Dude, are you kidding? Of course I did. Twice, actually. The cat has moved northeast several miles. Personally, I think he got wind that you're coming for him," Hank joked.

Sebastien could tell that Hank's laugh was tinged with nervousness.

"That's good. I'm leaving the hotel now."

Fifteen minutes later, Tiffany emerged from her small house as Sebastien sat in his car in the driveway, trying to decide whether he should go knock on the door, or just honk. Her medium-length dark hair had been curled into sepia waves, lining her freshly blushed cheeks. A cotton tank top with lace neck and thigh-length denim shorts accentuated her athletic yet graceful build. Sebastien swallowed hard.

"Who's this?" Sebastien asked, referring to the cat that Tiffany planted on the passenger seat, along with her purse, before climbing in herself.

"This is Mist. Kirby loves him. Hank asked me to bring him with—I hope that's okay? You aren't allergic or anything, are you?"

"Oh, of course it's okay. No, I'm not allergic at all." The dark gray feline stared up at Sebastien, its bright green eyes shooting suspicion.

"Oh good. Kirby would be upset if I didn't bring Mist with me. I'm not joking; that kid wouldn't talk to me for a week last time I showed up at Hank's house without him. I had to ask her to cat sit for me just to get in her good graces again. I wasn't even out of town or anything."

"Well, that is a very pretty cat, and unique. What breed?"

"It's a Nebelung," Tiffany answered, as she situated the cat on her lap and stroked his thick coat.

"You're kidding?"

"No, I'm not. Why?"

"Do you know that *nebel* is the German word for fog?"

"Of course I do! Why do you think I named him Mist? We're not all bumpkins up here, Dr. Grey."

"Oh, that's not what I meant at all. It's just…wow!"

"Did you just say 'wow'?"

"I'm sorry, you're just…so…"

"You can't be smitten with me, Dr. Grey. You've only been here two days." Tiffany had turned herself in the passenger seat, leaning her back against the door. She was smiling broadly and nuzzling Mist on the cheek with her nose, all the while looking directly and mischievously at Sebastien.

A momentary jolt of reproach shocked him, but Sebastien killed it quickly. He was getting the hang of Deputy Reese, and so he caught himself before going over the edge. "I wish you wouldn't call me Dr. Grey," he said, as he put the Rover in drive and consulted the directions on his navigation screen.

Mist began to purr. Tiffany poured the cat's long body across her pale thighs. "That's not much of a denial, is it, Sebastien?"

As they turned from the long dirt road onto the curved driveway of the ranch, a pigtailed flurry of purple and pink came charging out of the open garage. The little girl squealed "Tiffaneeee" and hugged the detective as she alighted from the Range Rover. "Where's Mist? Where's Mist?" she demanded, jumping up and down. Tiffany retrieved the cat from the front seat and handed her over. "Yay!!!"

Sebastien came around from the driver's side at about the same time Hank and Melissa appeared through the front door. The little girl looked perplexed as she saw the apparent stranger approach.

"Kirby, you remember your Uncle Sebastien, don't you?" Melissa said, as she offered him a hug.

Sebastien embraced Melissa, then crouched down and put out his hand. Kirby studied her uncle carefully for a moment, then shouted, "Yes!" She wrapped her free arm around Sebastien's neck and gave him a peck on the left cheek.

"Of course she remembers him," said Hank. "Come on in, little brother, I'll show you around."

"No, I want to!" The six-year-old took Sebastien's hand and led him through the garage and into the back yard. Hank followed while Melissa and Tiffany went in through the front door.

The evening was a little chilly, and the smell of the nearby pine trees competed with the odor of burning cedar from the firepit. The four adults were sitting around the fire and admiring the stars in a semi-silence—Kirby and Mist had been tucked in an hour ago. The breathtaking view of the sky cast a ponderous mood and lulled their conversation.

Dinner had gone fairly well, Sebastien considered. There was far too much talk about him, but he always felt that way. Melissa had inquired about the Block, his work, and his personal life—was he still teaching? Any significant others? He wondered what significance that phrase might hold. *Significant others.* Why not *girlfriend*? Was she implying something? Good opportunity for a resounding disclaimer, though, wasn't it? *No. I don't have a girlfriend at the moment.* Did Tiffany allow a petite smile into her wine when he said that? *I must remember to thank Melissa for being nosey*, he would later conclude.

Aside from the insubstantial sorties into his personal life, most of the conversation amounted to small talk—which meant that Sebastien was largely silent. He could not keep up. It is impossible to rehearse being spontaneous. This was one of his troubles. Thank goodness for Kirby, who had all manner of things to offer the table. She was quite the authority on ponies, princesses, chickens, and her little brother. *I must remember to thank Kirby for being so talkative.*

"Little brother! Melissa, you're pregnant?" Tiffany had

exclaimed. "I was wondering why you weren't drinking! You're usually such a lush!" She laughed.

"Oh ha, ha!" Melissa mocked in return. "We actually don't know the sex yet, but Kirby is rooting for a boy."

Tiffany turned to Kirby, who had been sitting next to her, and pulled a face. "Boy! Yuck!"

Kirby giggled.

"Congratulations, Hen—Hank!" said Sebastien. "That's really great for you all."

"Thanks, little brother. The stable is not the only thing I've been working on," he said, with a jump of his eyebrows.

"Should have put more men on the job; you might have gotten it done sooner," Tiffany said, laughing, a forkful of steak staged at her lips.

"I assume you're talking about the stables?" replied Hank. To which all but Kirby erupted into laughter.

So, as he summed it all up in his mind, Sebastien concluded that the evening had been a very pleasant one. He did not get much—or any—time with Tiffany. But what would he do with that anyway? It was better this way, he knew, as he secretly watched the flames from the firepit throw yellow-orange shades across Tiffany's pretty face.

Hank spoke up, breaking the stillness. "So, before we all fall asleep out here, let's game plan for tomorrow."

"Uh oh, Sebastien, we're being kicked out," Tiffany joked, as she worked her way to a sitting position.

Sebastien marked her figure as Tiffany stretched—curves and cambers pleasantly manifesting against the light of the fire.

"Oh, shut up!" replied Hank, flicking Tiffany on the crown of her head. "I'd like for us to meet in the morning—that includes you, Sebastien. You're all in now, Doctor. Let's level set the three cases."

"Three?" asked Sebastien.

"Yep. I'm including the truck on Deer Gap Road."

"You think they're connected somehow?" asked Tiffany.

"I think it is very possible. I've been reading reports—you should try it sometime, Reese—and the Hot Springs PD report on that stolen motorcycle makes for curious reading."

Tiffany looked up at Hank with interest. "How so?"

"The make and model, specifically. It was a Harley Davidson Fatboy."

Sebastien was tracking. "The motorcycle in the back of the truck was a Fatboy, right?"

"Yes, and that's another thing, which we'll get to later. Can you imagine Mickey getting that bike in the back of the truck by himself? Anyway, Tiffany, do you remember the message left with Val—the one meant for Mickey, I mean Tiny?"

"You're losing me, Hank."

"I don't suppose you have your notebook in your purse?"

"Ah, yep. Sure. It's right here." Tiffany fished through her capacious canvas bag and produced a tattered spiral notepad.

"Okay, read to me what that message said. Word for word if you have it."

"Of course, I do. Can we get some light?"

Melissa went to switch on the patio lights as Tiffany flipped through the pages.

"This is what I wrote down: Hey you Fatboy maggot. The boys in Rapid are waiting. Those other fellas won't be the only ones."

"See what I mean?" Hank asked.

"It must run in the family," Tiffany said with a straight face, looking from one brother to the other. "This can't be a coincidence."

"I don't think so. Tiny was anything but fat. The *Fatboy* must refer to the motorcycle. Of course, that's not even the part that connects Mickey's death to the remains we found."

"Those other fellas won't be the only ones," repeated Sebastien.

"Exactly. I know there is a lot to do tomorrow, but we need to hit the gas on this caper with Mickey. Specifically, you and I, Tiffany, need to pay the RO of that truck a visit. We'll do that while Sebastien works on the remains."

"Can we do that before Sebastien starts his examination? I was going to, uh, attend those autopsies."

Hank grinned knowingly. "Sure. The earlier the better anyway."

"Can I come with?" asked Sebastien.

Hank thought for a moment.

"I think it could be useful to have him there," said Tiffany.

"Let's meet at the station at six thirty. Sebastien, I'll pick you up. Now get your filthy cat out of here and get some sleep."

Tiffany rose and hugged Melissa, congratulating her once again on the pregnancy, then punched Hank square on the shoulder as she made her way to Kirby's room to extricate Mist.

"Sebastien, it has been so good to see you," Melissa offered. "I hope you'll be around for a bit and come visit again."

Sebastien put out his hand. Melissa took it with a smile. "Thanks for having me over," he said. I'm sure I'll be by again. Oh, and that's really great, too, about you expecting, I mean."

Hank and Melissa waved the Range Rover out of the parking lot. Sebastien waved back and wondered what they were thinking—about him, about whether or not he and Tiffany were about to go back to the hotel together. The trio drove along in silence for a few minutes. Sebastien noticed Mist kneading at Tiffany's legs, as if to make a bed.

"Are you cold? Do you want me to turn the heat on?" he asked, reaching his hand toward the dash.

"Nope, I'm okay. Thanks, though. Well, that was a fun evening. A lot better than hanging out with forensic dorks at the Rented Mule."

"Yeah, I'm glad we did this. It was a nice break."

"Speaking of breaks, we're going to be glad we got it. Should be pretty crazy the next few days. I'm really anxious for your examinations of the bodies. Hopefully, you can give us even more to work with."

"I'm really looking forward to that, too," he said, for an entirely different reason.

Sebastien walked her to the front door; he wasn't sure what the protocol was in these instances but figured it would be rude to leave her in the driveway in the dark of night. Later on, it would occur to him how stupid that was. After all, she's a cop. And a fit one at that. She could certainly take care of herself.

"Thank for driving, and for putting up with Mist," she said, as they stood at the front door. Mist mewed his assent, or perhaps because he'd heard his name.

"It was my pleasure. I really did have a great time."

Tiffany gave him a cursory hug, filling his nose with the smell of her perfumed neck.

"Thank you for the ride, Dr. Grey."

"Of course. You're very welcome."

With that, Tiffany unlocked the door and went inside. The clicking of the deadbolt echoed as Sebastien walked back to his car.

WORD ABOUT THE RECOVERIES—AT both sites—spread quickly and inevitably. Salacious news was difficult enough to keep under wraps, but in a small town, it was doubly difficult. It even hit the ten o'clock news out of Rapid City, which blasted rabid speculation over the entire region. The Sheriff's Public Information Officer did a pretty good job of keeping things vague though—two bodies recovered; yes, they look to be connected to the remains that were found last week and last month; no, we don't know their identities or cause of death; yes, please do contact the sheriff's office if you think you know who these individuals could be; no, there is absolutely nothing to indicate that mountain lions had anything to do with these individual's deaths—but still grand theories were beginning to be offered. Some were, of course, completely ludicrous. Others were pretty darn near the truth.

Kyle Corcoran had no need for speculation, or wild theories, or even reasonable conjectures. He knew the truth, the fulsome truth. And he was not the only one either. By Kyle's count, six men knew the facts. And two of them were dead. Very dead. The one, though, the missing one...

Kyle had a bad feeling about all this. This was not good. No Bueno. There is no way the cops could have found the bodies of Jimbo Milford and Dale Davis on the same day without being led to them. And there were only two people who knew where the bodies were dumped. Hell, *he* didn't even know where those two idiots left them. Not exactly, anyway. So, which one was it? Who was talking to the cops? It was a bit of a coin flip, but the odds, he reasoned, were a little better in one direction. He turned off the television and dialed up JT.

"Well?" he spat into the phone.

"Good news, Kyle. We found his girlfriend and put the fear of death into her. It's only a matter of time until we find him."

"What girlfriend? Where?" Kyle was not placated by this news in the least.

"Her name is Susan something. She works at a store in Hermosa. Me and Rudy followed her to her trailer. No one else is in there that we can tell."

"You check the mom's place again?"

"Roger that. We even talked to the old broad."

"You what?"

"We knocked on the door and asked her where we could find Tiny. She ain't seen him for a few days, she said. I think he's dodging us, Kyle. I don't think he's going to bring you another bike."

"Well, guess what, Pumpkin. The bike is the least of my—
our—troubles. Are you watching the news?"

"No Kyle, we're, uh, staking out that Susan lady's place."

"Listen, you dimwit. I can hear that you're in a bar. You just
figure out where he is because, guess what, you know who's no
longer missing? Dale and Jimbo."

"You mean the two guys we—"

"That's right. By some incredible stroke of luck, some abso-
lute coincidence, the cops found both bodies on the same day.
But you know I don't believe in coincidences; I certainly have
no reason to believe in luck either. So how do you think they
managed to pull that off? Hmmm?"

"Geez, Kyle. I don't know. Maybe a hiker, or something?"

"That's one long hike, JT."

"Well what did it say on the news about how they
found 'em?"

"All they said was a human jaw had been found off a fire
road on Custer Mountain few weeks back and they searched
area today. Does 'fire road on Custer Mountain' ring any bells?"

"Jimbo."

"Yep. But that does not explain how they got to Dale. The
only explanation I can think of is that someone is leading the
cops to the bodies. Somebody is talking. Are you talking, JT?"

"Oh, hell no! No way, Kyle. You know I wouldn't do that. I'm
in this as much as you are."

"You got Rudy there with you, right?"

"Yeah, he's right here. Want me to put him on?"

"No, I don't want you to put him on! I want you to keep an
eye on him. You got me? Don't let him out of your sight, and
don't let him talk to anyone."

"Oh man. You really think Rudy..."

"It's either Rudy or you. Take your pick."

"Okay, okay. I'll keep an eye on him."

"Good. And find Tiny."

Corcoran tossed the phone back onto the coffee table and walked out to the back patio for a smoke. He needed to think a bit, plan his next move. He'd clearly made his share of mistakes in this whole thing. He never should have let Tiny live. That was dumb. And maybe he shouldn't have reacted so violently in the first place. So what if Dale and his boys stole the bike back? They should be admired for that. But there was also the principle of the thing. You don't take from Kyle Corcoran. You don't screw with the West Side Silverbacks. People need to know that.

His bigger mistake, of course, was Rudy. He should have tried the guy out a bit more. Sure, the dude was eager to be part of the club, but he was too new to bring into such a high-risk enterprise—an enterprise that would never have been launched if it weren't for his own hair trigger temper.

Too many should haves. Should haves are for suckers. Kyle tilted his head back and blew chalk white smoke into the ink black sky.

22

Susan Whitebear lived in a trailer home community a half mile east of Hermosa, across the road from a small cattle ranch. The stench of manure, heaved by the early morning breeze, accentuated the dismal nature of the place. Hank was fairly sure he had served search warrants in this trailer park before. And he could only imagine the number of dots on the parolee map that were claimed by the Royal Meadows Mobile Home Community.

Number forty-two was a tea-green single-wide with a gravel roof and a narrow, dilapidated porch. In the yard of the next trailer to the left—number forty-four—two manic Dobermans came rushing toward the trio, barking madly, and scraping at the chain link fence that separated the properties.

"Hang on a sec," ordered Hank.

Tiffany and Sebastien waited as the sergeant approached the door to forty-four and knocked. The dogs turned and attacked the fence nearest forty-four's front porch, clearly trying to rip apart the interloper.

A man with a heavy beard and shaved head, wearing only

purple sweatpants, answered the door. His abdomen, chest, and arms were heavily inked.

"Good morning," Hank said, pleasantly. "I'm Sergeant LeGris of the Custer County Sheriff's Office. I was wondering if you could answer a couple of questions for me."

"I'm not on probation anymore." The man pulled his shoulders back and stood a little more erect.

"Oh, I'm not here about your probation. I could care less if you were cooking crack in a baby's bath."

The man was taken aback by the response.

"Ha! I'm just kidding, man. Seriously though, I just want to ask you if you saw or heard anything Saturday night."

The man relaxed, let out a breath, reached into the front of this sweatpants, and scratched himself.

"What do you mean, like gun shots?"

"Well, I just mean anything out of the ordinary."

"Gunshots are pretty ordinary, man."

"Were you here on Saturday night."

The man pulled his hand out of his pants and rubbed his beard, thinking.

"Yeah. Yeah, I was. But I don't remember anything particular about that night."

Hank motioned to the man's front yard with a jerk of his head.

"Did your dogs notice anything? You know, bark or anything?"

"Not really. Well, they did bark at a motorcycle for a minute. Went kinda ape, actually. I had to shut 'em up."

"What time was that?"

"Definitely after midnight. I went to bed about midnight, and the barking woke me up."

"And you went out to calm them down."

"I brought 'em inside."

"Did you see anything when you did that? Like, did you see the motorcycle that was making the noise?"

"Sure. There was a motorcycle in my neighbor's driveway and a dude at her door. I figured that's what the dogs were barking at."

"Which neighbor?"

The man pointed toward Susan's.

"And did you get a good look at the man?"

"Not really."

"But you could tell it was a man."

"Yeah. I mean, a dude looks different than a chick. Even in shadow, or whatever."

Hank almost reached out his hand for a shake, then thought better of it. He settled for a polite, "Thank you very much, sir. You've been very helpful."

The man replied, "Cool," before slamming the door.

"What was that about?" asked Tiffany.

"I'll tell you later. I think we've been spotted." Blackout curtains behind one of the windows in forty-two parted slightly, then dropped back, as they approached.

Sergeant, deputy, and anthropologist stood on the front porch waiting for Tiffany's resounding knock to be answered. A woman in her forties, with poorly died brown hair and an olive face wrinkled beyond her age, opened the door. She bore the look of someone on their way out the door, with her purse over her shoulder and a set of keys in her hand. The rumpled black polo with "Lucky Stop" emblazoned in orange over her left breast looked as if it had been rescued from the hamper. Hank wondered whether or not she was only "out the door" in order to truncate this encounter.

"Susan Whitebear?" Tiffany asked.

"Yes, I'm Susan. Can I help you? I was just getting ready to leave for work."

"I'm Deputy Reese and this is Sergeant LeGris. We're with

the Custer County Sheriff's Office. We're just following up on your stolen vehicle report. We won't take long."

Susan looked at Sebastien.

"Oh, and this is Dr. Grey, with our forensics team."

Hank gave Tiffany a subtle look, as if to say, *That was smooth.* Tiffany raised the corner of her mouth at him in return.

"Well, come on in. But I really only have a few minutes. I have to walk to work, and I don't want to be late again."

"Where do you work?" asked Hank, as Susan introduced them into the small living room.

Susan spread open her arms and replied, "This ain't my bowling shirt."

Tiffany laughed hard, causing Susan to relax perceptibly.

Only Tiffany and Hank sat down on the couch. Sebastien opted to stand.

"This is a cozy place, you have. Do you live here alone?" This was Tiffany's case, and Hank let her do most of the talking.

"Yes. Yes, I do," answered Susan, curtly.

Tiffany got to the point. "When did you notice your truck missing, Ms. Whitebear?"

"Well, like I said to the deputy on the phone, I went to leave for work on Sunday, and it was gone."

Hank noticed Sebastien turn his attention to the dining area, then disappear into the kitchen. Susan's eyes followed him.

"What time was, that?" Tiffany produced her spiral notebook and was recording the answers.

"Well, I had the early shift, so that would have been about six."

"Six a.m. that you left here, you mean?"

"No, no. My shift started at six. Sorry. I left here about ten 'til. I mean, I tried to leave. When I came out to my truck being gone, I had to walk to the store." Susan fingered her keys as she spoke.

"And what time did you get to work, then?"

"About quarter after six."

"According to our records, you reported the truck stolen that afternoon, at about..." Tiffany flipped through her notebook. "...about two-thirty."

"That's seems right," Susan replied.

"Why did it take you so long to report it stolen?"

"Well I was working! It was busy as hell in the store that day. I didn't get a break at all. When was I supposed to report it?!" Susan set the keys next to her in her yellow recliner and began to rub her palms against her denimed thighs.

"Of course. That makes sense," agreed Tiffany, not making anything of Susan's minor outburst.

"Do you have any idea of who might have taken it? Could a family member, friend, or boyfriend, or girlfriend maybe borrow it without asking?"

"No one that I can think of. And I don't have any family. Not around here, anyway. But...cars are stolen all the time—out of here, too. It happens all the time. Why send the three of you out here? I don't get it. I'll file an insurance claim and remember to lock my doors next time."

Hank gave Tiffany the signal with his eyes.

"Do you know a Mickey McCallister? He also goes by Tiny."

The color drained from Susan's face. She broke Tiffany's gaze and looked down at the cheap green carpet below her feet. Beads of sweat began to form above her eyebrows.

"Yes, I know him. We've hung out a little bit. Why? Do you think he took my truck?" Susan was back to fondling her keys.

"Do *you* think he took your truck?"

"Well, I suppose it's possible. But..."

"When was the last time you saw him?" Tiffany readied her pen once more.

"Oh, let me see. Well, that would have been Friday night. We went for steaks in Rapid City."

"Can you tell us about that? Walk us through that evening? What time was that? Did you drive, or Mickey? Or did you meet him there?"

Susan bolted out of the chair, red-faced and pointing, interestingly, at Hank. "I don't know what damn time it was! What does it matter? You're supposed to be looking for my damn truck! Would you please tell me what is going on?"

Hank stood up and pointed his finger back at Susan. "Sit down!"

Susan's rage was quickly replaced by pale shock. She fell back into her chair, her mouth trying to form a response, but nothing came out.

"Take us through Friday, please," Tiffany repeated, speaking softly.

"I got off work at four that afternoon, went home, showered, and got ready, then met Tiny, er, Mickey in Rapid at six thirty."

"So, you didn't drive together?"

Susan shook her head.

"Where exactly did you meet Mickey?"

"Let me see. It was Sandy's Steakhouse."

"The one on Omaha?" interjected Hank, who noticed Sebastien re-emerge from the kitchen as he sat back down.

Susan nodded. "We were there until about eight."

"What next?" asked Tiffany.

"That's it. We left."

"Together?"

"No."

"Did you notice if Mickey was on a motorcycle that night?"

Susan wiped her forehead with the palm of her hand and shook her head lightly at Tiffany's question.

"How did Mickey seem when you were at dinner? Was he acting any differently? Did he seem worried, at all?"

"He was, actually. He seemed on edge. I mean more than usual. He kept looking over his shoulder. And he barely touched his food. It was really strange. Oh, and there was something else—now that you mention it."

"Please, go ahead," prompted Tiffany.

"Two bikers came by my work yesterday. They were looking for Mickey."

"Mickey, or Tiny?" asked Hank, before Tiffany had a chance to ask the same thing.

"Tiny. Definitely Tiny."

Susan went on to describe the two bikers—both big and hairy, both white, one with "Rudy" on his leather vest. As she spoke, Hank marked how odd it was that Susan was now speaking much more freely and with more confidence.

"I SHOULD HAVE PUSHED HER HARDER," remarked Tiffany, from the front passenger seat of the Tahoe.

"No, Tiff. You did great," Hank assured her.

Tiffany turned to look at both Hank and Sebastien, who was in the back seat. "Where does this leave us?"

"We need more evidence, and we need to corroborate some things. The guy next door told me that his dogs went crazy on Saturday night because they heard a motorcycle. He looked out his window and saw a man on Susan's porch and a motorcycle in her driveway. He couldn't describe the man though. He just knew it was a male."

"What time was this?" asked Tiffany.

"Some time after midnight. He couldn't be more specific. Did we ever get a time of death?"

Out popped Tiffany's notebook, once again. "Um, let's see... estimated to be between eleven pm Saturday and four am Sunday. Fits perfectly."

"The problem is, now we have competing theories, and both involve motorcycles. Who was here on Saturday night?

Mickey on his new ride? One of the bikers who were looking for him?"

"So, you think that story was legit?" replied Tiffany.

"I do," began Hank, "I saw the same two bikers that came to visit Susan. They were walking out of the café as Sebastien and I were going in yesterday morning. They were not local, and one of them definitely had the name 'Rudy' on his vest. We— you—will need to chase that down. Also, we'll need video."

"I know. I'll pay a visit to Sandy's and the Lucky Stop. I'm also going to canvas this place to see if anyone has external cameras."

"Good. Sebastien, you're awfully quiet." Hank twisted his torso to look at his brother.

"She killed him. She killed him along with the tow truck driver. Or, at least he helped to dispose of the body and the truck."

"Wait. What? Bro, even for you that is off the chain."

Sebastien didn't react to his brother's incredulity. "Last night you said that there is no way Mickey could have gotten that motorcycle in the back of the pickup by himself."

"Yeah, so? It's a long way from that to the tow truck driver. Especially since we now know he had bikers looking for him. They could have gotten the bike in the truck."

Sebastien gave his eyes a half-roll at Hank. "They were looking for him yesterday. He's been dead since Saturday night or Sunday morning. Why would they be looking for him if they killed him?"

Tiffany smirked

"Okay," agreed Hank. "You have a point there. But why the tow truck driver? That's totally out of left field."

"Not when you consider the fact that the guy's business card is on Susan's refrigerator."

Hank swung his head from Sebastien to Tiffany, whose face

had drained of its levity, then back to Sebastien. "We didn't use the local tow guy for that; he was tied up."

"Exactly," declared Sebastien. "That was very convenient. And did you watch that guy hook up the truck? He put his hands all over the tailgate, like he was going out of his way to leave his palm prints. He probably got less action on his wedding night."

"Sebastien, you have a sense of humor! I love it!"

Tiffany reached back and briefly stroked Sebastien's knee while she spoke.

"What was the name on the card, Sebastien?" Hank pulled his radio mic off the dash and was ready to push talk.

"Shermer Wreck and Tow. I couldn't see the entire address, but I saw Hill City."

"That's like thirty miles from here," offered Tiffany.

"Dispatch, this is 1Y7, can you look at the call log from the fatal on Deer Gap from this last Tuesday? I need to know the name of the tow company that responded."

"Stand by 1Y7." The radio chirped.

"I know from experience that I'm going to regret asking this, but, anything else on your mind?" Hank asked, while waiting for dispatch to reply.

"Just one thing," said Sebastien. "That lady's coffee maker didn't have a coffee pot on it. Aren't those things usually glass?"

"1Y7"

"Go, dispatch."

"The tow company was Shermer's Wreck and Tow. The driver was Colin Shermer. Do you want the contact info?"

23

T iffany stared at the little monitor in the dimly lit office of Sandy's Steakhouse as the restaurant manager, a man who seemed altogether too young to be in charge of anything, sat next to her, deftly turning a black knob to move the video forward and backward. Fortunately, the camera system was top-of-the-line (according to the man, anyway), and the images were clear and time-stamped. It didn't take long to pull up the video from last Friday and see Susan and Mickey walk through the front door at 6:37 pm. The pair were then led to a table in the dining area, where they were seen on video for the next hour and a quarter.

Tiffany asked the man to bring up the video from the parking lot. The man explained that there was only one camera, and this resulted in a "damn blind spot." But he queued up the footage, nonetheless. Susan and Mickey could be seen leaving out the front door and walking toward a small red truck—Susan's truck. The footage showed Susan getting in the truck and rolling down the window.

After a few minutes of talk through the open window, Susan could be seen driving away, while Mickey walked away and into the blind spot. It seems likely from the footage that Susan was possibly telling the truth about not knowing whether Mickey was riding a motorcycle that night. Tiffany watched the video for a further few minutes but could see no sign of a motorcycle, or any other vehicle leaving the parking lot.

Tiffany thanked the manager and exited into the parking lot, then spun around to look at the front of the restaurant. There, mounted to the soffit of the hip roof, just to the right of the entrance, was the single camera. Tiffany then walked the front of the building to the left of the entrance and saw no camera covering that part of the parking lot. But she did notice another parking lot exit to the west of the building. Mickey could have driven (ridden?) out this way without showing up on the video.

Tiffany thought through these minor developments as she made her way south to Hermosa. On the video from the restaurant, Mickey and Susan seemed somewhat close and chatty. There were no signs, one way or the other, of paranoia or concern on the part of either. Moreover, the times just about matched up to Susan's story. From the standpoint of the timeline for the murder, none of this mattered particularly. But it did show the relationship between Susan and Mickey, as well as somewhat corroborate the statement of Val's brother-in-law. Susan was likely the mystery woman whom Mickey had been seen with around Rapid City.

Less than an hour later, Tiffany was showing her badge to the young redheaded woman behind the counter at the Lucky Stop—probably unnecessarily, since she was wearing her Sheriff's polo and had her duty weapon strapped to her small hip. But asserting authority was one of the few perks of a job otherwise filled with stress.

"Excuse me, I'm Detective Reese with the Custer County Sheriff's Office. Is the manager here?"

"Sure. Just a sec," replied the clerk, who then left the counter and disappeared into a darkened back room.

While she waited, Tiffany scanned the small store for cameras. There were several throughout the space—all obvious with small flashing red lights signaling their omniscience to any potential bad actors. This was promising, Tiffany thought.

A few minutes later, the clerk returned alone.

"The manager will be out in a minute. He's finishing up a phone call."

"Perfect. Thanks," replied Tiffany. "Hey, while I wait, do you have time to answer a few questions?"

The young woman looked around the store, which was void of customers at the moment. Tiffany took this as a somewhat sarcastic yes.

"Were you working early Sunday morning?"

"This last Sunday?"

"Yes."

"Oh yeah. I was here. We were very busy—I mean, *I* was very busy," she answered with a roll of her eyes.

"You mean you were working alone?" Tiffany took out her notebook, sensing important information was about to be revealed.

"Well, I wasn't supposed to be. But, yes, I was. We had a whole busload of tourists stop in before I even got the coffee going. It was a circus."

"You said you weren't supposed to be working alone. Who was scheduled to work with you that morning?"

"Susan was on the schedule."

Tiffany tried to not to betray her growing sense of interest. She pulled the pen from the pocket on her sleeve and said, "I see. Do you know Susan's last name?"

The woman replied, and Tiffany wrote, "Whitebear" in her notebook.

"So, she never came in?"

"She did, but she was late. By the time she made it in the rush was over."

"What time was that?"

"A little after eight, I think. What is all this about anyway? Is this about those bikers who came looking for Tiny?"

Tiffany feigned ignorance. "Tiny? Who is Tiny?"

"That's Susan's boyfriend. They came around yesterday asking if I'd seen him. I told them to ask Susan. After they talked, Susan looked pretty rattled. I figured something was up."

"Can you describe these guys? How many and what did they look like?" Tiffany's pen was poised.

"Two of 'em. Both were white guys. One was freakin' huge. Maybe six-four. He had black hair and a bushy black beard with some sort of beads in it. He also had a patch on his vest that said...let me think...I think it said *Randy*. The other guy was a little shorter—under six feet. He was bald and had one of those mustaches that goes down the sides of the mouth—you know what I mean?"

"I think I do. Thanks. We'll look into that. So, back to Sunday morning. You're sure Susan didn't come in until around eight?"

"After eight. Yep. I'm sure."

"What about today? Is Susan here today? Or did she work earlier?"

"Nope. She's not on the schedule. It's just me and the manager until the night shift comes in."

Just then a man emerged from the back, shaking his head apologetically and offering his hand.

"So sorry, Officer. We had a mix-up with a vendor, and I had to straighten it out."

"No problem, sir. Your employee here...uh..."

"Evie," the clerk interjected. "Evie Granger."

"Evie has been very helpful."

"She's our best." The middle-aged manager winked lecherously at Evie as he replied. "Now, what can I do for you?"

"I was hoping to take a look at your security camera footage from last Saturday night and Sunday morning. And yesterday as well. I understand you had some bikers here causing trouble."

The man suddenly looked crestfallen.

"I was afraid you were going to ask me that. You see, our camera system is out of order at the moment."

Tiffany didn't bother containing her incredulity. "What do you mean out of order? This is a convenience store? How the hell do you have a camera system that doesn't work?"

"Officer, I promise, we have an excellent camera system. It's fully digital. It's just that, we suffered a virus attack a few weeks ago, and the hard drive became corrupted. My tech guy says it was a Russian malware thing—whatever that is. Anyway, I assure you it will be in working order soon."

"So, no recording for the last few weeks?"

"No, ma'am."

"What's your name, sir?" Tiffany was in full authoritarian mode now.

The man turned pale. "Toby."

"Okay, Toby. Here's the deal. You have this nice young lady here working in your store with no security cameras. That pisses me off. So, I'm going to send Code Enforcement out here every damn day until those cameras work. I'll make sure every violation gets documented and cited. You got me?"

Tiffany didn't wait for a response. She just walked out the door. Had she turned around, she would have seen Evie Granger smiling wider than she had in a long time, and waving goodbye like she was waving from the dock to a departing aircraft carrier.

. . .

IT WAS PUSHING MID-AFTERNOON WHEN, later that day, Tiffany picked up her phone and dialed in Hanks's number. He picked up on the first ring.

"Hey Tiff, what's shakin' bacon?"

"It's a big nothing burger on the surveillance cameras, boss. The video from Sandy's pretty much confirms Susan's version of events from Friday night. Except, Mickey did not seem agitated on the video. It wasn't obvious that anything was bugging him."

"Interesting. What about the mobile home park?"

"I just knocked on every door. Only a handful of people were home. No one who answered has a security camera or knows a neighbor who does. I also walked the entire street and didn't see a camera on any of the houses."

"Hmm. Did you knock on Susan's?" asked Hank.

"You really think she would admit to having a camera? Even if she did, she would have taken it down if she did something to Mickey—or if he were there on Saturday."

"You did, though, didn't you?"

Tiffany could hear the smile in Hank's voice.

"Yes, I did. No answer."

"Ha! Got ya!"

"There's more, though. I went to the Lucky Stop and found out that their camera system has been down for a few weeks."

"What the—"

"I know. I know. I chewed the guy out. Anyway, the clerk there said that Susan was supposed to be working early on Sunday, but she didn't make it in until eight or so."

"She told us she got there just after six."

"Exactly," replied Tiffany. "And not only that, Susan didn't work today. She wasn't scheduled. It was just a ruse to get us out of the house this morning."

"We kind of figured that, though."

"Yes, we did. And there's one more thing. The clerk told me

two bikers came into the store yesterday. They were looking for Susan. She said one of them had on a leather vest with a name patch that said Randy."

"Was she sure about the name?"

"A better question would be, were *you* sure about the name?"

"I'm a trained observer, Tiff. You know that."

"Yes, I do know that. And no, she did not seem sure about the name."

"So, what's next on your end?" asked Hank.

"I thought I would go check on your brother. What about you?"

"I'm on my way to Shermer's Wreck and Tow to follow up on Sebastien's hunch."

"Seems pretty farfetched."

"Yep. Almost as farfetched as a skull up at Wandering Hills matching with a body in French Creek. Or as farfetched as a whole team of searchers missing a skeleton that was a few feet away from them."

'Touché, boss. Hey, by the way, you're not talking while driving, are you?"

"Gotta go, Detective. Almost there."

Tiffany next called Sebastien to see whether he was still examining the remains found the previous day. He indeed was and still had more work to do. She promised to join him in an hour. First, she wanted to run home and freshen up. Of course, she didn't tell him that.

24

Hank hung up the phone just as he approached Hill City. The last bit of his conversation with Tiffany—about Sebastien's hunches—reminded Hank of a clogged gutter during a pounding rainstorm, the water spilling over the culvert wall and down the front of the house, converting the flowerbed into a churning lagoon. In those situations, the solution is oftentimes quite simple. You just have to pull out the single offending impediment—a clump of leaves, the neighbor kid's baseball—and whoosh, the water once again flows freely and in the intended direction.

In the case of Mickey-slash-Tiny, it was Sebastien who reached in and cleared the obstacle. It had all been one big *whoosh* since Sebastien arrived. Hank hoped that a few well-considered questions for the tow truck driver might keep the water flowing. As it turned out, it was far easier to pull the soggy, rotting clump of dead vegetation from the gutter that was Collie Shermer than Hank anticipated. Just one small lie did the trick. Well, two really. They weren't even lies, technically.

"Thanks for making time, Mr. Shermer. I know it's probably inconvenient—me popping in like this."

"Not at all. Happy to help our local cops. What can I do you for?"

"I have a few questions about the tow you did for us. The one on Deer Gap Road."

Hank was reminded how large Colin Shermer was. The man was shorter than himself and probably weighed around 280. He began to doubt that a person in such shape could be involved in a murder, then remembered how Colin climbed down the hill to hook up the truck. Although, despite Shermer's large belly, the man did look pretty solid in the arms and shoulders.

They were sitting in the small and cluttered office at Shermer's Wreck and Tow. Stacks of tow receipts, bills, and other administrative jetsam were piled dangerously on the corner of Shermer's desk, threatening to topple over onto the coffee- and grease-stained tile floor. As soon as Hank stated the purpose of his visit, Shermer began adjusting the paperwork skyscraper, trying to steady and rearrange the papers to prevent them from falling. Hank thought he might be detecting nervous energy in these histrionics. Maybe Sebastien was right about the tow truck driver—Shermer—being involved. It couldn't hurt to push a little.

"How often do you get tows down south? Deer Gap Road is a bit out of your patch, isn't it?"

"A bit. But if the local guys are tied up, they call another company."

Hank shifted in his chair, settling in.

"Tell me how that works. I mean, how does our dispatch know to call you as a backup? Is there like a list, or something?"

"There is, but sometimes they can't know if you're busy, too. You need to let 'em know you are available." Shermer looked to be settling in as well. The innocuous shop talk was loosening him up.

"You mean when something happens? When a tow truck is needed? Hmm. That's fascinating, Mr. Shermer. I'm usually on the other end of these things. I never knew the tow companies worked like that."

"Oh yeah. We gotta be really good with our time. We can't have the wrecker sitting around in the yard. You gotta move in before the other guy when there's an opportunity. There's a lot of competition in this racket."

"But how do you know there's an opportunity? Like the crash up on Deer Gap, for instance. How do you find out before another company does?"

"Easy," responded Shermer, pointing a pen across the office to a small credenza near the door.

Hank reproved himself for not seeing it when he came in.

"Oh, a scanner. That makes sense. I don't know why that didn't occur to me. I figured you guys didn't know we needed a tow until we called. Were you busy on Tuesday, Mr. Shermer? Did you have a lot of tows?"

"Not really. There was this family from Florida whose van broke down in their campground."

"When was that? Before you responded to the crash on Deer Gap?"

"Yep. That was in the morning. They had an old minivan. It smelled like boiling transmission fluid. I can't believe they brought that hunk of tin all the way from Florida. Good luck getting home in that thing. That's what I wanted to tell 'em, anyway."

"Then that would have left you a good chunk of time between jobs. Which, based on what you said earlier, means you found out about our crash by listening to the scanner, hoping something would come up. Would that be correct?"

Shermer lean forward in his chair, suddenly looking serious.

"What's this all about anyway? I've ain't never had to answer these kinds of questions before. I'm just the guy who yanked the truck out of the ditch."

"Mr. Shermer, the truck you pulled out of the ditch didn't get there by accident. And the guy behind the wheel didn't die behind the wheel." Hank made sure to speak with certainty and confidence.

"I still don't see what that's got to do with me."

"The truck you pulled out of Deer Gap yesterday—do you happen to know the owner?"

"No, but I got it somewhere if ya need it," Shermer answered.

Hank smirked. Shermer knew perfectly well that the sheriff's office had the registered owner of the truck—and the motorcycle that was in the truck's bed, for that matter.

"No, I mean personally. Do you know the owner personally?"

"I don't think so. The name didn't ring a bell, anyways."

Shermer's equivocal reply was accompanied by a gulp that jiggled his chin noticeably. Hank read this as an opportunity to strike.

"What about the dead man behind the wheel? Did you know him?"

"I don't know who that fella is. I didn't get a good look at him, and I didn't ask the cops who he was. That ain't really part of the tow, ya know?"

"Sure, sure. That's makes perfect sense," Hank conceded, before laying a haymaker. "Can you think of any reason why your fingerprints would be on the big rock that was found in the cab of the truck?"

"Oh...well..."

Shermer shifted in his chair uncomfortably. His jowls shimmied and his belly pushed at the blotter on his desk, which in turn tipped over a paper cup. A few drops of what looked—and smelled—like whisky moistened the blotter.

"I touched a lot of things in the cab of the truck. I had to. Part of the job, ain't it?"

"No, you didn't. I was there. You don't recognize me?" Hank forced eye contact to bring his point home.

Shermer averted his eyes, distracting himself with the stack of papers once more. His armpits looked like they had been sprayed with a firehose. Hank noticed Shermer's rapidly blinking eyes and pressed again.

"And what about your business card being found in Susan Whitebear's mobile home? It was on the refrigerator. You just told me that you didn't know the owner of that pickup. You didn't even recognize the RO's name, you said."

"Well, that's probably just a coincidence. I probably gave her a tow at some point or fixed her flat, or somethin'. I just forgot. Do you know how many people I deal with in this job?"

"We can check on all of that," stated Hank, coldly. "Cell phone records, cell tower dumps. It's pretty easy these days." Hank couldn't remember what a cell tower dump was, but he knew it was an actual thing, and it sounded good.

Shermer rubbed a few fingers over the rectangular-shaped object in the breast pocket of his shirt.

"What's going on here? Why are you talking to me like I'm a suspect?"

Hank ignored the question. "Or maybe you met Susan in a bar? Or maybe you were sleeping with her? Or maybe you were *hoping* to sleep with her? I'm sure we can check on those things, too."

Shermer's bushy eyebrows jumped about a quarter inch up his forehead at that ultimate question. Hank watched as the tow man turned to look out of the office window, rubbing his right temple—as if kneading a fiction into his brain that would fit the facts being heaved at him. He was also breathing more loudly at this point, emitting noisy extirpations, like a bulldog with a head cold. An odd thought suddenly popped up to the front of Hank's brain: is this what a mountain lion sees just before the prey takes its last breath?

"And another thing: if you don't know Susan, why would we have your wrecker on video in her driveway?"

Shermer suddenly turned from the window and faced Hank with a look of stern defiance. Hank braced himself for the volley of protestations and fist-shaking.

"Look. I don't know what you're talking about." Shermer's response was firm but strangely calm.

"So, you're telling me that you had nothing to do with the death of Mickey McCallister. And, keep in mind before you answer, we can and will check your story."

"Who's Mickey McCallister?"

"That's the name of the guy we pulled out of the truck. He also goes by 'Tiny.' By sheer coincidence, he happens to be—or was—the boyfriend of the lady who owns the truck, the lady who reported it stolen. Does any of that ring a bell?"

"Boyfriend! No, I didn't know he was her boyfriend! And I didn't do anything, anyway. I didn't kill that guy. That slut did!"

Hank was too shocked to respond. Had he heard all that right? Had he just heard that Sebastien's crazy theory was, in fact, correct? Sure, he was willing to entertain the idea for the sake of giggles. But the reality of it was just too—what was that word Tiffany used? Farfetched.

"Look. Okay. I did help her get rid of the body. But he was dead when I got there. She killed him."

Hank actually had to compose himself. He had to force himself out of his amazement as he stood up and pulled his handcuffs from his belt.

"Stand up and turn around, Mr. Shermer. You can tell me all about it down in Custer."

Once Shermer was handcuffed, the two men sat down, and Hank called dispatch for a transport deputy.

"I don't suppose I could have a cigarette and a bit of whiskey while we wait?" asked Shermer.

"No-can-do on the liquor, Mr. Shermer. Where do you keep your cigarettes?"

BACK AT THE STATION, Hank texted Tiffany with an update before joining Shermer in the interview room. When he did enter the room, he found Shermer with his arms folded on the table and his head resting against his hands. He looked to be asleep.

"Mr. Shermer, you alright?"

The man sat up and leaned back, rubbing his eyes. "Sure. And call me Collie, okay?"

"Okay, Collie. That's short for Colin, right?"

"I haven't gone by that since grade school."

"Well, why don't you tell me what happened with Susan and Mickey? How did this all start?"

"She called me on Saturday night—well, I guess it woulda really been Sunday morning—and told me that she offed a guy. She said he attacked her. Tried to rob her. Like a home invasion kinda thing."

"What time was that?"

"I don't know. Two or three, I think."

"So, she called you asking for help? Or did you offer to help?"

"She asked if I could come help her get rid of 'im. Like I told you, I didn't kill that guy. She did. And I'll be damned if I'm going down for it. I may be dumb, but I'm not stupid."

"Well, Collie, I'm not really sure what that means. But if you tell me how you know Susan, and about everything that went down that night, it might make it easier to prove that you didn't take part in killing Mickey."

"We met at a singles thing at the VFW in town."

"Here in Custer, you mean?"

"Yeah."

"When was this?"

"About a month ago."

"Are you a veteran, Collie?"

"Desert Storm '90."

"That's very cool. Thanks for your service," Hank replied with sincerity.

This evidently made Shermer relax a bit. Hank noticed the man's shoulders drop a centimeter or two.

"So, you met Susan at the VFW. Did you start dating after that?"

"I gave her my card, and she gave me her phone number. But we didn't date or anything."

"Did you call her after the VFW thing? Or see her?"

Shermer's forehead turned a pale pink, which made the island of graying hair on the top of his head stand out.

"I tried. But she never picked up."

"Oh, she gave you a bad number. Dang brother. I hate it when they do that," Hank said, smirking.

There was something in Hank's response that evidently triggered Shermer, who sat erect and once again looked defiant and angry. Hank braced himself.

"Oh no. No, man. She did not give me a bad number. 'Cause guess what? When she called me at three o'clock in the damn morning, it was from the same number that she gave me! The same number I'd been calling!" Shermer smacked his fist down on the table to punctuate his point.

Hank felt an acute sense of sympathy for Shermer. The poor man had been used. Of course, all of this could be—would be—easily verified in the phone records. If it were true, then Susan had played Shermer like a guitar. Hank made a mental note not to rub it in. He stayed on point.

"So, she calls you and asks you to come help her get rid of this guy who she said was an intruder that she had just killed. Correct?"

"Correct."

"Did she say how she killed him?"

"Not on the phone. But when I got there, she said she stabbed him."

"Did you see the knife she used?"

"She didn't use a knife. She said she stuck him with some glass or something."

Damn you, Sebastien, Hank thought.

"Whose idea was it to put the body in the truck and take it to Deer Gap?"

Shermer didn't answer. He just looked down at the table.

"You yourself said that you've pulled many vehicles out of that gap over the years."

Again, no response from Shermer.

"Then what?" Hank continued. "Did you go back and help her clean up?"

Shermer nodded.

"Let me ask you this, Collie. How did you get the motorcycle in the back of the truck? That must have been a bear."

Shermer smiled faintly and replied, almost proudly, "I keep a pair of aluminum ramps in my wrecker. I just pushed the bike into the truck."

As Hank nodded, Shermer's eyes narrowed and his forehead wrinkled in confusion. "Hey, if you had me on video, you musta seen that," he said.

"Well, Collie. Here's the thing: we didn't have you on video."

. . .

HANK EXITED the room and called Tiffany, who was on her way to the coroner's office. He filled her in on the details of Shermer's interview and instructed her to write a search warrant for Susan's house as soon as possible. All-in-all, he was feeling good about this investigation. Everything Shermer told him should be pretty easy to verify.

25

A thumbnail sketch of the aforementioned second-hand and first-hand accounts was shared with Sebastien as he sorted through the toe bones recovered from the slope above the wash. Tiffany was leaning forward against the autopsy table as she spoke, her white sheriff's polo untucking slightly from her tan cargo pants just above the right pocket. Her hair was now in a simple bun—it was down this morning—a few strands having escaped, like brown lightning shooting from a Tesla coil. But Sebastien noted with keen interest that her make-up seemed refreshed—the faint sweep of pale lilac above her eyes just a little darker than it had been earlier. This was the first time they had been alone since last night, and despite the decomposing bodies all around him, Sebastien still had the smell of her perfume in his nose.

"So, I wrote a search warrant on Susan's house, citing Colin Shermer's confession," Tiffany said, continuing her narrative. "We can't tell if he was just an accessory after the fact or took part in the killing. He claims Susan called him in a panic early Sunday morning, and he went over there to find a man—Tiny —in a bloody heap on the kitchen floor."

"Did he know Tiny?" asked Sebastien, as he put the terminal phalanx of the left big toe next to its proximal neighbor.

"He says no. Right now, we don't have any reason to believe, or disbelieve him. Susan told Shermer that Mickey assaulted her in the kitchen, and she stabbed him in self-defense. I have a feeling we'll know much more after we bring in Susan and search her house. Plus, we're going to release a statement to the press this afternoon, along with a plea for information. Once the public knows who the victim is and what really happened, we're hoping more information will come in."

"Do you have her in custody?"

"Not yet. We don't know where she is. Shermer said she called him this morning after our visit. He said she was losing it and probably took off. We'll find her. She has nowhere to go."

"Did Shermer say what Mickey was stabbed with?" Sebastien asked, revealing a look of anticipation.

Tiffany smiled knowingly. "No. But he said there was broken glass all over the kitchen floor when he got there."

Sebastien started to reply, but Tiffany interrupted.

"Oh, shut up, boy genius. Just tell me what you've figured out about our two skeletons."

There was that smile again. Such a happy soul. So much sunshine packed into one person, and in the middle of murder and mayhem. How did she do it? What a mystery! What a beautiful, beautiful mystery. Sebastien screamed at himself to stop looking at her face. *Stop wishing you could kiss her, right here and right now. Get to work, Sebastien. Shake it off. She'll notice. She'll think you're an idiot. Concentrate. This is all in your head, just like everything else.*

"Well, we may as well start right here," he said, indicating the table between himself and Tiffany. "This is the skeleton from the wash by the fire road. I've cleaned everything as best I could, and laid it all out in anatomical order, more or less.

Some things are missing, as we would expect. But we have the skull, and the jaw that was found several weeks ago fits it perfectly."

"As we also expected," offered Tiffany.

"Yep. Working down, as you can see, we have all cervical, thoracic, and lumbar vertebrae and the sacrum. All of the ribs, too. The shoulder girdles and all arm bones except the left radius—I'm making a list for Gerry, for when they go back out there for a second search." Sebastien raised up a pad of lined note paper and set it back on the table. "We have the pelvic girdle, too, which is helpful for estimating sex and age. Most hand and foot bones were not recovered—probably taken off by woodrats or other rodents. No hyoid—the bone in the throat that can show indications of strangulation. This doesn't surprise me, though, because scavengers often go for the soft area of the throat."

"Okay, that's charming," replied Tiffany, grimacing. "Any clothing?"

"Over there." Sebastien pointed with a gloved hand to the brown paper bag on the counter by the sink. "Just a pair of jeans, size thirty-four, and a blue T-shirt, size medium. No shoes, no socks. Forensics is going to come pick those up, according to Gerry."

"Well, that would be kind of weird to be all the way out there with no shoes, right?"

"I would think so. That's another good reason to suspect it was a body dump, or at least that there was a car involved. And here, check this out."

The ribs, left and right, were nested next to each other on the table, to either side of the vertebrae. Sebastien picked them up a few at a time and showed them to Tiffany, who leaned in to study them closely.

"Look at the cracks in these ribs. The fifth through ninth ribs on the left side are all broken ventrally—the front of the ribcage, I mean. And on the right side, the eighth, ninth, and tenth ribs are cracked near where they attached to the transverse processes of the vertebrae." Tiffany pursed her lips and squinted her brown eyes. "I'm sorry. I mean, where the ribs connect to the spine. That indicates being hit from behind, or at least from the side."

"Kidney punch?"

"Possibly," answered Sebastien.

"So, you think these fractures are antemortem?"

"Oh, definitely. This guy was in a lot of pain."

"Guy?"

"Yes. Male." Sebastien put down the ribs and picked up the two hip bones, one in each hand. He pushed them together at the pubic bones and raised the articulated pelvic girdle so Tiffany could get a better look. "See the angle just below where the two bones are touching? That's called the subpubic arch. In females, that arch is really wide—about ninety degrees—to accommodate childbirth. In males it is much more acute, like you see here. There are other areas that indicate male, as well. Overall robusticity and rugosity, for example."

"Rugosity? That's a new one on me."

"It refers to the ridges and bumps for muscle attachments and insertions. Like I was saying the other day, men are usually more pronounced in that way. Not me, though." Sebastien hoped his joke would land.

"I'm rubbing off on you, Dr. Grey. You better get back home before it's too late."

Sebastien wanted to say so much in reply, but he didn't dare.

"What about age?"

"This person is fully grown, so we can't use formative changes to estimate age; we can only use degenerative changes, which are less reliable and have wider variation depending on lifestyle factors."

"Degenerative changes?"

"Oh, sorry. I keep doing that. Degenerative changes are the changes that occur in the skeleton as we get older. It's essentially wear and tear. Some people age more quickly than others. For example, if you worked on a crab boat, your forty-year-old skeleton would look a lot older than the skeleton of a forty-year-old accountant."

"Don't be sorry, Sebastien. This is actually fascinating. I really appreciate you walking me through this. I like learning from you." Tiffany touched his shoulder as she spoke these words.

Concentrate, Sebastien. "Okay, good. I really like showing you how this is done. I think most people find it pretty boring. It's not like on television, where you stick a skull in a box and a three-dimensional hologram recreation of the individual appears in the air. In reality it's less exciting, but more interesting."

"I don't know. I'm finding it to be extremely exciting."

Sebastien's mind worked extra hard to interpret that statement as appropriately as possible. It wasn't easy, as he traced her lithe movements around the autopsy table. She was leaning over the bones, now, examining them carefully.

"Oh good. Anyway, I'm thinking between forty and sixty-five for this person. I know it is a wide range, but that's really the best I can say based on cranial fusion and pubic symphyseal face shape."

Tiffany seemed to ignore these last big words. She was studying the skull now, pointing at it with a nitrile-covered index finger. "Is this what killed him?"

There was a large opening in the left side of the head. It was an oblong of about fifteen centimeters long and ten centimeters high.

"You might think so, but no. It actually did not kill him. It probably kept him alive."

"What do you mean?" asked Tiffany, looking up at him.

"This may be our best shot at identifying this person, actually. Do you see these little divots along the margin of the hole?"

Sebastien pointed with his pinky at five shallow circular depressions that were spaced evenly along the edge of the opening. Tiffany nodded.

"They are—were—the connection areas for a plate that was attached to this man's skull."

"So, he had a metal plate in his head?"

"Well, probably not metal. Methyl methacrylate is the material they most likely used. It's a polymer used in a lot of reconstructive surgeries. My guess is that this person had a hematoma on his brain, and they had to drain the blood. They then replaced the removed portion of the skull with the plate. I've seen it a few times before."

"You said it could aid in identifying him? Is there like a serial number or something?"

"No, nothing like that. But, yes, it could help. The plate itself was not recovered—unless forensics has it. But you could check the hospitals to see if you can locate the records of anyone who had his procedure. Or, at very least, it will help corroborate identity if we do get a potential name for this person."

"So, essentially check the hospitals to see who might have had one of the plates put in?"

"Exactly. There shouldn't be too many. Especially around here—if the surgery was done here—where the population isn't huge. Oh, and there's one more thing that might help us." Sebastien led Tiffany down the table to the right knee of the skeleton. "This little bone here is the patella, the kneecap." Sebastien picked up the small bone and placed it in Tiffany's hand. It looked like a triangle that aspired to circlehood.

"And?" Tiffany was staring into her palm as if she were holding something that was getting ready to bite her.

"See those raised ridges along the bottom of the bone?"

"Which side is the bottom?" she asked, rolling her eyes.

Sebastien showed her.

"You mean those parallel lines? Those look man-made, don't they?"

"They do, but they're not man-made. Those lines are where the patellar tendon connect to the kneecap. This person had arthritis in the knee. These bony projections are from the knee trying to repair itself."

"So, also something that we might be able to use for identity."

"Exactly."

"What about race?"

"Biological ancestry?"

"Whatever."

"All of the measurements from the skull come out Caucasian, as do the non-metric traits."

"You mean like ear canal shape and that thing on the back of the skull where the muscle attaches?" Tiffany asked.

"Very good! You remembered!" Tiffany wasn't quite right, but she had the gist of it, and there was no point in parsing the details.

Tiffany smiled at this. "Anything from the teeth in the skull?"

"Not much. There was another gold filling in the upper jaw. And a couple of teeth were missing antemortem, but the sockets have not remodeled all the way. So, although this person did have decent dental care at some point, like I gathered from the jaw, it would appear that has not been the recent case for him."

"Okay, we have a Caucasian male, forty to sixty-five, with a bad knee, a plate in his head, and poor recent dental care. What about—"

"Five feet nine to six feet."

"You're a smart ass." She laughed. "And no indication of a mountain lion attack?"

"Well, I'm no expert, despite what your boss says. But I do know that in Africa, cheetah predation on primates is indicated by severe crushing and severing trauma to the cervical spine. I see none of that here."

"Okay. So, then, if the big hole in his head is not what killed him, can you tell what did?"

Sebastien put down the kneecap and picked up the skull, turning it so the back faced Tiffany. "The little hole in the head killed him. He was shot in the back of the head. The bullet exited through his right eye orbit."

"Well in that case, I agree," laughed Tiffany. "It probably wasn't a mountain lion."

Sebastien and Tiffany moved to the other end of the autopsy suite to the remains from French Creek and the skull from the RV park.

"So, what about this one? What kind of trauma did you find in the rest of skeleton? Was it smashed like the skull?"

"Not at all. The ribs are in good shape, not like anything you see on the other guy—no cracks or breaks." Sebastien indicated the table with the remains from the wash. "No stab wounds to the vertebrae or scapulae. The hyoid was recovered, thank goodness. But no signs of fracture there. And, most importantly, look at the lower arm bones." Sebastien picked up the radius and ulna from each side and held them in front of Tiffany. "I disarticulated them—that is, separated them—and cleaned them to get a better look. Each of these bones is essentially pristine. No marks, cuts, breaks—nothing."

Tiffany noticed that "U" shape in two of the bones he showed her. She also saw where Sebastien was now headed. "No defensive wounds. Which means this person let his or her face get beat to pieces without lifting their arms to block the blows?"

"It's male. And, yes. Or, he was unable to lift his arms to protect himself. We call those parry fractures, by the way." Sebastien hoped he wasn't sounding pedantic.

"You mean, he was incapacitated somehow?"

"The only other time I have encountered a Lefort fracture like this, the victim had no other trauma—like this guy. It turns out he was tied to a chair and beaten. As unlikely as it should be, I think I've now seen that same thing twice. I think this guy was tied up and beaten in the face."

"Are you sure the skull goes with the rest of the remains from the creek? Could it be a coincidence? Maybe there are more body parts out here."

"Yes, I am quite sure. The atlas—the first cervical vertebra at the top of the spine—fits perfectly on the occipital condyles on the inferior surface of the skull. See here?" Sebastien demonstrated by taking up the inverted skull and the ring-like atlas and putting them together. "It would be a monumental coincidence if they did not belong to the same person. DNA will confirm it, of course. And remember the adipocere on the skull—that fatty tissue that indicates it had been in water?" Sebastien put down the atlas and turned the RV park skull in his hands, showing Tiffany the back of it again. "There is also adipocere on the skeleton from the creek," he said, as he pointed to the underside of the leg bones and the shoulder blades. "This skull was in the water for about the same length of time as the rest of the remains were. That is also pretty compelling."

Tiffany began studying the two hip bones on the table, still connected at the pubic symphysis, the silty brown and white leg bones protruding from the hip sockets.

"Are you checking me on the sex?" Sebastien asked, smiling, and feeling proud of his erstwhile pupil.

"Subpubic arch seems pretty narrow to me." She winked, still leaning over the bones. Tiffany's graceful, fit, and lively body offered a strange counterpoint to the stinking corpse on the table. "Is this an adult? Like the other one?" Tiffany stood up and stretched her back.

"Yes. Also fully grown, but with a lower end of thirty-five years old. Upper end around sixty. This guy was quite a bit shorter than the gunshot victim—between five-four and five-seven. Like I said before, race is difficult to assess with the skull being so damaged. But looking at the femur, I think we can rule out African ancestry."

"No gunshots on this one?" Tiffany asked, scanning the bones on the table once more, as if she would recognize something.

"Nope. COD is massive blunt force trauma to the face. A horrible death."

26

When Kyle Corcoran was a child, growing up in Denver, he had a fascination with science—dinosaurs, chemistry, astronomy, geology, and the like. His favorite toy was an electrical set that his father bought him one Christmas—the Christmas before the old man left to become a lifetime guest of the Colorado Bureau of Prisons. That was also about three years before Corcoran's own first arrest. He had taken the neighbor lady's Plymouth for a joyride and crashed it into a portable toilet at the fairground. Like father, like son.

It seemed like so long ago that his path twisted into the misty darkness of crime and violence. Nevertheless, the former student of science had not forgotten all of his learning. For instance, Corcoran certainly knew that those thin wisps of white against the blue sky, far above him and the others at Canyon Lake Park, were cirrus clouds. But, as it was, he probably did not care, even on such a beautiful day. In fact, unlike the dozens of other people at the park—families, dog walkers, arm-in-arm couples—Corcoran was likely unaware that this Wednesday in August was arguably the most beautiful day of the summer, so far. He was just too distracted to consider such things. But surely those park-goers were aware of him, aware of the large man with the long, stringy blond hair and bushy beard; the man wearing the leather jacket and chunky black boots, sitting sternly on the bench with his arms crossed and legs out, laced at the ankles, staring fixedly forward.

It might have been the skinniest squirrel he had ever seen —Corcoran had been watching it, fascinated, for the last ten minutes. Twiggy—as he decided to call it—was trying to sneak up on a picnic table that was presently occupied by a large, multigenerational family. They were making a hell of a mess— bread, chips, grapes, cookies, and other squirrel temptations covered the entire surface of the table and dusted the ground around it. Twiggy would creep slowly from the base of the tree, over the open grass, toward the table. Each attempt to retrieve an abandoned morsel was inevitably thwarted by noise or movement by someone at the table before Twiggy got to the halfway point—just about where the bike path bisects the wide, deep green lawn. The squirrel would then scramble back up the tree and gather his courage for the next attempt.

Corcoran was starting to regard Twiggy with vile contempt. He would never let fear get in the way of taking something he wanted. What that pathetic, emaciated squirrel should do, should have done already, is bite and claw his way to the food, draw blood. That's what Kyle had been doing since crashing that Plymouth—biting and clawing, drawing blood, taking the offensive, removing all obstacles. Fear is for the weak, and the weak don't get fed.

Corcoran scanned the sky to see whether any eagles or hawks had taken notice of Twiggy. He didn't see any. Just a matter of time, though. The strong always overcome the weak and timid. And if you are going to take something from someone else, it's best to do it like a raptor—without hesitation or fear. Dale and Jimbo were just like Twiggy. *Were.* And Tiny, too. Corcoran wondered what tree that little rodent had climbed.

"Watcha looking at, boss?" Rudy sat down on the opposite end of the bench, leaving room for JT to sit next to Corcoran.

Corcoran ignored the question, scanning the sky one more time, briefly, before he spoke. "Well?"

"We can't find Tiny anywhere. And the cops were at that lady's house," Rudy answered.

"Which lady?" asked Corcoran. "Tiny's mom, or the lady you two went and threatened?"

This is exactly why Rudy took the other end of the bench.

"Tiny's girlfriend. We got no idea why they were there, though. Could be something totally different. I mean, it wasn't just one cop car there. It was a bunch of cars and crime scene people. They were definitely searching the place," said JT.

"Were they now?" Twiggy caught Corcoran's attention once more, dashing toward the picnic table. He made it three-quarters of the way this time before darting back.

"Yep. Something definitely went down. Looked pretty serious," Rudy offered.

"Either of you ladies know of a way to find out what happened there?"

"Not that I can think of," replied JT.

Rudy fingered the beads in his beard, looking thoughtful. "I could go back down there; maybe pretend to be a friend, you know, just dropping by. I can ask the cops what's up."

Corcoran tried to hold it together. It was his fault anyway. Rudy was too stupid to blame. He may be good at crushing skulls; but when it comes to thinking things through, he might as well be in a coma. Corcoran knew this when he enlisted Rudy to help him get the bike back.

"You know what, Rudy? That's a good idea. You go down there," Corcoran said. "And find Tiny!"

Rudy evidently felt pleased with himself. He sat back on the bench, closed his eyes, and let the sun hit his face.

"What are you waiting for?" Corcoran said stridently.

"Oh, you want me to go now?" Poor Rudy looked confused.

Corcoran didn't answer. He just sat there, arms still crossed, ankles still crossed. Rudy got up and lumbered toward the parking lot. The two remaining men sat in silence for a few moments. A Coopers hawk materialized high above Twiggy's tree, circling casually, scanning the ground below. Corcoran looked for Twiggy, but the squirrel was nowhere to be seen. He took his sunglasses off, leaned forward, and squinted into the pine.

"I don't know, boss. He's getting to be a liability," JT said.

"Yes, my friend. He certainly is living on the edge."

"He's putting us all on the edge. He knows too much. He's going to go down there and try to buddy up to some stupid cop, who will immediately start asking questions. What if they bring him in?"

"Calm down."

"But Kyle, he could lay it all on us. Why did you tell him to go?"

"Well, I'm not planning for him to make it down there, Sally."

"Oh." JT looked questioningly at Corcoran for a few moments, then asked, "You want me to kill him?"

Corcoran replaced his sunglasses and leaned back on the bench.

JT stood and made for the parking lot. "Hang on, Rudy. I'm coming, too," he called.

JT HOPPED in the Cadillac just as Rudy was reversing out of the parking lot.

"I'm going with you, man," JT said, as he closed the door.

Rudy felt like something about this was odd. He and JT had arrived at the park to meet Corcoran in separate vehicles. This didn't make sense.

Once inside, JT fished a CD from the glove box and inserted it into the stereo. The two men rode without speaking for about twenty minutes and listened to the twang of country music. They were well out of the city and into the brownish green prairie on state route 79 before anyone spoke. It was JT who broke the silence.

"So, what's the plan? We just go down there and ask the cops what's up?"

"I was thinking we could act like we're visiting a neighbor or something. You know, say 'Hey man, what's all the ruckus about?'"

"Okay, that's pretty good."

Rudy heard the words, but it looked to him as though JT was doubtful.

"What's the matter?" he asked.

"Nothin. I'm just thinking—you know. What if they ask you for ID or something? What if they ask you which neighbor you're visiting? I'm just a little worried they might bring you in."

"Is that why Kyle told you to come along? To make sure I don't do nothin' stupid? To babysit me?"

"We're all in this together, man. Remember, I didn't want to kill those guys in the first place. I don't need you getting hooked up, then ratting me out. You feel me?"

"What do you mean you didn't want to kill them? You tied that prick to the chair, didn't you? And you are the one who shot Jimbo. Wasn't the plan to just leave him out there? Teach him a lesson?"

"Are you really that stupid? Do you really think we could let Jimbo live after we took care of Dale?"

Rudy was tiring of this pattern. Kyle and JT were constantly belittling him, making him feel stupid. They were stupid. This whole thing was stupid.

"Hey look," demanded Rudy, "I didn't steal Dale's motorcycle, so I could care less if him and his idiot friends stole it back. I did what I did to help Kyle. So, yeah, if I do ever get hooked up, you better believe I ain't going down alone. But we need to find Tiny. He's the only one left who knows. And why am I the stupid one if Kyle is the one who decided to let him live?"

JT shook his head in exasperation. "Do you really think Kyle was going to let Tiny live? You don't think that once Tiny replaced the motorcycle we were going whack him? That's how this stuff works, man. Or didn't they teach you that in prison?"

Rudy felt it coming, the rage of the bullied, the abused. He'd had enough. The stress of having Tiny out in the wild and always being blamed was working his last nerve. They had underestimated him, and it was time JT knew that.

"Tell me something, JT. Are you and Kyle planning on using me as a scapegoat here? Because, if you do, I'll kill ya. I'll kill you both."

Just then, JT leaned forward and pulled his revolver from its ankle holster. He pointed it at Rudy.

"You don't threaten me. Or Kyle. You're a punk, and we all know it. And you ain't going to Hermosa to get the attention of the cops either."

Rudy smiled, breathed in deeply through his nose, and kept driving.

"You hear me?" growled JT.

Rudy continued to look ahead and continued to smile. "Is that why Kyle told you to come with me? So you could kill me?" he asked.

JT ignored the question. "See that dirt road up there? Pull off there."

Rudy took another deep breath, then said, "I can't, there's a rabbit in the road."

"Wha—"

Just as JT began to speak, Rudy turned the speeding car to the left sharply, causing JT to smack his head against the passenger window. Before JT could orient himself, Rudy gave him a right cross on the chin, which slammed JT's head into the window once more, and threw bloody saliva across the dashboard and onto the window. JT was out cold.

Rudy then did as he was instructed and pulled off the highway. He followed the narrow dirt road for a few hundred yards until it bent gently to the north, revealing a small copse of oak. Rudy parked, grabbed the revolver that had fallen onto the floorboard at JT's feet, then dragged the unconscious man into the trees.

THE WARM WATER spattered his back as Sebastien leaned forward with his forehead pinning his right forearm against the shower wall. The smell of decomposing flesh was just about gone from his skin—although he knew from experience that it would come back to him in the middle of the night, waking him up from even the deepest slumber. The phenomena was so regular, so reliable, that at one point he'd considered writing a paper on it, describing how the smell of decay worked its way backward, reversing course and traveling from the olfactory bulb in the brain back to the nostrils. He would have called it, *Tapho Memoria, the remembrance of death.*

Which reminded him: his only pair of jeans were now out of service, smelling of putrescine—the calling card of decay. He should probably make a quick run and buy some more, unless he wanted to wear one of the three pairs of cotton chinos he'd brought with him on the mountain lion hunt tonight. *What a dope!* Maybe it didn't matter. Maybe he was overthinking it.

And, why bother buying more pants if he was just going to leave soon anyway?

Leave soon? Yes. Why not? His work was pretty much done —except for tonight's excursion, which was, in his opinion, pointless. But everything else that he had been asked to do was complete. In fact, it was, in his humble estimation, an altogether successful trip. Hank now had more than he had before —by far. And knew more than he knew before—also by far. He was now reassured, for instance, that mountain lions were not the cause of the bodies in the wash or creek. It was good old-fashioned murder. *Homo sapiens aggressio*—the most dangerous animal on earth, and the most likely to do violence.

Then there was the matter of the body in the truck—which was really just a side project, so-to-speak. It was not an anthropology problem, and his involvement was fortuitous to say the least. And yet, Sebastien was able to help there, too. Maybe he had been misjudging himself, not giving himself enough credit. Perhaps he was more than just an awkward misfit, hiding away in his art deco fortress, aspiring to pomposity with the opera crowd, yet dodging all social engagement.

Though, to be honest, he wasn't quite sure. His head was swimming, going back and forth, replaying his every move since he'd arrived in South Dakota, dispensing judgement on each breath he took of the Black Hills air. There was a lot to digest, so much cud to chew. He felt himself starting to spiral. What was it that Tina—Dr. Lucas—had advised him to do in these situations?

Sebastien, when you find yourself obsessing about the events of the past, I want you to stop and write down all of the good things that happened. Pretend that you are writing a persuasive essay, trying to convince the reader that the events were actually positive. Will you do that for me?

Tina referred to this exercise as Positivity Journaling, and Sebastien had thus far avoided it like the plague. Somehow writing down his thoughts, his earnest impressions, made him feel exposed. *What if somebody finds it? What if after I'm dead, a distant relative opens a trunk and discovers The Positivity Journal of Sebastien Grey? What disaster! What shame!*

Something about his South Dakota trip made him feel differently now. He knew he had done well here, and there was much to be glad about, if he could just filter out the noise, uncertainty, and suspicion.

Sebastien wrapped a towel around his naked midsection and sat down at the small desk in his hotel room. The fans in his laptop whirred as it booted.

After twenty minutes of brooding and typing—with special emphasis on the former—Sebastien came up with what he felt was a reasonable representation of a positive spin on this trip for his first ever journal entry. He noted how everyone, to a man —and woman—expressed wonderful appreciation for his ingenuity and his analysis. Not the least of whom was Tiffany; she seemed genuinely impressed and interested in his quirky mental operations. And maybe not just that. Maybe she actually liked him—as a person.

Tiffany. What happened there? Somehow in Sebastien's mind, and in just a few short days, she had gone from an ordinary stranger/cop to a warm, funny, insightful, and compassionate woman. Woman! And how did a face, which did not catch his attention at first, imprint itself on his mind so vividly? He did not expect this when he set out to help his brother; he did not expect to be feeling like this at the end of the case. What was it she'd said? "You can't be smitten with me. You've only been here two days."

27

Sebastien turned to look back down the hill in the direction of Custer, wondering whether the pallid glow from the valley floor was, in fact, the small town, or if he had his bearings wrong. It was fully dark now, and the drive up here included a handful of switchbacks and side roads; his usually excellent sense of direction was failing him.

The GFP team were staged on a bluff overlooking Willow Creek—a Jeep and two pickup trucks were backed together about ten feet apart, forming a sort of triangle. The group of biologists and trackers were standing huddled at the rear of the Jeep, monitoring the radio receiver and watching a large monitor, which was hooked up to a laptop. Sebastien was standing a little further off from the group, isolating himself a bit. He didn't know any of these people—aside from Barry, whom he had met, briefly, the other morning at breakfast. He was feeling out of place, a bit unwelcome—Hank LeGris' spy.

From the preliminary briefing, Sebastien gathered a basic understanding of the operational strategy. M323 had been located—via radio collar—in the immediate vicinity of Willow

Creek, which itself was dotted with ranches, retention ponds, and even a couple of luxury estates. Livestock, wildlife, and pets were plentiful here—which fit the lion's *modus vivendi*. The team had set up three box traps and baited them with road killed deer. The traps where each about a quarter mile from the command post on the bluff, somewhat equidistant from each other. Trap one was located to the southwest in a stand of pine between three retention ponds. Trap two was set to the southeast in a forested area that butted up against a hayfield, beyond which was a long creek. Trap three was north of the command post, in the apex of a triangle formed by two private ranch roads, where the forest gave way to open grazing fields.

A game camera was set at each trap site. If the mountain lion became captured in one of the traps, or if he even approached any of them, he would be caught on camera. In addition, the entire watch area—as they called it—was circumscribed by six additional game cameras.

The radio collar was providing a sense of where the lion was and the direction in which he may head. Currently, M323 was to the south of them. He had been heading north up the ridge, through some ranchland, until about forty-five minutes ago, at which time he stopped moving. The debate amongst the group at the back of the Jeep was whether M323 had picked-off a calf from the ranch and stopped to feed, or he was just resting.

A woman broke off from the group and approached Sebastien as he scanned the lights in the valley. It was difficult to make out her features in the darkness, and with the glare of her headlamp in his eyes, but she appeared tall—as tall as he was—and a little stocky. She wore a knit cap over her short hair.

"Hey. I'm Diane." The woman put out her hand.

"I'm Dr. Grey," he replied, as he took her hand—thick and

calloused—in his own. His use of formality seemed somehow appropriate to the mission.

"So, you're the guy from the sheriff's office."

Sebastien wasn't sure whether the statement was meant to be taken as a question. He just nodded vaguely, squinting at the LED beam that shot into his corneas.

"Oh sorry," Diane said, reaching to her forehead to switch off the lamp. "So, what do you think?"

"I'm sorry, about what?" It was one of those moments where Sebastien wondered whether he was being too literal. Was there a subtext he was missing?

"Our mountain lion. Does the sheriff's office think we have a problem animal on our hands?"

"Well, I can't really speak for the sheriff's office." Sebastien pulled his down vest around his chest with his hands. The temperature was beginning to drop.

It was hard to read her face in the dimness, but Diane's tone was one of confusion. "I'm sorry. I thought you said you were with the sheriff's office?"

"Well, I'm more of a consultant, you could say," he explained. She tilted her head at this. "Barry invited me to join you all. Hope that's okay."

"What kind of consultant?" She sounded insistent.

"Anthropologist."

"You mean like Homo erectus and Neandertals?"

Sebastien was getting a little annoyed. She couldn't possibly be that narrow-minded, that stupid. Was she baiting him? Or was he overly tired from this long, eventful day and interpreting her the wrong way? He must remember to thank his brother for dragooning him into this. "Forensic, actually."

"Oh, I get it now." The silhouette of Diane's head bobbed against the moonlight. "Those bones that were found—the sheriff's office thinks a mountain lion left those. Ha!"

Sebastien was a bit confused. Weren't the GFP the ones

concerned? Suddenly aware that politics may be involved, he didn't know how to respond. *Thanks again, Henry.*

"You said Barry got you out here, right?" She turned briefly in the direction of the Jeep. "You should know, Barry is a good biologist—and he does a mean barbequed brisket—but he gets a little *enthusiastic* at times. The fact is, there has never been a single mountain lion attack on humans in the Black Hills. Well, there was one, but it was a captive lion, an accident."

"I think I can safely say that the sheriff's office agrees with you. So, where does the panic come from? I'm not from here, so I'm missing some context." Sebastien noticed himself slipping into interested interlocutor mode. It was his anthropological mind, he supposed.

"Oh, that's easy—the ranchers. Attacks on humans may be something of a myth around here, but lions taking livestock is a real thing. It's a buffet in the hills. Why do you think we're standing on this particular hill?"

"We got him!" A voice came from the area of the Jeep.

Sebastien and Diane hurried over and joined the others. "He's heading up the ridge—right between traps one and two," someone said, pointing at the monitor as they walked up to see.

On the large monitor were nine smaller screens—each showing one of the game camera feeds. Sebastien and Diane arrived in time to watch the hind quarters and long tail from M323 disappear casually off one of the smaller screens. Based on the apparent size of the trees, fallen branches, and bushes on the monitor, M323 appeared relatively huge.

A buzz of suspense settled on the group as they stood staring at the monitor in the back of the Jeep. The camera at trap one was showing M323's furtive movements—the lion would approach the trap for a moment, then back out of sight of the camera, then re-emerge. This went on several times. At one point, the lion lifted a bread plate-sized paw to the outside of the trap and scraped it down the metal caging. The lion looked to be trying to figure out why the deer was just lying there. Was it sleeping? As he watched, Sebastien wondered whether M323 could smell death. It was an interesting question. He should remember to ask one of the biologists.

After a few moments, M323 nearly entered the opening of the trap, eliciting mutters of encouragement from the team members at the monitor. Three times the cat stuck his head in, but each time something spooked him, and he backed out. Frustration was beginning to set in.

Finally, M323 altogether disappeared from the screen. After several minutes, Barry wondered aloud, "I think he may be gone. He's spooky. He always has been."

Ten more minutes went by without any sign of the mountain lion on any of the monitors. Barry checked the radio receiver. The cat was still in the area, but several meters farther down the ridge. "He's going back down," Barry announced. "Vern, Diane, we may as well set up some chairs. It might be a long night."

Sebastien stepped back to make way for Diane, and another man, to break from the group. They walked directly to one of the pickups and lifted out some folding camp chairs, then began setting them up.

Long night? Great, thought Sebastien. He looked around in the moonlight searchingly. He had to relieve himself and wondered what the best approach might be. Should he borrow one of the trucks and drive back down the hill? That's stupid, he thought. He's a man, after all. Nature gave him just the equipment to make do in such circumstances.

"I'm going to go take a leak," announced Diane, semiloudly. She then walked behind Sebastien and into the darkness on the east side of the command post.

"Me, too," proclaimed the man whom Barry called Vern.

"Find your own bush!" called back Diane.

Sebastien remained standing in the same spot for a few

moments trying to settle on a direction to head to accomplish his own urinary mission. Propriety dictated that he steer clear of the side of the hill that Diane was on. He settled on the west side, as Vern chose the south side.

It took him about thirty yards to find what he considered to be suitable cover—a small group of trees that surrounded a water trough—before he felt comfortable enough to unzip. Looking up to the night sky through the pine, it struck him just how much light pollution there must have been on the hill. It was much darker here, and the stars shone brilliantly against the pitch-black firmament as his bladder emptied into the grass.

Sebastien squinted his eyes to get a better look at the trough. It was really just a shadow in the dark, but its outline was unmistakable, and it triggered something Barry had said in the café: mountain lions are shifty bastards, ambush predators. What a great place to stage an ambush this would be—hidden in the trees while a cow or sheep or whatever came in for a drink.

A piercing shriek broke the air from over his left shoulder. Sebastien nearly bit his own tongue when he jumped at it. He zipped up as fast as his shaking fingers would allow and spun around. He saw nothing in the darkness but could hear commotion and more screams. "What's going on?" he yelled.

"He's here! He's here!"

It was Vern. Sebastien ran toward the voice and could hear the others doing the same. He was cursing himself for not bringing a headlamp or flashlight with him as he tripped and stumbled over the uneven ground. Stupid!

"Grab the gun," someone yelled. "Got it," someone else replied. Sebastien looked toward the voices, which were now on his left, and saw narrow beams of light bouncing down the hill in his direction. One of the rays briefly caught a figure standing stock still, trembling. It was Vern, about twenty-five feet ahead of him. A fulgid bar of light shot from his forehead. Sebastien ran toward it.

"Where is he? Where is he?" someone shouted.

In an instant, Sebastien found himself on the ground, rock painfully embedded into the palms of his hands and his mouth full of dirt. A whiplash of pain raced down his spine. He spit violently, then tried to flip onto his back and stand up again, but his foot was caught under an exposed root. Lying on his left side, he was working to wriggle his foot free when his eyes caught sight of two yellow orbs reflecting in the shaking beam of Vern's headlamp.

M323 lunged toward Sebastien, teeth exposed and making a hissing sound. Sebastien covered his face with his forearm expecting to be leaped upon. It did not happen. It was a bluff. The mountain lion had stepped back to his original position, hissing. Vern's lamp illuminated the billows of muscle that rose from its forearms onto its huge shoulders.

Sebastien pushed his foot forward a few inches, finally freeing it from the root, then flipped onto his back and up to his feet. M323 took this as an attack and lunged in again. Sebastien darted to his right in an effort to evade the collision. Several beams of light now illuminated the scene, and the onlooking team all shouted noisily trying to scare off the mountain lion. But M323 made the left turn and lunged at Sebastien again, grazing his shoulder and throwing him off balance. Sebastien found himself on the ground once more.

In the luminescence of the collective headlamps, he could see the mountain lion about ten feet away. The cat looked confused, not merely aggressive. The chaos of the lights and noise most likely made him feel trapped and defensive. He pawed the ground in agitation. In a move that, as Sebastien would reflect much later, appeared profoundly fluid and grace-ful, M323 dipped his shoulders slightly and sprang into the air straight at him. Sebastien crossed his elbows above his face and curled his forearms over his scalp, flexing his body into a ball.

A loud cracking sound echoed through the trees. At first, Sebastien thought it was the sound of his skull being crushed, but pain never came. Nor did the sensation of having a hundred-and-eighty-pound animal land on him. He uncovered his face and looked up, confused.

"Are you okay?" Barry shouted, as he ran up to Sebastien.

"Yeah. I think so. What happened?"

"I got him," said Diane, casually—as if it was another day at the office. "He ran off into the bushes." She was walking calmly toward them, carrying a rifle under her arm and pointing past Sebastien down the hill.

Sebastien's heart was pounding, the adrenaline surge just now peaking. He tried to stand but collapsed. Barry and Vern grabbed him by the arms to steady him.

"Sit down," said Vern. The two men lowered Sebastien onto his butt on the ground, but he immediately stood back up. He was too worked-up to sit. He limped around with his hands on his head, sucking the cool night air into his lungs.

"He should be out cold in a few minutes," said Diane. "Vern, can you help me bring down the carrier?"

"Sure thing," replied Vern.

"Wait," shouted Sebastien angrily. "Are you telling me that thing is still alive?"

"Of course he is. I was careful about measuring the dose," answered Diane, with a thumbs up. "Not my first rodeo, Doctor."

Barry and Vern made a timely catch as Sebastien fainted.

HANK, Melissa, and Tiffany were sitting at the LeGris dining room table. Kirby and Mist were puddled together in Kirby's bed, fast asleep.

"A drop more?" asked Hank, suspending the top of the whisky bottle a few inches above Tiffany's glass.

"No, no. I'm good," she replied, covering her glass with her hand. "Thanks."

Hank poured a half-inch of Johnnie Walker into his glass, put the bottle down, and continued to articulate his train of thought. "So, I just don't see Susan staying hidden for too long now that the murder has hit the news."

"I agree. Although, she certainly won't go home. The mobile home is all torn up now anyway."

"Yep. I expect some other jurisdiction will pick her up. Oh, speaking of the search warrant. You said there was no sign of a weapon?"

"Nothing obvious that could have caused the stab to the neck. The autopsy indicated a jagged cut, which does not match any of the knives in the house. And, no coffee pot was found—as Sebastien pointed out after our visit. It looks as though he's right."

Hank looked into his glass, nodded faintly, then drained the whiskey with a backward jerk of his head.

"You know what bothers me, though?" Tiffany continued. "A twenty-gauge shotgun was found under Susan's bed."

"Why does that bother you? Pretty normal around here," Hank said.

"Well, why kill Mickey with a broken piece of coffee pot if you could just blow his head off?"

"Messy? Loud?"

"Not any less messy than what forensics found. When they tore up the vinyl floor and sprayed Luminol, the place lit up like a parade. That must have been a real bear to clean. But, you're right about a shotgun being the louder option."

"Well, that's it for me. Good night, all." Melissa leaned over and hugged Tiffany, then kissed Hank on the lips emphatically. "You need a trim," she told him, as she scratched at his slightly graying goatee. Hank smacked her on the butt as she walked away.

"Oh, hey. Honey. Would you grab my bag off the couch on your way?"

"Take a look at this." Hank took the bag from Melissa and pulled out a thick file folder, placing it on the table in front of Tiffany.

"What am I looking at?" she asked, as she opened the folder and saw a stack of what looked to be medical records.

Hank slid the folder back over in front of himself and rifled through the papers. "Ah, here," he said, as he placed two stapled sheets in front of her. One was a medical form and the other was a photocopy of an x-ray.

Tiffany took up the sheets and flipped to the x-ray first, instinctively giving preference to the picture over the jumble of medical terminology. "Hey! Look at that! Where did you get this?"

"I went to the county hospital after they took Shermer to the jail. It was a hunch. Based on Sebastien saying that this guy would not have had good dental care recently, I figured his medical care would have been through County."

"That's brilliant," she whispered.

"I thought so, too." Hank smirked.

"Not you! Your brother!"

"Hey! A little credit, please?"

"Just kidding, boss. So, who is this guy?"

"James Milford, forty-eight-year-old white male. He lives with his sister in Blackhawk. That x-ray was taken seven years ago, about six months after he had the plate put in."

"Why the plate? Car accident?"

"Bar fight. According to his sister, he's a real piece of work.

Likes to fight any chance he can get. Apparently, he picked a fight with some college kid half his age and twice his size. He was out cold before his cranium hit the concrete."

"So, is this going to confirm ID for us?"

"I'm going to take this to Dr. Rose tomorrow and see what he says. I'm sure Gerry will track down dental, too. Oh, and according to his sister, Jimbo—that's what they call him—walked with a limp. ID is looking good."

"I'm assuming you asked her if Jimbo was missing?"

"Since last Fall," replied Hank, filling his glass again. Tiffany slid hers toward him. He drained the bottle's last quarter inch into it. "The last time she saw her brother he was hanging around with some bikers out of Rapid City. There seemed to be some argument over a motorcycle, and Jimbo and his buddy Dale Davis went to sort it out. No sign of either of them since."

"*The boys in Rapid are waiting,*" Tiffany muttered.

"Exactly what I thought."

"Something tells me that poor Mr. Davis got his face beaten to pieces." Tiffany puckered her own face in sympathetic pain.

"Me, too. Needless to say, I will have Gerry chase down those dentals as well."

"Why didn't the sister report Jimbo as missing? Or, did she?"

"No, she didn't. She said she's used to him leaving town unannounced—usually because he pissed off someone. He always comes back, she said. So, she didn't think to report it."

"Who did she think he pissed off this time?"

"You ever heard of the West Side Silverbacks?"

"Sure. They're an outlaw motorcycle gang, right? Out of Rapid City?"

"Right and right. I put in a call to crime analysis. They're searching their gang database and will get me a list of names."

"I know I've said this before, Hank. But we would be completely stuck if it weren't for your brother."

"And I know I've said this before. I think he has a thing for you."

"I like him. He's nice. And sensitive. It's sweet. And he's a heck of a lot better looking than you!"

"Fine with me. I'm taken. Speaking of that, I'm going to curl up with Melissa. You're welcome to take the spare bedroom if you want."

"Thanks, boss. I think I should."

28

Hank was sitting at his desk at the station when he heard a knock on his door, followed by Tiffany poking her head in.

"We got one. Interview room two."

"Corcoran?" Hank asked hopefully.

"Nope. A guy named Rudy Goodwin. He's on the list."

Hank looked at the list of gang members to verify.

"Seriously?" said Tiffany.

"Hey, calm down. I was just checking to see where he is on the hierarchy."

"He's not a shot caller. I think he's pretty new, based on when he was validated as a member. But, if it makes you feel any better, we found him at Corcoran's house. He was leaving when we got there."

"But no Corcoran?"

"No. We're still looking."

Hank picked up the file folder that was sitting on his desk and headed into the hall.

"Alright, let's do this," he said.

"Wait." Tiffany grabbed his arm as he passed her at the door, stopping him.

"What?"

"I'm worried about Sebastien. I haven't been able to reach him."

"He's fine. He's probably just sleeping in. He was out late last night with the GFP team, remember? Now, get your head in the game, Detective."

Rudy Goodwin looked up as Hank and Tiffany entered the interview room. He didn't appear concerned, or the least bit moved by the fact that the police rolled up on him as he walked away from Kyle's house that morning. The three exchanged handshakes. Hank took the seat across from Rudy on one side of the small metal and wood table. Tiffany stood by the door, leaning against the wall with her arms folded. There were only two chairs in the tiny interview room.

Hank read Rudy his Miranda rights, and Rudy agreed to speak with them.

"Well, I bet you're wondering what this is all about?" Hank asked, with an affable tone and pleasant smile.

"Not really. I'm always gettin' harassed by cops. Part of life."

"Really? Why do you think that is—the harassment, I mean?"

"No clue. I'm a law abetting citizen."

Tiffany snickered at the ill-chosen word, but Rudy didn't notice.

"Do you get down here often? I've looked but couldn't find a record of you causing problems in this county."

Rudy appeared to relax a little. His arms dropped to his bellybutton; his fingers knitted together loosely. "Nah, I ain't never been down here. And I don't cause problems."

"Not even been to Custer? Lots of cool stuff going on in this town."

"Nah," the man answered diffidently. "So, what's going on? Why am I here?"

Hank opened the file folder that sat in front of him on the table and took out a piece of paper with two headshots printed on it. He slid the paper across the table and asked, "You know either of these guys?"

The faces of James Milford and Dale Davis stared up from the page. Rudy's eyes pinched as he studied the photos.

"Nope. Never seen 'em. Should I know 'em?"

Tiffany watched the man closely. His arms tightened around his chest once more. His heavily booted right foot began silently tapping against the blue institutional carpet; the fingers of his right hand ran through his thick beard, causing the copper beads to jingle.

"It's my understanding that these two guys had a beef with the Silverbacks a while back. I'm just wondering when you saw them last."

"Like I said, never seen 'em. Don't know 'em from Adam Ant."

More snickering from Tiffany. This time the man caught it.

"What the hell? Can you just tell me what you want so I can get out of here?"

"Don't worry, we'll get you back up to Rapid City soon. I understand you were leaving as our detectives got to Kyle Corcoran's place this morning. What were you doing there?"

"Just visiting. You know."

And where were you going from there? Anywhere in particular?"

The man replied with a flat, "No."

"Hmm. Have you seen Kyle?"

"No."

"But you were at his place?"

"I knocked on the door. But he didn't answer. That's when

the cops pulled up. So, what do you want, anyway? What's this all about?"

Hank placed his open hand palm down on the folder. "It's really simple, actually. We just want to lock down your story for when we charge you and your buddies for killing these two guys."

"I ain't killed nobody. You're full of it."

"Oh, I think you did. You know what the bummer is? For you, anyway. You just happened to dump their bodies in a county that has the latest DNA technology. Did you know, we can get DNA from a bone? Not the victim's DNA, mind you, but the perpetrator's DNA. That's right—from the victim's bones. Brand new technology. It's called 'external bone DNA.' And we got lots of bones in our freezer right now. The bones of Davis and Milford, to be precise. These two guys." Hank lifted the piece of paper and shook it. "So, yes. You will be charged, along with the others. The question is, what do you want to be charged with? There's a hell of a big difference between murder and accessory-after-the-fact, or even just tampering with a body."

Tiffany marked the man's reaction to this information. By the look of him, he did not understand that half of Hank's statement was utter bull, a complete fabrication. Not that it mattered. The man's fingers froze, buried in his beard, mid-comb. He turned to look at the stark white wall of the interview room, breaking his eye contact with Hank. His mind was clearly turning. Tiffany was enjoying this.

Hank left it there, giving the man a few minutes to bite the hook.

Tiffany looked at her watch: ten forty-five. She was starting to pull her phone out of her back pocket when she heard the interview room door open behind her. She turned to face one of the patrol sergeants, who waved her into the hall with a curled index finger.

"What's up, Paul?" she asked, once the door to the interview room fell closed.

"I don't know if this has anything to do with what you and Hank are working on, but another body has been found."

"You're kidding?" Tiffany's eyes widened, and her head jolted in shock. "French Creek?"

"Nope. This was off of Seventy-Nine, just north of Hermosa. A group of horseback riders found it."

"Is it another skeleton?"

"No, this one is fresh. Well, kind of fresh. And the coroner found an ID on him. His name is JT Stahl." The sergeant handed a piece of yellow notepaper to Tiffany.

"Well, I'll be.... Thanks, Paul. I owe you a beer."

"Darn right you do. How about I get your personal number, and we can work something out?"

Tiffany winked and said, "Your wife already has it. Thanks again."

The sergeant turned red and chewed his tongue as Tiffany turned toward the door to the interview room. In a sudden epiphany, she paused, pulled her phone out of her pocket, saw that there were no calls or texts, then punched in a number.

"Hey Sommermire, how's it going at Corcoran's?"

"So far, we got zip. I was just doing the rock-paper-scissors with Larson for who has to climb into the attic."

"And no indication of where Corcoran might be?"

"Not really."

"How does his house look? Any indication of trouble there?"

"Ah, it's a little bit of a mess. A lamp is knocked over, and there's something spilled on the carpet, with an empty glass near it. Smells like cheap bourbon. Probably nothing out of the ordinary for a biker's place, you know?"

"Okay. Hey, I understand that Rudy Goodwin was there when you arrived."

"Yep. We sent him down to you all. Isn't he there?"

"Yeah, we got him in the interview now. Is his car there?"

"There's a Cadillac in the driveway. I think it's his. I can run the plate."

"Do me a favor," replied Tiffany. "Check the trunk."

"Do we have a search warrant for Goodwin's car?"

Tiffany rolled her eyes. "Is it on Corcoran's property?"

"Yeah, like I said, it's in the drive—oh, I see what you mean. We'll check it."

When Tiffany re-entered the room, Hank and Rudy were still sitting in silence—just as they had been when she'd left. It was a real standoff, apparently. She gestured for Hank to step into the hall.

After about five minutes, Hank and Tiffany stepped back into the room.

"Well, slap my butt and start the rodeo. This is just fine! Looks like I'm going to get a weekend after all," exclaimed Hank.

Tiffany did her best not to laugh. She hadn't heard that one before.

"Whatever. Can I go now? I got nothing to say."

"No, sir. You cannot leave."

Rudy laughed nervously. "Well then you damn well better charge me."

"Good idea. How does two counts of murder sound? I mean, for starters. We can probably push it to four by dinner time."

The man's face turned beat red, and his eyes widened as he clenched his teeth.

"So, I have to say, it's not often we find an actual body in a trunk." Hank sounded matter-of-fact, like he was talking about the weather. "I mean, sure, you see it on TV a lot. But not in real life."

"What are you talking about? I ain't got no body in my trunk," the man said.

"I didn't say it was your trunk."

"Oh," the man said, with relief.

"But it is. It is your trunk. Sorry, man. I couldn't resist."

The man's rage returned. "You're full of it. Screw you!"

Tiffany approached Rudy with her phone in her hand and called up the picture that Detective Sommermire had just sent her. It was a photo of a man face down, somewhat fetal, stuffed into a trunk. "What do you call this?" she asked.

"You must've planted it."

"Seriously? Is that what you're going with?" asked Hank, with a snort.

The man did not answer.

Tiffany once again took her spot against the wall by the door.

"You don't seem very surprised by this little development," Hank continued.

"I couldn't be more surprised. Seriously," the man said, lifting his hands pleadingly.

"So, you didn't know it was there?"

"That's what I said. Are you deaf?"

"Isn't that just the craziest thing?" replied Hank, ignoring the attitude and looking toward Tiffany. "Somebody just came along and stuck a dead guy back there without you knowing."

"I tell ya, people are nuts these days," replied Tiffany.

Again, the man did not respond.

Hank decided to play along a bit, just to lock him in. "Well, fine. Let's just say—for the sake of argument, I mean—that that is what happened. Can you retrace your steps for me? Was there any time your car was left unattended in the last day or so?"

"Last night. I didn't sleep in the damn thing." His arms once again crossed against his chest.

"What time did you park the car for the night?"

"About ten."

"Where were you headed to this morning when our guys rolled up? Back down to Hermosa? Or maybe even back down to Custer?" Hank emphasized *back* in both phrases.

"I told you, I ain't never been there."

"Well see, that's a lie. You're full of them, my amigo. I saw you at the café on Wednesday morning. Don't you remember me? You practically knocked me over on the way out."

Rudy's face turned pale.

"So, what were you doing down here?"

"I was in a mood for a walk around the lake."

"Which one?"

"Stockade."

"Why Stockade? Plenty of lakes up north."

Tiffany thought she might have detected the man's face twitch.

"I uh, don't know. I mean, it's pretty this time of year."

"Well, that is certainly true." Hank nodded firmly. "That is certainly true. Of course, it has been a little, you know, crazy down here lately. People stumbling onto all kinds of things in this part of the county—having their pretty days spoiled."

Rudy tilted his head and began to speak but stopped himself.

"What? You hadn't heard?"

Rudy shook his head.

"Well, no matter. So, let's recap: sometime last night someone broke into your Caddi, popped open the trunk, and stuck a dead guy in it. Then, this morning, you went to pay Corcoran a visit, but he wasn't home. Am I leaving anything out?"

"Nope."

"Detective Reese, what was it that the guy from the coroner called the temperature thing? Alvin morris?"

Tiffany instantly detected that Hank was slipping into his

dumb cop, ah shucks, role. She smiled and pushed herself vertical from the wall. "Algor mortis, he called it."

"Oh really? Geez. I've been telling people it's alvin morris. Well, hell. Anyway, our detective took the temperature of the body in your trunk—the algor mortis—and do you know what he said? I bet you can guess."

Tiffany admired how readily Hank could lie when the case called for it.

"I don't even care, man."

"I'll tell you anyway because it might jog your memory a bit. Anything helps, right?"

The man resumed fingering his beard.

"Based on the temperature of the body in your trunk, the guy's only been dead an hour at the most."

Rudy gave a look of confusion. "What? What are you talking about?"

"I'll tell you what I'm talking about. But first, is there anything else you want to ask me?"

"Like what?"

"Rudy, I just told you about a body found in the trunk of your Cadillac, and at no point did you ever ask me the name that goes to that body."

Rudy pushed his chair back from the table and put his elbows on his bouncing knees, his thumbs holding up his chin, his forehead beginning to moisten.

Hank continued, putting the West Side Silverbacks hierarchy in front of Rudy on the table. "I think you'll recognize these guys. These are your biker pals. We can just go ahead and scratch off two of the names, though. You'll know which ones."

"I don't know nothing about any of these guys."

"Are you sure?" asked Hank, his voice feigning incredulity. "That's really weird because, see here, your name is on the list also."

"That don't mean nothing."

"Well, okay, then. Let me help you out. This guy was found taking a dirt nap down off of Seventy-Nine this morning—you know the area, I think." Hank tapped JT Stahl's name with his finger. "And this guy, he's currently folded up in your trunk. But you already knew that because you killed him. You killed Corcoran, and you were on your way to dump him in the same area where you dumped JT. Or maybe the area where you dumped James Milford. Or down in French Creek, where you dumped Dale Davis. French Creek, as you know, flows out of Stockade Lake. It's pretty there this time of year, I hear."

Rudy lifted his head from off his thumbs and shook his head unconvincingly. "I didn't do anything to anyone. You're full of it."

"That's a compelling argument, Rudy. You should remember that for the trial. In the meantime, tell me what you have against JT Stahl and Kyle Corcoran."

"I w—"

"Wait, I'm not done. I still want to know why you killed James Milford and Dale Davis. Oh, and there's one more person I want to ask you about. Hank began to pull a blank sheet of paper from the file.

"Hey, I didn't kill Tiny! That Indian broad did! I saw it on the news."

"Now we're getting somewhere, Rudy. See? This isn't that hard." Hank let this sink in for moment, then continued. "Detective Reese here is going to walk us through what we know, or what we think. And you are going help fill in the blanks. Detective..."

Tiffany was caught off guard for a moment, but she knew what Hank was doing and knew that he didn't have to do it. This was the kind of investigation that could result in a promotion, and Hank had been telling her, for months now, that she was ready.

"Okay, Mr. Goodwin, this is what we know. We know that

last fall Mickey—AKA 'Tiny'—McCallister, Dale Davis, and James Milford got into a beef with the West Side Silverbacks over a motorcycle. We know that this resulted in the murder of Davis and Milford. We know that Davis was tied up and beaten in the head until he died." Tiffany watched Rudy's eyes widen to half dollars. "He was then dumped in French Creek. And we know that Milford was shot in the back of the head and dumped off a fire road halfway up Custer Mountain."

"Or, he was shot *on* the fire road," added Hank.

"Yes," said Tiffany. "You could have shot him before or after you took him to the road."

"I didn't shoot him at all."

"Who did?" asked Tiffany.

"I don't know. I keep telling you. I don't know what you're talking about."

Rudy's posture had softened. He faced the floor and rubbed his forehead as he spoke. He was clearly dejected, resigned. Tiffany could sense imminent collapse. It was starting to feel like the end.

"Okay, Rudy. We'll just test the gun in your trunk against the fragments found in Milford's skull." As she spoke, Tiffany shot a quick glance toward Hank. He smirked just enough for her to know that he recognized, and appreciated, her own ability to flex the truth.

"That ain't my gun! That's J—" Rudy threw his hands up, leaned back, and covered his face with crossed arms.

"That's JT's gun? Is that what you were going to say?"

There was no response, so Tiffany continued, taking a different tack. "Well, that would make sense, wouldn't it? You didn't shoot Milford. You're just a pawn, right? What? Did they force you to help dispose of the bodies?"

Rudy lowered his arms and looked directly at Tiffany. "Exactly. JT shot Jimbo. For all I knew we were just going to leave him out there. Teach him a lesson."

"So, he was shot here, in Custer County?"

"Yeah. We were going to leave him up there. We were just supposed to park, open the trunk, and let the dude wander off. But JT popped him. I didn't know that was going to happen. That wasn't supposed to happen."

"What lesson were you trying to teach him? Was this about a motorcycle?"

"Kyle stole Dale's motorcycle, then bragged about it. Dale and his buddies broke into Kyle's shop and took it back."

"So, you smashed Dale's face in. Or was it somebody else who did that?"

Rudy opened his mouth, then closed it without a word.

"And what about Tiny McCallister? How does he play into this?"

"Like I said, his old lady killed him."

"We know that, Rudy. But we also know that you guys were looking for him. Was he involved in stealing back the bike?"

"Kyle heard that Tiny was the lookout when they broke into his shop. But we never knew for sure. Anyway, he left town right after, and Kyle just kind of forgot about it. Then, when he came back, we grabbed him and brought him to Kyle."

"Who's we?" asked Hank.

"Me and JT."

Hank nodded, then look at Tiffany to continue.

"Okay, you grabbed him. Then what?"

"Kyle told him that if he didn't find a replacement bike, he would disappear like the other two."

"That explains why Tiny was seen riding around on a motorcycle. Why didn't Kyle just take his bike back after Dale was killed?"

Rudy twisted his lip, like a little kid thinking about whether or not to tell a lie.

"He did. But I, uh...I crashed it."

Tiffany approached the table and kneeled, placing one hand on the table and another on Rudy's knee.

"Rudy, what I'm hearing here is that you and the rest of the Silverbacks may not have been as close as we thought. It seems like JT was going off half-cocked and getting you into all kinds of trouble. And maybe Kyle Corcoran had a thing against you for wrecking his—Dale's—motorcycle."

Rudy nodded faintly as he spoke. "Kyle sent JT to kill me. That's why I shot him. It was self-defense. He pulled a damn gun on me in the car."

"That's the gun in your trunk?" she asked softly.

"Yeah."

"That must have pissed you off. Did you then use the same gun to shoot Kyle?"

Rudy looked down but did not answer.

"Rudy, look at me," instructed Tiffany, evoking a soft, even maternal concern. "Did you then use the same gun to shoot Kyle?"

"No. I broke the bastard's neck."

29

"That was brilliant. Absolutely brilliant," offered Hank, as they stood in the rear parking lot of the sheriff's office and watched Rudy Goodwin get driven off to jail.

"Thanks. I learned interviewing from the best," Tiffany said, as she put her sunglasses over her eyes.

"I wasn't really talking about that—but yes, you did great in there. I was referring to the audible you called about checking Rudy's trunk."

"I'm sure they would have checked it soon enough."

"In detective work, timing is critical. And having the trunk checked while we were in the interview made all the difference. I can imagine that car being towed down here with a body in the hot trunk and us never being able to pin down time of death."

"Well, we technically don't know time of death. You were lying about Kyle's body temperature."

"I was only lying about knowing the temperature, but not lying about when I thought Rudy killed Corcoran. There's a difference."

"So, where do we go from here?" asked Tiffany.

"This thing has gone multi-jurisdictional on us. Stahl and Milford were certainly killed in the county. Corcoran and Davis were both killed in Rapid City. And, Mickey, of course, is all ours."

"Hey, that reminds me. Your brother may not be so smart, after all. Didn't he say the skull in the RV park had Asian traits? Davis isn't exactly an Asian name, is it?" Tiffany said.

"I think the good doctor said, Asian, Native, or Hispanic—to be technical, anyway," Hank reminded her.

"Well, sure. But still."

"While you were out looking for Corcoran, I had crime analysis do a full workup on our victims. Davis's mother was full blood Blackfoot Indian."

Tiffany shook her head in amazement.

"Hey, you should know better than to doubt a LeGris. We have a gift." Hank put his left arm around Tiffany and gave her playful punch to her right shoulder.

Tiffany looked at her sergeant and said, "He's a Grey. Remember?"

"So am I. LeGris mean 'the gray.' I'm surprised you didn't know that."

"Very funny, boss. Any word about Susan?"

Hank shook his head. "Nope. But she can't go far."

"Do you think she really killed Micky in self-defense?"

"I absolutely do. The guy was a piece of work. Like you pointed out earlier, why did she use a weapon of opportunity to kill Mickey, a broken piece of coffee pot, instead of the shotgun to kill him? That bodes well for her."

Tiffany looked at her watch. It was almost three o'clock already.

"You're excused, Detective. Let me know when you find out where he's been."

❧

"GOOD AFTERNOON, I'm Detective Reese, with the sheriff's office." Tiffany showed her badge to the woman behind the registration desk.

"How can I help you? Is everything okay?" The woman looked mildly alarmed. It was seldom that the police had to pay a visit to one of the nicer hotels in the Southern Black Hills.

Tiffany chose to take the stairs to the second floor, rather than the elevator. She needed to stretch and flex a bit after all that time in the interview room.

Room 207 was halfway down the hall, on the left. A "Do Not Disturb" sign had been inserted into the keycard reader. This was at least a sign that Sebastien was probably in the room, she figured. Tiffany found herself straightening her bangs a bit before knocking, which made her feel a little foolish—like a schoolgirl hoping to be kissed. Tiffany knocked on the door firmly.

"Sebastien? Are you in there?"

She heard rustling from behind the door, as if Sebastien were rushing to get dressed or something.

"Where the heck have you been?" Tiffany demanded, as she barged past him into the room, looking around for clues that might answer that question. "I've been calling you all day!"

"Sorry. I, uh, slept in a bit."

"A bit? Geez, what happened to you? You look awful. And why are you limping?"

"Oh, it's nothing. I tweaked my foot last night. I'm glad you noticed how awful I look, though. That's the look I was going for."

"Very funny, Doctor. How'd that go, by the way?"

Tiffany sat on the edge of the bed as Sebastien searched for a shirt with which to cover himself. She couldn't resist giving his naked torso a surreptitious once-over. He was much fitter than she realized. There was a slight indentation in his upper arms, defining his deltoids and biceps. She could just make out his spine against his fair skin, which reminded her of the spine she'd uncovered on the bank of the wash. She wondered to herself, as Sebastien fished through his suitcase, how rugose he was, what his mastoid processes might look like. How much would they protrude?

"It went fine. We found the problem mountain lion and relocated it."

"Really? That's awesome. Good job!"

The now mostly clothed anthropologist sat next to Tiffany on the bed. "Well, yeah. I also found out that the only person at the GFP who thinks it was a man-eating mountain lion is Barry Van Lowe."

"Barry Van Lowe? Do I know him?"

"Oh, sorry. Maybe not. He's the biologist that Hank and I met with the other day."

"Well, Hank will be happy to hear that. Once word gets out that the mountain lion has been moved, and that the unidentified bodies are now identified and were the result of homicides, the mountain lion panic should dissipate." Tiffany glanced down and noticed the large purple bruise on the inside of Sebastien's ankle. "Oh man. That looks bad. How did it happen?"

"Oh, it's not a big deal. I just caught it on a tree root in the dark. So, have you made some progress on the skeleton cases."

Tiffany laughed. "Progress is putting it lightly. Things are pretty well wrapped up."

"Really? Well, that was quick."

"It's all thanks to you."

Sebastien gave a sheepish shrug and half smile.

"No, seriously. Think about it. Without you, we would only have a smashed skull and a jaw. But now we have enough to identify the remains."

"Have you identified them?"

"We have a positive ID on the body from the wash. You were right about the hole in the skull—it was the result of a plate. Hank went to the county hospital and found only a handful of patients that had had that procedure done. And only one person matched the approximate height and age you came up with from the skeleton. It was a guy named James Milford. His post-procedure x-rays match the x-rays of our skull. We tracked down Milford's sister and, sure enough, she said that he's been missing since last October. She also told us that Milford's friend, Dale Davis, has also been missing. It turns out, they had a run-in with some outlaw bikers. We're chasing down Davis' dental records now so we can compare them to the skull from the RV park. Hopefully, there is enough for a comparison. We're pretty sure it's him, though."

"There is," Sebastien said. "Have you identified the bikers?"

"You're never going to believe this."

"Try me. I've seen some crazy stuff."

"We sent detectives to bring in the head of the gang this morning. He wasn't there. But our guys ran into one of the club members leaving his house. He had just killed the guy we were looking for and stuffed him in the trunk of his car—which was sitting in the driveway as they searched the place."

"Okay. I've never seen anything that crazy."

"Hold on. It gets better," said Tiffany. "He killed another member of the gang yesterday and dumped him off of the highway.

"Wow. Did he dump him near where the other bodies were found?"

Tiffany shook her head and said, "No. It was just north of Hermosa. That's the town where Susan Whitebear lives. But it was in our county, as opposed to up north where all these goons call home. Anyway, we brought the guy in, and after feeding him a bunch of bull, he cracked."

"What do you mean bull?" asked Sebastien, looking confused.

"Hank told him that we could get *his* DNA off of the bones from the two dump sites. He told the guy it's a new technique. I think he called it external bone DNA."

"Are you kidding me? And the guy believed him?"

"Apparently," Tiffany said, laughing. "Of course, we had no idea if this was one of the bikers who murdered Davis and Milford. But when I told him that Davis had been tied to a chair and beaten, he definitely looked like he knew what I was talking about. In the end, he told us that he and the two bikers he'd just killed were the ones who'd committed our murders. And, to tie it all together, they were also the ones looking for Mickey. The guy we interviewed is one of the guys you and Hank ran into in town the other day."

Sebastien stood up, limped to the window, pulled back the curtains, and gazed out toward the tree-covered hills.

"I guess my work here is done," he said, as he looked out.

Tiffany thought for a second before speaking. "No, you have one more job to do."

Sebastien turned around, looking confused.

"You need to buy me dinner."

"Oh, do I? Is this part of the official investigation?" Sebastien leaned against the windowsill and smiled.

"No. It's part of my investigation into the mysterious Doctor Grey. I'm going home to change. I smell like felon. Pick me up in an hour and bring a jacket."

AS THE DOOR CLOSED, Sebastien felt a surge of energy and boyish excitement. He rifled through his remaining clean clothes—there wasn't much; he hadn't planned on being here this long—and pulled out a pair of dark grey slacks and an oatmeal henley shirt. He examined his vest and concluded that it was just too filthy from last night's assault by M323. But he had a cotton field jacket that he hoped would suffice for whatever Tiffany had in mind. These, together with his brown leather sneakers, should render him reasonably assembled. He was now prepared to shower and shave.

30

Hank slammed on the Tahoe's brakes, sliding at least fifty feet down Custer Street before coming to a stop within inches of the man.

"Geez, Mike! I almost ran you over. What are you doing running into the street like that?"

"Sorry, Colonel. You're just the man I was looking for." Homeless Mike ran around to the passenger side, threw open the door, and climbed in.

"Excuse me, Mike! County vehicle! You can't just get in it like it's yours."

"I don't have a car, Chief. You know that. Drive up a little way and make a left. I wanna show you something."

Hank decided to let it go. He didn't smell alcohol on Mike's breath. Maybe this was a legitimate issue. He called in the "hailed by citizen" to dispatch and continued down the street, making a left on Second Street, as prompted by Mike.

"Park here, by the power station."

Hank and Mike got out of the Tahoe, and Mike led them on foot westward onto Mickelson Trail.

"I thought I told you to stay off the trail?"

"I am staying off it. I just keep my tent and clothes here, Corporal."

"Where are you taking me? I need some info here, Mike."

"We're almost there."

Hank rested the ball of his right palm on his holster. Stories of ambushed officers played through his mind as he looked at the low bushes and dense woods that lined the trail.

"It's up here." Mike pointed to a spot about twenty yards off the trail. A filthy blue tent stood in between some pine.

Hank looked around Mike's makeshift camp and saw only the tent, a bicycle leaning against one of the trees, a clothesline with nothing on it, and a two-burner camp stove next to a large, flat rock.

"In here." Mike walked directly up to the tent and started to unzip the door.

Hank unsnapped his holster and stood back a good ten feet as Mike folded back the tent door.

"I believe you've been looking for this, Chief," Mike announced triumphantly, pointing into the tent.

Hank could see a person lying on a brown sleeping bag— the same sleeping bag that Mike had been dragging through the street on Monday. He cautiously approached to get a better look. It was a woman wearing a black shirt and jeans. She had her hands up to her face, her grayish brown hair falling between her fingers.

"How in the heck did you get all the way out here?" Hank asked, as he knelt onto the dirt-covered tent floor.

A sobbing Susan Whitebear pulled her hands from her tear- and snot-covered face. "I'm so sorry," she cried.

TIFFANY HANDED the binoculars over to Sebastien. "There, across the lake. See that big tree over there? The one closest to the shore, on the left side of the cove. Focus on where the trunk meets the ground and then go straight up."

Sebastien adjusted the binoculars to get a clear view of the tree and scanned upward. "Oh, hey. There it is."

"Pretty cool, huh? This pair of bald eagles has called Deerfield Lake their home for the last few years. Last year, I was lucky enough to see one of their fledglings take its first flight. "Do you see anything in the nest?"

"I think I see a little head sticking up. Maybe a baby eagle?"

"It's called an eaglet," Tiffany provided. "If you scan the tops of the trees near the aerie—that's what the nest is called—you should be able to find one of its parents. One is usually keeping an eye out while the other looks for food."

Sebastien swept the binoculars across the horizon, resting the barrels on anything that looked like a bird. "I don't see anything."

"Let's just sit and listen for a minute. We should hear a call when the food gets near the nest."

Sebastien handed the binoculars back to Tiffany. They were sitting on a picnic table with their feet on the bench, looking over the lake. It was not yet dusk, but there were only a handful of people in sight—a couple of kayakers in the middle of the lake, paddling peacefully, and a man and boy fishing off the dock near where they sat. The breeze off the water pushed a chill onto the shore and made the pine trees whisper.

Tiffany looked lovely tonight. Her clothes were casual— blue jeans and a grey regatta jacket over a white cotton shirt— and her make-up was sparse, the sunset reflecting dully off her nude lipstick. But her long bob hair was once again curled into subtle waves, contradicting the unconsidered effect of the rest of her appearance.

"What?" She caught him staring at her.

"Nothing. I was just thinking about the case."

"You're a damn liar," she replied with a smirk.

Sebastien looked out over the lake, fixing his eyes on one of the kayakers.

After several minutes, Tiffany spoke. "So, when do you leave?" She lifted the binoculars to her eyes and scanned the water for nothing in particular.

"Tomorrow morning, I think. There's nothing left for me to do here. I'm not needed anymore."

"You'll have to come back for the trial. If it comes to that, I mean."

"That's true."

"What's next for you? Do you have other cases waiting?"

"Not at the moment."

"But you have your building to run?"

Sebastien was not sure where she was going with this line of questioning. "That's true," he repeated.

"Hank told me that you don't have any family in California —not since your mother died."

Sebastien nodded in reply, hoping he wouldn't be pressed into a conversation about family. "I do have my dog, if that counts."

"Pets always count. But they aren't quite the same as family."

"Sometimes they're better," he said.

"I know you don't believe that. Your brother and his family are terrific. Great people."

"I know. You're right," Sebastien agreed.

"So, what's keeping you in California?"

It wasn't a bad question. What was keeping him there? Was it the Block, which, as Hank pointed out, ran itself? His forensic work, which was sporadic? His friends? What friends?"

"I guess nothing is keeping me there. Now you're making me depressed."

Tiffany turned to look at him, setting the binoculars in her lap. "Sorry, Sebastien. I'm not trying to make you depressed. I'm only curious."

Sebastien felt authorized to ask his own questions now. "Why? Why are you curious about that?"

"It just seems to me that you have more up here than you do down there. I mean, for starters, look how beautiful this place is." She indicated the lake with a sweep of her hand. "Plus, you have Hank, Melissa, Kirby."

"No job."

"Do you need a job?"

"No forensic work, then."

"Excuse me, Doctor. What exactly have you been doing all week?"

"Are you telling me there's always this much murder and mayhem up here?" Sebastien laughed at his own sarcasm.

"Hey, you know what I've been thinking about?" she asked him, as she rested a gracile hand on his knee, causing him, once again, to swallow hard. "You'd make a heck of a detective. It's not just the bones and bodies. You're a good investigator. You see things, little things, that most detectives don't."

"I think Hen—Hank would disagree."

"I think you're wrong about that." She squeezed his knee. Sebastien no longer noticed the cool breeze.

"Are you trying to recruit me? I'm not the police officer type. Probably couldn't even pass the psyche exam."

Tiffany giggled out loud.

"No, I'm serious," Sebastien said.

"Do you want to know what I think?" Tiffany took up both of his hands and looked him in the face. Sebastien's eyes froze into hers. "I think you're full of crap. You think you're awkward, but you're not. I think you're fascinating and brilliant. Sure, you're a bit different. But, so what? One day I hope you give yourself permission to be different, Sebastien. You'll be happier."

Sebastien was stunned as she held his gaze in some sort of mesmeric trance. He would normally feel reprimanded, would normally be mortified that such a person as Tiffany had figured out his insecurities, his deficiencies. He wanted to tell her that she was wrong, that he was not at the level she thought he was. But he found himself unable to form those words, unable to believe them.

"Do you know what I like best about you?" Sebastien said, surprising himself.

"Oh please? I'm dying to hear this."

"I don't have to guess what you really think. You tell it like it is. You tell me things I need to hear."

Tiffany laughed. "Well, I was hoping you were going to say how pretty I am, but I guess I'll take that."

"Do you need to be told how pretty you are?" Sebastien was looking back over the lake now.

"You definitely know more about bones than you do about women, Sebastien."

"I just meant—"

"I know what you meant. And thank you."

"So, do you really think I should be a detective?"

"Well, maybe not an official one. Ooh, I know. Maybe we could talk to the lieutenant and see about bringing you on as a consultant?" She had let go of his hands now.

"I'm fairly sure that's only a thing on TV," he replied.

"Yeah, you're probably right."

"So, let's recap." Sebastien ticked off his list with the fingers of his right hand. "I'll have my brother, his wife and his daughter, my dog, and the beautiful scenery."

"Yes, and the beautiful scenery," she agreed. "Don't forget that."

"Check. Beautiful scenery. But," Sebastien raised his left hand, "no job, no friends, bloodthirsty mountain lions who will probably eat my dog, murderous bikers..."

Tiffany nodded along playfully, ticking off the list with her own lithe fingers. "True. True. Definitely. True."

They chuckled together for a moment before falling silent. A portentous air enveloped the picnic table.

Sebastien couldn't take it any longer. He had to know. "Are you trying to get me up here to be nice, or because you want me up here?"

Tiffany lifted her right hand and rested it gently on his newly shaved left cheek. "We may need to work on those detective skills, after all, Dr. Grey," she said, before reaching her lips up to his.

EPILOGUE

Sebastien attached the documents and hit "send" on the email to Dr. Rose, Gerry Good Crow, and his brother. With the delivery of his reports, his forensic work in South Dakota was now officially done. He stowed his laptop in its bag, grabbed his suitcase from off the bed, and made his way to the lobby.

Hank, Melissa, and Kirby all stood up from their seats when they saw Sebastien exit the elevator. Kirby ran up and grabbed him around the legs, nearly throwing him off balance.

"Hey. What are you all doing here?" Sebastien asked, smiling.

"We couldn't just let you skip town, bro."

"We were afraid you might not come by the ranch and say goodbye. We didn't want to miss you," Melissa said into his ear, as she hugged him and pecked him on the cheek.

"That's nice," he said. "I was definitely going to stop by on the way out," he lied.

Hank reached out his hand, and Sebastien took it. "I can't thank you enough, Sebastien. I just really can't. I'm so glad you came up. And it was really great to see you."

Sebastien was taken aback. His brother seemed genuinely moved—almost teary. "Well, of course. I'm really glad I came up, too. To be honest, I actually didn't have much going on, case-wise. So, this was good."

"Daddy said you're coming to live here," Kirby announced, while jumping up and down on one of the chairs in the hotel lobby.

"Honey, come down from there," Melissa instructed.

Sebastien's look of confusion prompted Hank. "I talked to Tiffany this morning. She told me about your conversation last night. I think that would be amazing if you came here. We would really love having you. I'm serious. It's about time we got the band back together."

When were we ever a band? Sebastien said to himself. "Yeah, well, I didn't make any promises. I just said it might be a good idea."

"We think it would be a great idea," said Melissa. "It would be so nice to have family close by. You're Kirby's only uncle. And I know Tiffany would be excited." Melissa gave him a wink and a wry smile.

"Just think about, will ya?" pleaded Hank. "We can work out the details of a job and everything when you get here. Or you can just keep the Block and run it from here. Think about it, okay?"

"Okay, I'll think about it," he replied, not telling them that he had been up half the night researching commercial real estate agents in the Bay Area.

Hank gave him a tight hug, and Sebastien whispered into his ear, "What if I get up here and she doesn't like me?"

"We love you, bro. That's all that matters."

THE END

ABOUT THE AUTHOR

Ryburn Dobbs taught biological anthropology and forensic anthropology at several colleges throughout the San Francisco Bay Area and spent ten years as a forensic anthropologist, working dozens of death investigations. In addition to his anthropological pursuits, Ryburn also worked as an investigative analyst specializing in homicides and unsolved cases.

The Comfort of Distance is Ryburn's first novel and the first in the Sebastien Grey series. For more information about Ryburn, his blog, and updates on new books please visit www.ryburndobbs.com.